JESSICA WATKINS

Love,
OBSESSION
AND POWER

HONEY

ISBN-13: 978-1517309107
ISBN-10: 1517309107

Dedication

This book is dedicated to my one and only child, Solomon III. I also dedicate this book to my wonderful and supportive parents, Billy and Lauretta. The three of you are truly the wind beneath my wings.

Acknowledgements

I am thankful to God for blessing me with the gift of creative writing and the ability to tell great stories. I am grateful for the talent He has entrusted me with. It is indeed my passion. Thank You, God. Thank you, Solomon III for your love, support, patience, and understanding. With every project I write, you prove to me just how much you really love me. You never complain about the insane amount of time I spend writing, and for that I am appreciative. Mommy loves you to the stars and back. Mama and Daddy, I wouldn't be the successful woman I am today if you two hadn't raised me to work hard and believe in myself. I owe you an endless debt that I'll never be able to repay. I love you guys from the bottom of my heart. To Big Solomon, my husband of nearly eleven years, I say thank you for allowing me to write. I couldn't do it if you weren't a *real man* who takes care of his household and provides generously for his family. I love you so much. Thank you. My oldest sister, Dawn, and my baby sister, Nikki, are always in my corner no matter what. I appreciate all you two do for me. We are the troublesome trio. LOL! Thank you, Lance and Shirley for your support. Andra, my cousin, manager, and confidant, is responsible for so much. I can't list everything she does for me because it's a lot. Thanks for just being present whenever I need you. There would be no Honey without you. A special shout out is due to every member of the Randall, Fults, and Berewa families. I love every single one of you. I have the greatest screen team on the planet. They are the reason why I don't release garbage to the public. Every serious author needs a screen team like mine. Thank you, Dawn, Nikki, Andra, Ashley, Ingrid, Diann, Deborah Anne, Christan, and Cherell. You sistahs are hard on a chick, but I wouldn't want you to be any other way. Finally, thank you, Ms. Jessica Watkins for the incredible opportunity to share this amazing story with the world. God bless you.

Chapter One

"Congressman Day! Congressman Day! Over here, sir!"

Emmanuel scanned the crowd of reporters through flashes of light from dozens of cameras. His eyes zoomed in on the beautiful face behind the sexy voice. He paused, attempting to compose himself. The woman was too damn fine. Her good looks had caught him totally off guard. Whoever the gorgeous creature was, she had definitely captured the congressman's undivided attention. Every manly fiber in his being was on high sexual alert. With a subtle nod of his head and a half smile, he prompted the pretty reporter to ask her question.

"I'm Jazz Dupree from Black Diamond Television. Best wishes on your re-election bid, sir."

"Thank you, Ms. Dupree."

"You're welcome, Congressman. Your opponent is quite popular in Georgia. She's unlike anyone else you've squared off with in your previous races over the years. Give us a hint. How do you plan to defeat State Senator Divinity Davis in your upcoming primary? She's a pretty tough cookie. Is it possible for you to battle a female opponent without looking like a big bad bully?"

"I'm a gentleman, Ms. Dupree. Everyone knows that. No one has ever accused Emmanuel Day of being a bully, especially not toward a *woman*. As usual, I plan to run a squeaky clean campaign and stick to my platform. Equal justice in our legal system for all citizens, affordable healthcare, and quality education for every American child are the basic reasons why I came to Capitol Hill. I'll debate Senator Davis on those issues any day of the week, but I refuse to stoop to petty bickering and personal attacks."

"Your opponent has raised globs of money, Congressman Day. Do you have a plan to match her financial windfall?" a young male reporter shouted above the buzz of the crowd.

Emmanuel smiled and waved his hand at the throng of media vultures, dismissing them. He was done answering questions for the day. He turned to Tyrell, his nephew and personal assistant. "What do you know about Jazz Dupree?" he whispered.

"Not much, Unc. I heard she started off as a sports reporter at another network before she moved to Black Diamond. She is sexy as *sin*."

Tyrell was correct. Jazz Dupree was smoking hot in Emmanuel's eyes too. It should've been a crime for her to wear the color red. Her golden complexion appeared flawless against it. Emmanuel immediately imagined eating strawberries dipped in creamy caramel when he first laid eyes on her. Her three-piece pantsuit hugged every defined curve of her slender frame to perfection. Jazz Dupree was walking seduction. Her full pouty lips, brown almond shaped eyes, and high cheekbones were a hypnotic combination. The brightness of her smile and her short, curly afro added to her exotic features. The woman had an unforgettable face and a killer body to match. Emmanuel nearly fell under the spell of her beauty as she grilled him about his approach to defeating his female opponent. He was no different than any other full-blooded, virile, heterosexual male. Congressman Day appreciated the sight of a gorgeous woman.

"Yes, Ms. Dupree is eye candy without a doubt," he agreed with his nephew after some time. Then it suddenly occurred to him. "I knew I had seen that face and that banging body somewhere before. She used to cover the National Football League for Sports World International some years ago." Emmanuel glanced at Tyrell out of the corner of his eye as they walked side by side toward the private elevators reserved for members of congress and their staffs. "Get the scoop on Jazz Dupree. I want the full deal. She's not married. I already know that much."

Tyrell smiled. "How do you know that, Unc?"

"There's no wedding ring on her left hand. It was completely bare. If she was *your* wife, wouldn't you have her finger blinged out with the biggest diamond you could afford?"

"Point well taken. I'll see what I can dig up on the pretty reporter."

*****

Jazz studied the two pictures that Jackson, a photographer from Black Diamond Television, had captured of Congressman

Emmanuel Day at the press conference earlier that afternoon. *Not bad*, she silently admitted to herself. His dark chocolate skin was the first thing that had awakened her feminine senses. It was as smooth as silk. Jazz had seen the brother on TV several times before, and his face had graced the covers of a few African-American periodicals. But nothing had prepared her for the personal encounter. The congressman was slap-your-mama fine. He was much taller than he appeared on the small screen and in print. His long, chiseled physique towered a few inches above six feet, and the muscles in his chest and arms looked rock solid. Jazz drew in a deep breath and exhaled it slowly when her eyes fell to rest on his set of full lips. She imagined they were soft, moist, and kissable. The well-groomed mustache above them put the icing on the cake.

Emmanuel Day was a very handsome and charming man. If he wasn't a prestigious member of the United States Congress and the senior partner at the most reputable law firm in Metro Atlanta, Jazz would've possibly considered him a serious candidate for her affections. But the truth was she didn't fraternize with subjects that she interviewed. Basically, that meant all ballers, actors, musicians, producers, writers, or other wealthy public figures were off-limits. And because of Jazz's hectic work schedule, she didn't have much free time for romance anyway. She encountered many attractive charismatic brothers while she raced around the globe in hot pursuit of the latest scoop, but none of them had been able to penetrate the wall she'd built around her heart. However, as her eyes took in the raw masculinity of Congressman Day, she couldn't help but wonder how it would feel to be touched, tasted, and loved by man of his caliber.

Jackson waved his hand before her eyes to get her attention. "Jazz, did you hear what I just said?"

Jazz blinked a couple of times and shook her head from side to side. Her thoughts had plunged so deep into a pool of lust that she hadn't heard a single word her friend and coworker said. "I'm sorry, Jackson. My mind drifted away. What did you say?"

"The big dogs just decided to add Congressman Day to the list of subjects to be featured in that special political documentary. A lot of people think he'll be the country's next African-American president. But for now, his goal is to become the first black United

States senator from Georgia someday. Personally, I think he'd make a great governor for the Peach State."

"Which reporter have they assigned to cover the congressman?"

"No one yet, but Gigi wants him bad. And I'm not just talking about for the assignment either. She *wants* the man."

"Are you serious?" Jazz sat straight up in her chair and folded her hands on top of her desk.

"Yeah, I heard that Gigi virtually stalks Congressman Day all over Washington. She has kissed up to a random group of congressional aides and staff members all over Capitol Hill, so she's often invited to major political events. The chick is shameless."

Jazz smiled and nodded her head in agreement. "Gigi is aggressive. She'll move heaven and earth for the opportunity to cover Congressman Day's segment of the documentary."

"She volunteered for it already," Jackson said flatly. "Mr. McConnell hasn't made a decision on it yet, though. If he doesn't give the assignment to Gigi, she will torture whoever gets it. That person will have my sympathy."

Chapter Two

"Excuse me?" Jazz bolted from her chair and started pacing the floor in front of her boss's desk. Her heart was beating at triple speed inside her chest. Mr. McConnell's spacious corner office at Black Diamond Television's headquarters in Washington, D.C. suddenly grew warm. It seemed to be spinning in slow motion too. "You want *me* to cover Congressman Day's segment of the documentary?"

"I sure do. I think you'll do an excellent job. Congratulations, Jazz," the older gentleman said, leaning back in his chair. "You crushed a lot of hearts with this one. Every unattached female reporter at the network wanted the assignment, especially *Gigi Perdue*."

"Why did you give it to *me*, sir?"

Mr. McConnell chuckled lightly. The youthful twinkle in his eyes defied his age of seven decades and six years. "I trust you, Jazz. You're the ultimate professional. I know you'll capture the very essence of the congressman and give us a great story. *And* there's no doubt in my mind that you will conduct yourself appropriately with class and integrity during the assignment at all times."

*****

Emmanuel stood from his seat behind the massive cherry wood desk. He walked around it with his hand extended. "It's a pleasure to meet you, Ms. Dupree. When Tyrell, my personal assistant, informed me that *you* would be the reporter following me around for the next six weeks, I was pleasantly surprised."

"I'm honored to have received this assignment, sir."

Jazz took the congressman's offered hand and shook it. She was nervous. He felt it in her weak and shaky grip. He also noticed how soft and petite her hand was. The smooth flesh caused his hand to tingle from the friendly contact. A warm sensation shot through Emmanuel, and he released Jazz's hand abruptly.

"Have a seat." He nodded to the pair of scroll back chairs facing his desk. "Before we map out our agenda, may I offer you something to drink, Ms. Dupree?"

"Sure. What do you have available?"

I'm available and I'll give you anything your heart desires, baby. Just tell Papa what you want. Emmanuel dropped down in his seat, completely shocked by his lustful thoughts. Yes, he was one hundred percent attracted to Jazz, but he had always been able to separate business from pleasure. It was the most valuable lesson he'd learned from his disastrous relationship with Maya Durant all those years ago.

Emmanuel eased back into professional mode quickly. "Every beverage imaginable is available here. Name it and it's yours."

"I'll take a cup of hot tea please."

*****

"Hurry up, Ramone!" Jazz wrinkled her nose and frowned at her best friend. "You've never taken this long to do my hair and makeup before."

"And you have never been out on a date with a fine, fudge-covered congressman before either. Okay?"

"It is not a *date*!" Jazz fired back.

"Is he picking you up from your condo?"

"Yes."

"Will you be dining with him?"

"Of course, we're going to eat, Ramone. It's a *dinner* party and dance."

"Are you going to allow him to take you in his arms and twirl you around on the dance floor like a princess, darling?"

Jazz released air from her cheeks, completely annoyed. "I'm sure we will dance."

"Can I go with you?"

"No!"

"Well, then it *is* a date, sweetie pie."

It wasn't a date because Jazz did not date any of the hundreds of men that she interviewed. That was the ultimate no-no on her personal list of professional do's and don'ts. Ramone knew that better than anyone. He and Jazz had been best friends since she moved from Dallas, Texas to the nation's capital seven years ago. It was love at first sight for the newly hired reporter at BDT and D.C.'s premier hair stylist for the black elite. Jazz had been referred to Fabulous & Fierce Salon and Boutique by Gigi during her first week on the job. Ramone, a true football fanatic, recognized the familiar face he'd seen on the sidelines of football fields across America right away. He and Jazz clicked the moment her bottom hit his styling chair, and they had been tighter than skinny jeans ever since.

That's why it irked Jazz that Ramone had been referring to her upcoming outing with Congressman Day as a date. He was totally aware that she was only spending time with the congressman socially to obtain information for the documentary. Her career as a journalist was important to her, and she wanted to do a top notch job on her current assignment. So far, her close interaction with Congressman Day had been smooth and quite productive. Jazz had spent lots of time in committee meetings and in the galley high above the house floor observing the legislative process. Her comfort level was strong when the camera crew was there filming Congressman Day engaged in various activities. But whenever Jazz found herself alone with the brother in the privacy of his office or seated across from him at a candlelight table for two, she felt as naked as a newborn baby. The way he looked at her never ceased to set every inch of her flesh on fire. It was almost like his midnight irises held a never-ending blaze. And every time the cool congressman smiled at Jazz, she became acutely aware that God had created her woman. Plainly put, she was attracted to Congressman Day, and there wasn't a damn thing she could do about it.

"Okay, you're done, sweetie." Ramone gave his styling chair a push. It turned slightly and stopped at an angle where Jazz could see herself in the huge wall mirror inside his spacious work station. "I know you like it. I gave you extra *everything*, boo. I couldn't have you on the congressman's arm looking like a reporter. Ramone had to transform you into a fashion model."

Jazz was utterly speechless, which was so out of character for her. She was a broadcast journalist for heaven's sake. Talking came as natural to her as breathing, but Ramone's handiwork had locked her jaws—*literally*. The soft curls in her short afro sparkled with a soft sheen. Ramone had enhanced her flawless complexion with just a hint of foundation and dusting powder. A pale shade of pink to her lips and high cheekbones added perfect touches to her skin. Bronze highlights had been applied to her eyelids, and her curvy lashes fanned out gracefully with light strokes of mascara.

"I love it, Ramone," Jazz whispered in awe.

"Of course you do. Ramone is the ultimate beauty connoisseur. *Okay?*"

Chapter Three

Emmanuel lost his train of thought the moment Congressman Jared Abernathy from Virginia approached Jazz. The arrogant young man took her by the hand as soon as she returned to the ballroom from the ladies' room. He had been flirting openly with her all evening, very much to her displeasure. Jazz, an elegant and refined woman, had politely rejected each of Congressman Abernathy's advances. But at the moment, she appeared helpless and flustered as he invaded her personal space.

"Excuse me please," Emmanuel told a group of his colleagues he'd been chatting with. He placed his half empty champagne flute on a passing server's tray and left the huddle. His gaze was so intensely fixated on Jazz as he made a hot path in her direction, that he was unable to avoid Gigi's clever interception. Before the congressman had time to fully process what has happening, the chick had wrapped him in her arms and was swaying to the live music from the rhythm and blues band.

"I've been waiting to dance with you all evening," Gigi purred seductively. "I'm going to have to teach you how to *play*. You work too hard and way too much. You were over there talking politics with your associates for more than an hour when you could've been having a good time with me."

Emmanuel ignored Gigi's comments and allowed her to lead him in a slow dance. He wanted to escape from her clutches so he could go and rescue Jazz from Jared Abernathy, but he didn't want to be rude. They too were now on the dance floor swaying and twirling about. The sight of Jazz in Jared's arms made Emmanuel break out in a cold sweat. He was actually *jealous*, which only made him angry. Green was not his color, but for some strange reason, he felt possessive of Jazz. Maybe it was because of all of the time they'd been spending together recently. He was very fond of Jazz, and he enjoyed her company. They had unbelievable chemistry. His attraction to her was physical, mental, and *sexual* for sure.

Gigi tightened her hold around Emmanuel's neck and pressed her body closer to his. She was a relentless hunter. From the moment they'd met at a Black Diamond Christmas party his freshman year in congress, she had been on his ass like black on a cast iron skillet. Emmanuel had been attracted to Gigi initially, but soon found her aggressive behavior repulsive. She was a good-looking woman, and she reeked of raw sexuality. She used her light brown eyes to cast erotic spells on men. Her curvy petite figure and long dancer's legs were hard to resist. And the way she tossed her long sandy curls over her shoulders whenever she laughed was a complete turn-on. Emmanuel had fallen prey to Gigi's bold advances *once* in a moment of sheer weakness. The one night stand must've meant a whole lot more to her than it had to the congressman, because she had been chasing him for a repeat performance ever since.

Like a hawk's, Emmanuel's sharp eyes zoomed in on Jared's hands. He was squeezing Jazz's tiny waste a little too snuggly, and she didn't seem to like it at all. The expression on her face was not a happy one. Jazz, like Emmanuel, had been trapped by an undesirable dance partner, but she was too polite to walk away. The popular Luther Vandross ballad the band was performing seemed to be the extended version. Emmanuel couldn't wait for the song to end. He was sure Jazz felt the same way. As stunning as she looked tonight in her bronze, beaded evening gown, her face was very somber. Jared was smiling like he had just struck oil. He had a gem in his arms, and although it was against Jazz's wishes, the idiot seemed to be enjoying it.

The long drawn out song finally ended just as Jared leaned down and whispered something in Jazz's ear. Her eyes stretched wide and she grimaced before she shoved him in his chest, breaking free from his hold. Emmanuel excused himself from Gigi and ran after Jazz who was trying desperately to get away from Jared. The fool was making persistent steps behind her.

"What's your problem, Abernathy?" Emmanuel called out, on the brink of rage.

Jared stopped and turned around slowly with a smirk on his face. "I don't have a problem, old man. I was just having fun with the lady, but she's too stuck-up to have a good time."

Emmanuel looked down the long hallway leading to the hotel lobby. Jazz was still walking as fast as she could in her high heels away from Jared. "Young cats like you make me sick. You need to learn how to respect a lady. Better yet, stay away from women altogether, especially *that* one." He yanked his thumb in the direction of the lobby. Jazz was nowhere in sight now.

"She's a little too young for you, isn't she, Congressman?"

"She may be, but she's definitely too much of a woman for you."

With that said, Emmanuel hurried to the lobby in search of Jazz. He found her watching television and sipping chardonnay in a cozy bistro located near the hotel's gift shop. A sportscaster's report on some major off-season football trades on her former network had lured her into a trance.

"Hey, you," Emmanuel said, sliding onto the vacant bar stool next to her. "I saw what went down between you and that lowlife punk, Abernathy. I wanted to save you, but I got tied up."

"I'm a big girl. I can take care of myself. I've handled butt naked defensive linesmen bigger, stronger, and tougher than Congressman Abernathy in NFL locker rooms. He just caught me off my game, hiding behind his title and expensive tuxedo. I guess anybody can serve in congress, huh?" Jazz chuckled softly.

"I guess so. I've been there almost a decade."

"But *you're* not like Jared Abernathy or some of the other ones I've come in contact with. Not once over the past two weeks have you treated me like a piece of meat."

"What did that thug say to you?"

"It doesn't matter." Jazz waved her hand, dismissing the subject. "Don't you think you should be heading back to the party? You're in the middle of a hotly contested re-election campaign. There are thousands of dollars in donations in that ballroom. You better go get some of it."

"I'd rather stay here with you."

Jazz licked her lips seemingly self-consciously and studied her wine glass. Emmanuel hadn't intended to make her uncomfortable or nervous. He simply wanted to spend some time with her alone. He looked forward to their one-on-one conversations. They provided him the perfect opportunity to drink in her beauty and pleasant personality.

"I've been your ball and chain for two weeks. You should be tired of spending time with me, Congressman."

"Only a mentally challenged man would grow tired of spending time with a woman as fine as you. Besides, all the hours we've spent together were for the documentary. It was *work*. Tonight it's all about pleasure. You've been picking my brain to learn everything you can about me. I want to get to know you better, Ms. Dupree."

"What exactly would you like to know about me?"

"*Everything.*"

Chapter Four

Tyrell typed the last few notes on his electronic tablet and stood. "Is that everything?" he asked Emmanuel.

"Yeah, I think that covers it for today. Tell everyone I'll be unavailable for the next hour or so. I need to finalize my speech before Ms. Dupree arrives."

Tyrell gave his uncle a knowing smile.

"What's so funny?"

"You like her."

"Why wouldn't I like her? She's nice, very professional, and—"

"Fine as hell and very sexy too."

"That's true, but Jazz Dupree doesn't date public figures, Tyrell."

"Really? According to my research, she was once engaged to Super Bowl MVP, Mario 'The Blaze' Thomas. That dude is the most popular running back in the NFL. He's the Dallas Stars' franchise player."

"I had no idea. She must've met him while she was a sports reporter. It doesn't matter. Ms. Dupree has made it perfectly clear that she will *never* date a man she has interviewed or intends to interview one day. And because she works for the largest black-owned television network in the country, most of her subjects are celebrities. So no athletes, entertainers, or *politicians* will ever get any love from her. That includes your uncle."

"Well, *I'm* not a public figure."

Emmanuel frowned and pointed his index finger stiffly at Tyrell. "Don't even think about it. Jazz Dupree is off-limits to you."

"Why is that, Unc? She's single and closer to my age than yours. Sources tell me she's only thirty-two. I'm thirty."

"I don't care," Emmanuel growled.

Tyrell continued his spiel, adding, "I love jazz music. She loves jazz music too because her mother, who died just days before her tenth birthday, was a *jazz* singer. That's why her parents named her Jazzlynn. She hates the name, so she shortened it to just Jazz."

"That's not true. Ms. Dupree loves the name her mother gave her. She only hates the last part of it because she blames her father, a jazz pianist, for her mother's death. His name was Lynn Dupree, and he introduced his wife, Inez, to heroin. Sadly, she died of a drug overdose in Paris at the height of her career. Mr. Dupree died years later from an addiction-related condition."

"*Wow*! Who told you that, Uncle Manny?"

"Ms. Dupree did."

Jazz had shared those very personal and painful tidbits about her life with Emmanuel that evening in the hotel bistro. She'd been quite candid about other things as well. Emmanuel had had a wonderful time listening to Jazz's alluring voice as she spoke openly about her childhood and rowdy college days. Her maternal grandparents, who raised her in Jacksonville, Florida, had encouraged her to pursue a career in broadcast journalism. They'd discovered her golden speaking voice at a very early age and they knew right away that the whole world needed to hear it. Emmanuel and Jazz had shared a hearty laugh when she'd recalled her first live television interview as a young intern from Florida A and M University. It was a hot boiling mess, or so she'd claimed. But Jazz had come a long way since then, having landed a dream contract with a major sports network as a NFL correspondent. Then she hit the jackpot when she was selected over hundreds of others to join Black Diamond's reporting team.

In Emmanuel's eyes, Jazz was a very successful and accomplished woman with good looks and a magnetic personality. He'd told her as much that evening while they enjoyed cocktails. That's when she crushed his ego, informing him that he and no other man living in the limelight had a snowball's chance in hell to date her. Even now, Emmanuel still felt the sting from Jazz's words as he tried to polish up the speech he was scheduled to deliver later that day. He was somewhat distracted too because of the bombshell Tyrell had dropped on him before he left his office. Of all the things Jazz had shared with him in the hotel bistro, she'd never mentioned that she had been engaged before. In fact, other than laying down her rule regarding dating high famous men, she'd kept a tight lip about her love life. Suddenly, the nosy bug bit the congressman. He wanted to know why Jazz hadn't become the wife of football star Mario 'The Blaze' Thomas. He was also curious about her present dating situation. She had told Emmanuel that she was very much single, but she hadn't explained why. His interest in Jazz instantly rose to another level. He wouldn't be satisfied until he learned *everything* about her.

*****

Gigi sucked her teeth and rolled her eyes to the ceiling in disgust. She'd enjoyed Emmanuel's fundraiser speech. The brother was charismatic to a fault, and he looked more delicious than a slice of double chocolate cake in a brown five-button suit. The food had been superb and the drinks too. Some of Washington's political heavyweights were in attendance, so Gigi was having a great time. But her jolly mood took a nosedive when she noticed how affectionate and attentive Emmanuel was toward Jazz. He kept her close by him at all times during the event as if she were his companion instead of a reporter covering him for an assignment. Something about the way the congressman looked at Jazz with his sexy brown eyes gave Gigi the impression that he was attracted to her. He was guiding her around the room with his hand in the small of her back while he greeted his guests. Gigi didn't miss the lazy smiles Emmanuel flashed at Jazz whenever he introduced her to one of his VIP supporters. He couldn't keep his hands off of her. The subtle touches to her shoulder and hand while they whispered in each other's ears made Gigi's blood boil. All of Emmanuel's warm gestures toward Jazz ticked her off. She was jealous because he had never treated *her* that way.

Sure, they had shared some hot, juicy, toe-curling kisses in the past. And Gigi would never forget the night that Emmanuel had *finally* melted under her feminine heat. It had taken her more than six months to get him in her bed, but it was well worth her patient efforts. Just thinking back on that rainy night caused Gigi's juices to flow. She actually squirmed in her seat, lusting. Visions of her and Emmanuel sipping Cristal at a Congressional Black Caucus function almost nine years ago drifted slowly through her memory. She had asked him for a ride home, and when he agreed to oblige her, she began plotting her sexual shakedown. Her hardest task was getting Emmanuel inside her condo. He had declined her offer for him to join her for a night cap three times on the drive to her place, explaining that he had reached his alcohol limit for the night. But Mother Nature had Gigi's back. By the time they reached her spot in Silver Springs, Maryland, the weather had grown extremely severe. The windshield wipers on Emmanuel's black Jaguar XKR-S Coupe could barely handle the torrential rain. The wind was blowing so hard that it rocked the car from side to side. With limited visibility and lightning crackling ferociously across the sky, it only made sense to go inside and wait out the storm.

Both Gigi and Emmanuel got soaking wet when they made a swift dart through the heavy downpour to her front door. Once they were inside, he removed his drenched tuxedo jacket, dress shirt, and tie. She excused herself to her bedroom where she was *supposed* to have exchanged her wet red evening gown for something more comfortable. Emmanuel hadn't expected that something more comfortable would be her birthday suit, but it was all a part of Gigi's scheme. The congressman couldn't resist her. He was a thoroughbred brother with hot blood pumping like lava through his veins. And standing before him was a gorgeous enticing woman as naked as Eve in the Garden of Eden. But what she offered him was much more tempting than any apple. Like ice cream on a hot stove, Emmanuel was weak, mushy, and of no good use. He became a victim of Gigi Perdue's sex trap just as she had hoped. That single night of raw, wild, unabashed passion was the highlight of her life, and she would give her next paycheck for a second round. She had been on a quest to get another piece of Emmanuel ever since then, but he had told her several times that in no uncertain terms would it ever happen again.

Nevertheless, Gigi had remained hopeful about having her way with the congressman again, and even possibly capturing his heart someday. But now watching him stroll coolly around the room, as proud as an African tribal chief with Jazz at his side, she wasn't so sure anymore. Emmanuel Day wanted that woman. Gigi's feminine instincts confirmed it. And if he whipped out his charm on Jazz like he had done on her nine years ago, he would reel her in without any resistance. He would make her forget all about her vow against dating rich and powerful men. Emmanuel had the skills to make any woman forget her name. Gigi could testify to that sure enough. She tucked that thought in the back of her mind for the time being, because there was no way in hell that she would allow Jazz to snatch Emmanuel out of her reach.

Chapter Five

Emmanuel held the spoonful of spicy homemade chili before Jazz's pouty lips. "Taste it. Go ahead. I dare you."

She made the ugliest face he had ever seen. But even with her eyes crossed, her nose wrinkled, and her lips twisted, she still looked incredible. And she smelled like heaven. The flowery scent of her perfume was wickedly intoxicating. Emmanuel had never smelled that particular fragrance before he met Jazz. He found it amazing how she made a simple pair of black slacks and a crisp white blouse look like an outfit suitable for a runway in Paris. Her svelte body was one of God's most magnificent creations. It was perfect, and Emmanuel would never do anything to cause it harm. The chili he was daring Jazz to taste was a little peppery, but he was sure she could handle it. He moved the spoon closer to her mouth, urging her once again.

"I don't tolerate spicy food well," Jazz whined like a little girl.

"It's not *that* hot. You helped me prepare it. I let you chop up the peppers so you could control the spice level. You only added a few, plus a small amount of the cayenne seasoning. I've tasted already it, woman. The kick is mild at the most."

Jazz closed her eyes and parted her lips reluctantly. Emmanuel eased the spoon inside her mouth and watched her facial expression closely. He was waiting for her reaction. They'd prepared dinner together at his home located in an exclusive suburban community right outside of the District. A camera crew had filmed the activity as a part of the documentary. The network wanted to capture a more up close and personal glimpse inside the life of the congressman in his bachelor pad. Although he had a fulltime housekeeper, he prepared his own meals every once in a while, using some of his mother's down home recipes. With Jazz's assistance, Emmanuel had shown off his culinary skills as he answered a series of questions about his private life away from Capitol Hill.

"Mmm…it's good," Jazz admitted, smiling.

"I told you." Emmanuel got up from his seat at the table. "I'll fix you a bowl and pour us a couple of glasses of wine."

"Oh, no, let me," Jazz insisted, shaking her head. "You cooked with very little help from me. I was too busy getting all up in your business. By the way, thanks for being so candid. I know you weren't prepared for some of those questions, but I wanted candid unrehearsed answers. The audience will appreciate the natural flow of our conversation. You delivered. Thank you."

Emmanuel nodded his head as he watched Jazz move around his kitchen like she owned the place. "I aim to please. I want my constituents to know that I'm a *man* first and then a member of congress. My life isn't much different from any other man's. I'm crazy about my mother. We speak every day on the phone. My father is my hero. I argue with my siblings about silly stuff all the time. There is absolutely nothing that I wouldn't do within reason for my three nieces and two nephews. And my golf game is nothing to brag about."

"And you're a hard-nosed bachelor who is too indulged in his career to settle down," Jazz added smoothly, as she returned to the table with a glass of chardonnay in each hand. She placed them on the table and went to the stove to fill a bowl with chili before she reclaimed her seat across from Emmanuel.

"I don't remember saying that. You asked me why I'm still a bachelor at the age of forty-two. I told you that my career as a politician slash attorney has not allowed me the time to find Mrs. Right yet. I'll admit that I haven't put up much of a search for a wife. Call me a foolish romantic, but I believe God will drop her right into my arms. In fact, He may already have."

Emmanuel was amused by Jazz's sudden interest in the spicy chili and wine, than the conversation that she had initiated. He had purposely put her in the hot seat, and she was now burning in the flames. He'd flipped the script on Jazz. When she deflected, it was obvious that she no longer wanted to discuss his bachelorhood, because it had opened the door to her life as a single working woman. Emmanuel had expressed a personal interest in her a few nights ago. They had met at his office to review a stack of photos that were taken for the documentary. The atmosphere was laid back, so Emmanuel took a very direct approach. He'd asked Jazz out on an official date for the day *after* his election, which would also be the end of their working relationship. He wanted her to trust him to be the first, and possibly the only, public figure she would allow into her private world since her broken engagement. The invitation was still in the air, because Jazz hadn't given Emmanuel an answer yet. She'd requested some time to think it over. Apparently, she was still processing her decision.

*****

Jazz was going *through*. Emmanuel was in Atlanta for two days stomping on the campaign trail. He had invited her to join him on the short trip, but she'd declined. She was afraid to be alone with him in certain nonpublic settings. At least at his office Tyrell was usually someplace close by. His nephew's presence gave Jazz a sense of security. Dining alone with Emmanuel at five-star restaurants didn't bother her either. She actually looked forward to those intimate moments. But sharing the small compartment of a private jet with him, or sleeping in the guest bedroom at his suburban Atlanta home would put her directly in the path of temptation. The dynamic between them had shifted drastically. Jazz had become addicted the congressman's masculine magic. God knew she hadn't meant to get hooked, but the brother's swagger, charisma, and irresistible good looks had totally depleted her resistance. Emmanuel had more charm and sex appeal than an entire army of men. He was smooth, confident, and mysterious—a superior gentleman. And his smile was lethal. It killed Jazz's ability to think rationally every time he flashed it. Therefore, for the sake of her sanity, she believed she had made the right decision by remaining in Washington while Emmanuel flew down to Atlanta.

Unfortunately, now that he was gone, Jazz was missing him terribly. Her heartbeat quickened every time her phone rang, hoping it was him. Emmanuel had called her when he'd reached his law firm earlier. They'd spoken briefly. He promised to call her after a meeting at one of his congressional field offices later that evening, and she was anxiously waiting to hear the silky tone of his voice. In the meantime, Jazz had watered all her plants, thoroughly cleaned her condo from top to bottom, and held a long conversation with her grandparents. Now she was watching edited footage of Emmanuel's activities over the past few weeks. The first portion of the DVD included snippets of their various one-on-one conversations at his congressional office and other locations. There was also a clip from his speech at the fundraiser. Jazz particularly liked scenes they had captured of Emmanuel arguing in committee meetings. The congressman was overly passionate about fair treatment of young black males in the criminal justice system. He believed they often received harsher punishments than their white counterparts for committing the same crimes.

The next section of footage gave Jazz tummy bubbles. She and Emmanuel were in his kitchen preparing chili and chatting it up. The conversation about his family back home in Metro Atlanta was carefree. He and Jazz appeared to be a pair of really close friends discussing the very personal details of his life. They were relaxed and comfortable with each other. The chemistry between them was fogging up the television screen. It was undeniable.

Jazz held her breath when Emmanuel paused on the footage, looking deeply into her eyes after she had inquired about his love life. The sparkle in his gaze made her shiver. Jazz wanted him. She hated herself for feeling the way that she did, but she couldn't help it. Her desire to have Emmanuel Day went against her principles and the commitment she'd made to herself after Mario broke her heart. Brothers of means and popularity were *dangerous*. They walked around with a sense of entitlement. Women were like toys to most of them, especially the ballers. Jazz didn't want to be hurt or taken for granted ever again. But if she were to allow Emmanuel into her world, giving him access to her heart and body, she'd risk the possibility of becoming a victim of love a second time.

Matters of the heart were risky. Jazz knew that better than anyone. She had gambled once, by getting involved with a football star against her better judgment. But like Emmanuel, Mario Thomas was fascinating and super attractive. He wooed her and treated her like a queen, trying his best to win her affections. After weeks of rejecting his repeated come-ons, Jazz finally let her guard down and they became an item. Their relationship was a hot and steamy one from the very beginning. It was snatched right off the pages of a modern-day fairytale. They were a power couple in the sports world. Life was good. The Super Bowl MVP went in for the kill when he took his lady home to meet his parents in Boston after romancing her consistently for just eight months. Mario popped the question at a huge family dinner and gave Jazz a ten carat canary diamond engagement ring to seal the deal. Of course, she agreed to marry the fastest running back in the NFL and started planning the wedding of the century. Jazz was so happy to have finally found true love. The future Mrs. Mario Thomas was counting down the days until her grand stroll down a snowy white beach aisle.

Sadly and unexpectedly, Jazz's world got turned upside down before her big day arrived. It was a day she would never forget.

Mario padded toward the foyer on bare feet after the bell's third chime. He and Jazz reached the massive oak wood and beveled glass door at the same time. She wiped her damp hands on the bottom of her apron and watched her man open the door for their unannounced visitor.

"Are you Mario Thomas, sir?"

"Yeah, I'm The Blaze. Who are you?"

The extremely tall gentleman dressed in a dark suit shoved a brown legal envelope in Mario's direction, and apparently, on instinct the popular baller reached out and grabbed it. "You've been served," the mystery man announced before he turned and walked away.

"What is it, sweetie?" Jazz asked, peering around his muscular build as he tore into the envelope. Her eyes were locked on the documents as he removed them. The heading of the first page nearly caused her heart to stop beating. "Oh, my God...it's...it's a paternity suit!"

"This is bullshit! It's not true, Jazz. I haven't been with another woman since we've been together. You've got to believe me, baby. It's not true."

It was indeed true, and Jazz found out how painfully so two weeks later in a courtroom when a judge revealed DNA results, declaring Mario the biological father of a baby girl. He had lied about his weekend affair with a Dallas Star cheerleader consistently up until his court appearance, and Jazz had believed him with all her heart. After the cold hard facts slapped her in the face, she felt like such a fool. She ended her relationship with Mario immediately and called off their elaborate Aruba ocean-side wedding ten days before they were scheduled to fly to the island. Two hundred of their family members and closest friends felt the sting as well, especially Jazz's grandmother who had never liked Mario in the first place.

Jazz was so devastated after the breakup that she went into seclusion before finally quitting her job and returning home to Jacksonville to regroup. The comforting care of her grandparents gave her the strength and determination to make a fresh new start. After a few months, Jazz began distributing her résumé and audition tapes all over the country. It didn't take long for her to generate a response, and her phone started ringing off the hook. Several networks and television stations flew her to their cities for interviews. Out of all of the offers she received, Black Diamond seemed to be the perfect fit. Jazz bid Florida farewell and headed for the nation's capital, leaving the pain of her past far behind her.

Chapter Six

"Congressman Day, what are you doing here?" Jazz left her desk and met him in the middle of her office. "I didn't expect to see you until Monday afternoon."

Emmanuel smiled. "I needed to see you *today*."

The man made her weak, and set off warm vibrations that snaked all over Jazz's body. His very presence caused her to dream about things she hadn't experienced in almost eight years. Jazz had concentrated so much on protecting her heart from getting hurt again that she had neglected the needs of her flesh. *Damn, I want this man!* The wanton woman within shouted out. Jazz swallowed those words and asked a simple question. "What do you need to see me about?"

"Have dinner with me."

"I...I can't. My friend, Ramone, is having a hair show this evening. He expects me to be there."

"Where is the show? I'll pick you up afterwards. I need to see you tonight and I won't take no for an answer. I can't. Give me the address to where you'll be."

"Come to the Rainbow Theatre around nine o'clock."

*****

Gigi slammed her office door shut and pressed her back against it. She was pissed. She hadn't expected that when Sierra, one of the secretaries downstairs, had called to alert her that Emmanuel was in the building, that it would be to see *Jazz*. Upon hearing that he was there, Gigi had quickly sprayed a little bit of perfume behind her ears and squeezed a few drops of Binaca on her tongue. She was about to step out of her office to track Emmanuel down when she saw him walking up the hallway. He stopped directly in front of Jazz's office, knocked once, and entered. He was careful to close the door behind him apparently to ensure their privacy. Reeling from the shock of the scene, Gigi nearly hit the floor. She saw blood red. Obviously, Jazz and the congressman's working relationship had evolved into a more personal one. Gigi had expected it to happen eventually. She had witnessed the sparks flying back and forth between the two of them firsthand. But she had no idea that Emmanuel would work his magic on Jazz so quickly. He must've broken her off real proper. The former sports chick had sworn off famous men for life, but evidently, she had reneged on that nonsense. Clearly, she and Emmanuel had spent more time playing than working. Gigi walked to her desk and picked up the phone. She dialed the production department.

"This is Ms. Perdue. Connect me with Adams." She blew out an impatient breath. "I'll hold, but not for long. Tell him it's *me*. Hurry up!"

Gigi peered out her window as she waited for her little boy toy to come on the line. From time to time she would call on the young production assistant to do her dirty work. Rashad Adams was always willing to snoop around the network and feed Gigi information about her colleagues in exchange for a hot sexual treat. This would be the first time she'd ever asked the young handsome stud to spy on Jazz. Up until now, the little prim and proper reporter from the Sunshine State had never reached Gigi's radar. But now that she had stolen her assignment *and* her dream man, she considered Jazz as more than her arch rival. She was a major pain in the ass.

"Set up a viewing room for me," Gigi barked as soon as Adams answered the phone. "I want to see all of the edited material from Jazz Dupree's project with Congressman Day. I'm curious about what they've done so far."

*****

Ramone snatched a lavender handkerchief from his breast pocket and wiped his shiny bald head. Then he waved it in the air dramatically, fanning himself as if he were having a hot flash. "A tall glass of chocolate milk just walked in the room. Help me, Jesus! I'm about to faint."

The fine hairs on the back of Jazz's neck bristled. A sudden chill followed, which caused her to shiver. She knew without turning around that the man Ramone was having a fit over was Emmanuel. It had to be him. Ramone was crazy and sensational, and his description was way over the top, but it fit the congressman like a glove. Jazz's belly flip flopped when Emmanuel's rich baritone voice whispered her name. He touched her left shoulder, and her knees buckled.

Jazz regained her composure and turned around slowly to face him. "You're early."

"If you're not finished here, I'll wait."

"I'm Ramone Sanchez, Jazz's best friend," he interrupted with his hand reaching for Emmanuel's. "I have followed your career since the day you landed on Capitol Hill. You're a shot caller. I admire your political game."

"Thank you, Mr. Sanchez," Emmanuel said, shaking his hand. "I'm here to serve the people of my district." He released his grip on Ramone's hand and looked at Jazz. "Are you ready? Or should I hang around for a while?"

"I need to—"

"She's ready," Ramone interrupted *again*. "Take her. She's all yours."

Jazz smiled at her BFF, but she really wanted to punch him in the face for his selective lingo. There were no secrets between them. Ramone was aware of Jazz's deep crush on Emmanuel. If a sistah couldn't confide in her closest buddy, who the hell could she confide in? Jazz had told Ramone all about the chemistry between her and the congressman. He knew she'd had dreams about him kissing her passionately and making love to her all night long. Those dreams had snatched Jazz from her sleep every night that particular week. She was very much attracted to Emmanuel, but she feared what that meant. Ramone had encouraged Jazz to take the man up on his proposal to go out on a date with him the day after his election. She had been considering it with great caution, but she still hadn't made up her mind yet. She was so confused, and Emmanuel's presence only complicated the situation.

A soft pat on the back from Ramone shook Jazz from her jumbled thoughts. He handed her the designer purse he'd given her last Christmas and pecked her on the cheek.

"Have a good time, sweetie. Call me tomorrow."

"Okay."

Emmanuel took hold of Jazz's hand and led her out of the theater. They walked to the parking lot in complete silence. She had no idea where they were going or why he'd insisted on seeing her tonight. Once they reached the car, Emmanuel made sure Jazz was comfortable and secure in her seat. He walked around to the driver's side and got inside.

"Why are you nervous?" Emmanuel asked after he started his engine. "You've been alone with me several times before tonight. What have I said or done to frighten you all of a sudden?"

"I'm not afraid of you, Congressman Day."

Emmanuel laughed. "That's not what your body language says. Your hand was trembling when I held it. I swear I heard your heart beating while we were walking to the car. You're on edge, Ms. Dupree. Why is that?"

I'm afraid that I'll fall in love with you and you'll break my heart, was on the tip of Jazz's tongue, but she refused to let it spill out. Instead, she cleared her throat and whispered, "I am not afraid of you or any other man. It's just that I'm curious about why you wanted to see me tonight. That's all."

"You'll find out soon enough."

Chapter Seven

Jazz closed her eyes and leaned back in her seat. She tried to relax as Emmanuel guided his luxury car toward the northwest section of D.C. He leaned over and turned on the stereo, and to Jazz's surprise, Earl Klugh was doing his thing as only he could. He was one of her favorite jazz musicians of all time. She had interviewed Mr. Klugh at least three times for Black Diamond. He was a very interesting man and an incredible guitarist and composer. Ramone had surprised Jazz for her birthday a few years ago by taking her to a concert featuring Earl Klugh and George Duke. It was an amazing night that she would never forget.

"We're here," Emmanuel announced twenty minutes later. He killed the engine and looked at Jazz.

She sat up and stared back at him. Nothing in his eyes gave her any clue as to why she was sitting in his car on a Friday night without an interview outline in her hand. Jazz tore her eyes away from his and checked out their location. Emmanuel's Jaguar was parked in front of Pookie's Pool Hall and Grill. Jazz was totally confused.

"You wanted me to come and shoot pool with you? Are you serious, Congressman?"

Emmanuel exited his car without a word. He removed his beige suit coat and paisley print power tie and tossed them on the back seat. Then he walked around to open Jazz's door and helped her out.

"This is a spot where I come to escape the political scene and just chill. Very few people who hang out here know who I am. So I don't have to talk about the economy or gun control or national security. I'm a regular dude here. My favorite waitress, Betty Jo, knows me as Manny, and she serves me my choice of beer and club sandwich just the way I like it. I don't even have to place an order. At Pookie's I get the most privacy I'll ever enjoy in a public place in Washington, D.C."

Jazz and Emmanuel walked hand in hand into the dark pool hall. They met a moderate size crowd of people scattered about the place. The bar stools around the circular counter were all filled with patrons sipping spirits and watching a professional women's basketball game on a big screen television. Most of the booths and tables in the dining area were occupied. The aroma of greasy food lingered in the air. Everyone seemed to be enjoying their Friday night at the down home establishment. Jazz peeped out a few card games in progress. Each of the five pool tables was surrounded by competitors and onlookers. Jazz smiled at all the excitement and trash talk buzzing around them.

"What's up, Manny?" A light skin, full-figure woman in tight jeans approached them. The tag attached to her red apron said her name was Betty Jo.

"Hey sweetheart," Emmanuel said before his kissed her plump cheek. "I've missed you."

"I've missed you too and your *big tips*." She belted out a raspy laugh from deep within her gut. Then she got serious and checked out Jazz from her curly afro down to her wedge heel Trojan sandals. "Who do you have with you, Manny? She reminds me of that chick from BDT."

She offered the woman her hand in a friendly shake. "My name is Jazz. It's nice to meet you, Betty Jo."

Betty Jo clapped her beefy hands together. "I knew it! I knew it!" she exclaimed excitedly, ignoring Jazz's hand and grabbing her into a bear hug. "You *are* that reporter from Black Diamond. Welcome to Pookie's, honey! Let me find y'all a table!"

Emmanuel and Jazz followed Betty Jo to a booth in the back corner of the room. She handed them menus and took their drink orders. "I'll be back with a glass of chardonnay for the lady and a Corona for the gentleman," she promised before she left them alone.

"I thought bringing you here was a better idea than inviting you to my house," Emmanuel explained. "I didn't want to invade your privacy at your place either. This is a neutral location."

"For what?"

"I need an answer to my proposal, Ms. Dupree. I've been patient and understanding long enough. All of the suspense is driving me crazy. It's an annoying distraction. How can a brother concentrate on a campaign with uncertainty hanging over his head like a dark cloud? Tell me right now. Are you going to let me get to know you on a personal level after my primary election or not?"

Emmanuel's boldness slapped Jazz in the face. Once again, he had pushed her into the spotlight. Only this time, she had no way to escape or hide. Time was up. The man deserved an answer, but Jazz hadn't made a decision yet. "I don't know," she mumbled, lowering her eyes to the table between them.

"Why are you willing to deny yourself the pleasure of spending time with a man you're obviously attracted to?"

"Who said I was attracted to you?" Jazz snapped. Emmanuel's cockiness had ticked her off.

He laughed. "*I* did. You're attracted to me just as much as I'm attracted to you. I bet I interrupt your sleep every night the same way you interrupt mine. You daydream about me too. I know you do. I'm not ashamed to admit that you're constantly on my mind throughout the day. There is something magnetic between us, and neither of us can truthfully deny it. So stop this madness, Ms. Dupree."

"I have no idea what you're talking about."

"Really?" Emmanuel's eyes held Jazz prisoner for a brief moment before she looked away. "If I had taken you to my house instead of this pool hall, you know as well as I do that the heat between us would've set off smoke detectors all over the District, Maryland, and Virginia."

"Stop it, Congressman Day," Jazz hissed, narrowing her eyes. She patted her chest with an open palm and panted for her next breath. "I don't like this side of you. Where is the gentleman I've been spending time with for the past few weeks? Or was it all just an *act* for the camera?"

"That was Congressman Emmanuel Marcus Day, baby. If you would stop playing games, I could introduce you to Manny, the *man*. Hell, he'll be whomever or whatever you want him to be. And he will do anything it takes to please you."

*****

"Ugh!" Jazz yelled in frustration.

Ramone stifled a laugh and watched his girlfriend burn a path on the rug in front of his styling station. Jazz had arrived at his salon before he did early Saturday morning. It was only minutes after seven, and Ramone's first client wasn't due until eight o'clock. Jazz was in a foul mood over her meeting with Emmanuel last night. His blunt speech about her attraction to him had knocked her off of her game.

She hadn't seen it coming and she was extremely annoyed over it. Ramone was quite amused by the whole situation.

"Girl, sit down! I'm getting tired of watching you waste so much energy over nothing. The man told you the truth. You want him, and he wants you. What's the problem, darling?"

"I am *attracted* to him, Ramone. That does not mean that I want to sleep with him."

"You've thought about it," he reminded Jazz. "And you've had some spicy and sweaty dreams about it too."

"It doesn't matter. Emmanuel Day had no right to speak to me that way last night. It was very disrespectful and unprofessional. I don't think I can work with him any longer. I'm going to ask Mr. McConnell to assign another reporter to complete my project. Gigi would be more than happy to step in."

Ramone stopped spinning in his styling chair. "Please don't do that, Jazz. You are a *professional*. The documentary is a major production that every reporter at your network was dying to be a part of. They all wanted the opportunity that McConnell entrusted to you. Don't blow it. Yes, the congressman might've been a little bit too straightforward with you, but he was honest."

"I know, but why did he have to throw it up in my face like an arrogant jackass?"

Ramone got up and wrapped Jazz in his arms. "There *is* something going on between you two beyond a shadow of a doubt. You owe the man an answer. How long did you expect him to wait? Maybe he took a razor sharp approach to help you make up your mind."

"I can't risk it, Ramone," Jazz whispered, shaking her head. "He might break my heart."

"You can't afford *not* to take the risk. That fine hunk of a congressman might just be the one to make your heart sing. You owe it to yourself to find out one way or the other. For some of us, love only calls *once*. Others are lucky enough to get a second shot. No matter what, though, when love calls, you better answer, girl. Give the brother a chance. He may be worth it."

Chapter Eight

On the flight to Atlanta for the big debate, Jazz kept her distance from Emmanuel aboard the private plane. She sat reading the latest edition of Ebony magazine surrounded by the camera crew from Black Diamond. Everyone seemed hyped about the debate between Emmanuel and his opponent, State Senator Divinity Davis. Jazz was trying her best to downplay it, telling herself that she was just a reporter tagging along for her job. Her attempt at self-hypnosis wasn't working out so well, because every time she caught Emmanuel staring at her, the truth struck her like lightning. Although she was still upset with him for the cockiness he'd displayed at the pool hall, Jazz wanted to be wherever Emmanuel was. Somehow the very essence of the man had seeped into her pores and penetrated her veins. He was in her blood, making his way to her heart.

Ramone had forced Jazz to admit the truth before she left his salon Saturday morning. Everything Emmanuel had said to her was unquestionably on point. Albeit spiced with arrogance and great assumption, it was a reality that Jazz needed to come to grips with. For the first time since she had called off her wedding to Mario, she had come face to face with a man who rang her bell. Everything about Emmanuel Day sent her womanly senses off the chart. It wasn't just a physical attraction either. The way he carried himself with confidence, coolness, and control was a complete intellectual turn on. His voice and articulation of words demanded any woman's attention. Jazz was drawn to Emmanuel like a tissue to tears, and it was driving her insane every waking minute of the day. And it only got worse at night when she was all alone in her cold lonely bed with thoughts of him keeping her awake, denying her much needed sleep.

Jazz wanted to explore the possibilities of what could happen between her and Emmanuel. Pride and fear had kept her from accepting his proposal. She now realized she had acted like a fool Friday night when she demanded that he take her home even before Betty Jo had served them their drinks. Emmanuel had boldly confessed his interest in Jazz and attempted to make her take ownership of her attraction to him. No crime had been committed. The take-charge congressman had simply acknowledged that there was a mutual connection between them, and he'd suggested that they tap into it.

As soon as the debate was over, Jazz planned to apologize to Emmanuel for her craziness at the pool hall. Then she was going to accept his invitation to go out on a date with him the day after his election.

*****

The audience erupted with applause when the announcer introduced Emmanuel. He appeared on the stage decked out in a sharp navy blue five-button suit. As the incumbent, who had represented his congressional district for nearly a decade, Emmanuel was quite popular. And as a smooth and handsome bachelor with lots of power, he had a huge female following. His smile was infectious. He waved several times to the crowd and the applause swelled. A few whistles and shouts mixed in with sounds of voices mumbling throughout the gym. After he took his place behind the podium on the left side of the stage, the announcer introduced State Senator Divinity Davis. She was a well-respected politician from East Point, Georgia hoping to replace Emmanuel on Capitol Hill. According to the polls, she was currently running fifteen percentage points behind him.

Ms. Davis was attractive and shapely. She was a petite sistah with a cinnamon complexion and long, black, curly hair. Her gray pinstripe suit hugged her hourglass figure snuggly. The skirt was too short, exposing more of her thighs than one would consider tasteful. Emmanuel took note of it as he walked toward the middle of the stage to greet the senator. He took her by the hand.

"After I kick your butt in this debate, maybe you and I could hook up and go for a wild ride under the sheets for old times' sake. I used to really put it on you back in the day."

Emmanuel was stunned by Divinity's brazenness, but he didn't show it. He gripped her hand firmly and smiled for the cameras. "I'll pass on your offer, Senator Davis. I'm cool in that department. And as far as this debate goes, you might win it, but you won't win the election."

"Are you sure about that, Manny?"

"I'd bet my firstborn on it. Short skirts and bed hopping may help you win state senate races, but that type of behavior doesn't work in the big league, baby."

While the cameras flashed continuously, Emmanuel smiled one last time for the audience, before dropping Divinity's hand and winking at a group of his supporters waving his campaign signs. He did a graceful about face and returned to the podium. His eyes settled on Jazz sitting in the second row on the right side of the gym. He swallowed hard a few times. She was wearing the hell out of an orange jumpsuit. And the tangerine lipstick spread smoothly across her lips was teasing him to leap off the stage and kiss her into submission. Jazz's presence was required at the debate because of the contract Emmanuel had signed with Black Diamond to cover his primary re-election campaign. However, she was a major distraction that he had no use for at the moment. Their eyes met and locked for a brief moment. Emmanuel let his gaze drop to the stack of index cards covered with notes on top of the podium. He needed to stay focused on the task before him or Divinity would win the debate for real. He couldn't allow that to happen. Emmanuel took a few deep breaths and released them slowly. His eyes wandered over to Jazz one last time for good luck while the moderator explained the debate rules and format. Opening greetings came next. The stage was yielded to Divinity first as the challenger, which was political protocol. By the time she finished to a moderate response from the audience, Emmanuel was poised and prepared for battle.

*****

"Yo, Unc, Ms. Dupree would like a word with you."

Emmanuel looked up from his laptop screen to face Tyrell. He'd been responding to email messages since he took his seat on the plane. His debate performance had been phenomenal according to the audience's enthusiastic reaction as well as the post commentary from the media. Divinity had seemed flustered at times, but Emmanuel had shown her no mercy. He was surprised by her lack of knowledge about the president's healthcare reform bill and the exchange program's impact on the state of Georgia. That particular topic and national security, especially the United States' relationship with Iran and Afghanistan, had shaken Divinity up—*literally*. She had appeared clueless and frustrated. Unfortunately for her, Emmanuel and the audience had watched her unravel before their very eyes. Now congratulatory messages and financial pledges were coming in from everywhere. Emmanuel was skimming through some of them when Tyrell approached him with Jazz's request.

"Did she say what she wants to speak with me about?"

Tyrell shook his head. "No, she didn't. The only thing the lady said was she needed a brief word with the congressman tonight. Then she kindly asked me to arrange the meeting for her."

"When is my next scheduled appointment with Ms. Dupree?"

"Let me check," Tyrell mumbled, scrolling through his tablet. "She'll be with you most of the day Thursday. She and a camera crew will attend your special judicial committee meeting. There's a healthcare luncheon at noon, and you invited her to the Veteran's Administration ball for that evening."

"If Ms. Dupree can't wait until Thursday to speak with me, have her make an appointment to see me tomorrow or Wednesday. I'm busy tonight."

Chapter Nine

"He blew me off, Ramone! Can you believe him? He said I needed to make an *appointment* to see him. Who does he think he is?"

"Congressman Emmanuel Day, I suppose," Ramone answered sarcastically.

"He is an arrogant, self-absorbed, stuck up jack—"

"Mmm, mmm, and you want him. But you may have pushed him away. The man expressed an interest in you, sweetie. You strung him along for weeks without giving him an answer to his proposal. Then when he asked you to go out with him again to put a little fire under your ass, what did you do?"

Jazz flopped down on her bed with the phone wedged between her ear and shoulder. "I got upset and made him take me home."

"Correct."

"What should I do now?"

"Are you ready to explore your attraction to the man?"

"Yeah, I'm ready."

"Well, you need to put your big girl panties on and swallow your pride. Then you should call Tyrell and schedule an appointment to meet with the congressman as soon as possible."

Jazz checked the clock on her nightstand. "But it's two o'clock in the morning."

"So what? Call Tyrell, honey. Text him. Fax him. Just make the damn appointment. And when you come face to face with Congressman Day, tell him you would love to spend some private time with him. Make it clear that you want to take things nice and slow, but give him the green light on the romance."

*****

Gigi's eyes had grown blurry. She'd stayed up well into the night watching footage from Emmanuel's segment of the documentary. She hated to admit it, but Jazz was one hell of a journalist. Her approach to inquiry was subtle, natural, and sharp. She knew how to get the scoop without appearing pushy and desperate.

Then again, she and Emmanuel did have unbelievable chemistry. It made their interaction come across very personal like two good friends, or even *lovers*. Gigi couldn't help but wonder if they had been intimate during the course of their project. No doubt, there was something more than work going on between them. A blind man could see it.

A sound technician on the crew that had accompanied Jazz to several functions and interview sessions with Emmanuel reported to Gigi often. He'd told her that the congressman and reporter were quite cozy with one another. The entire crew believed they were having a fling because of their touchy-feely interaction. One night at a political dinner, Emmanuel fed Jazz crème brulee from his dessert plate. Then he dabbed crumbs from her lips with his white linen napkin as if it was something he did every day. The sound tech described the gesture as more intimate than foreplay.

At this point, it was a foregone conclusion. Emmanuel would never be Gigi's man. That one night of blazing, wild sex would have to last her a lifetime. She had finally wrapped her mind around the fact that the congressman simply did not want anything to do with her. But just because Gigi couldn't have him, it didn't necessarily mean that Jazz had a right to all of that chocolate masculinity either. *Oh hell no!* The little green monster inside of her was about to take over. Emmanuel could be with any other woman on the planet besides Jazz Dupree. She and Gigi were coworkers and often competitors for certain assignments. The walls inside Black Diamond's building had sharp ears. All of the gossipers would turn the situation into a soap opera. Plus Gigi would see Jazz all the time prancing around, smiling happily because of all the good loving Emmanuel would be giving her. She refused to be reminded on a daily basis that she had lost her dream man to some stuck-up reporter from alligator territory. That just wouldn't work. Gigi could live without Emmanuel, but she would make sure that Jazz lived without him too.

*****

"Ms. Dupree is here."

Emmanuel turned away from the beautiful view outside his office window. It was a pretty day in late July. He faced Tyrell, who was grinning from ear to ear. "Send her in." He loosened the knot in his teal and purple striped tie and sat down behind his desk.

Emmanuel was excited about seeing Jazz, but he turned his inner cool control all the way up and relaxed while he waited for her to enter the room. The familiar scent of her perfume greeted him first. Then the *woman* in all of her glory appeared and frazzled his five his senses, but in the most pleasant way possible. The sight of Jazz in a simple lavender knee-length sheath caused tightening in Emmanuel's loins. A vibrant floral print scarf tied neatly around her neck added flair to the outfit. She looked like a super model.

"Congressman Day, thank you so much for taking this meeting with me. I know how busy you are."

Emmanuel motioned with his hand to the pair of chairs facing his desk. "Please have a seat, Ms. Dupree." He'd been tempted to pat his thighs, inviting Jazz to rest her tight round ass on his lap, but his better judgment kicked in.

"Thank you again. I won't take up very much of your time. I'll get straight to the point. I'm sorry for the way I acted Friday night at the pool hall. It was very silly of me. Please accept my apology."

"Apology accepted."

"Great." Jazz licked her lips luscious and paused as if she were gathering her thoughts. "I would love to go out with you the day after your election victory. You were right. Something *has* sparked between us since we've been working on the documentary. It only makes sense for us to try to find out exactly what it is."

Emmanuel smiled. "I agree."

"I'd like for us to take it slow if you don't mind."

"Slow is my speed, Ms. Dupree. I'll be slow, gentle, and thorough. I'm a man who aims to please the woman he's involved with."

Emmanuel had turned up the heat on purpose. He watched Jazz go from cool and comfortable to warm and uneasy in a matter of seconds. All those weeks of waiting for her to accept the truth about her feelings for him had only heightened his desire for her. Now with the election only seven days away, Emmanuel had something else to look forward to besides a political victory. He was going to introduce Jazz to more romance and passion than she could handle.

Chapter Ten

"I have to find the perfect outfit for Congressman Day's victory party and a knockout dress for our first date. My goal is to look sexy but not slutty. I want to be fly but not over the top."

Ramone pulled a red cocktail dress from the rack and smoothed it across his long lanky body. "How do I look?"

"What size is it?"

"It's not for you, darling, it's for *me*." Ramone winked an eye and rotated his narrow hips. "I would look fierce in this at the masquerade ball in New York in October."

"Get serious. You're supposed to be helping *me*. I want to look hot and classy when I meet the congressman's family. I'm going to stay with his parents, you know."

"You're going to meet his mom and dad so soon, sweetie?"

"I will be introduced to them as Jazz Dupree, the reporter from Black Diamond Television who's covering their son's primary re-election campaign. No one will know that the congressman and I have the hots for each other."

"*Humph*, I've seen the way the man looks at you. His eyes heat you up like a firecracker, honey. His parents will know he wants you for sure."

Jazz didn't want to accept Ramone's prediction, but only a fool would dismiss it altogether. She removed the red dress from his grip and inspected it. "I hope you're wrong. I want Congressman Day to enjoy his big night with his family without any distractions from me. When the clock strikes midnight, things will evolve between us, but not a moment sooner."

"When are you two heading for the ATL?"

"We're leaving Saturday afternoon."

"You and the crew will be covering him all that time?"

Jazz shook her head. "He and I are flying to Atlanta alone on one of his wealthy supporter's private plane. The crew will join us early Tuesday morning, Election Day."

"Oh my."

"What does that supposed to mean?"

"Do you think you'll be able to keep your hands off of each other before midnight Wednesday morning with no camera crew to run interference?"

"Of course, we will. We're sticking to the plan, Ramone. Until the final vote is counted, we will keep a safe distance from each other. I will continue to call him Congressman Day, and he will refer to me as Ms. Dupree."

"And when the clock strikes midnight, he'll be all over you calling you baby, sugar pie, and sweet thang. I'm sure you'll be screaming *big papa*!" Ramone did a suggestive slow shimmy and then doubled over laughing.

Jazz rolled her eyes at him and stomped off in the direction of the dressing rooms. She heard Ramone's laughter behind her back. She wanted to turn around and snap his neck, but she knew it would be useless.

*****

"Has anyone seen Jazz this morning? There's something I need to ask her."

None of the members of the glam squad answered. It was six o'clock in the morning. And it appeared that no one was in a very talkative mood. The makeup artist continued stroking Gigi's eyelid with a unique shade of green shadow. All of the stylists were busy hanging new inventory on the clothing racks inside Black Diamond's wardrobe room.

Liza, one of the seamstresses for the network, walked over to Gigi. "She left for Atlanta yesterday. I had to alter a hot pink pantsuit for her before she took off. Her waist is so tiny I had to take in an inch and a half on both sides."

"That can't be true. The crew that's been recording Jazz's project is still here. I saw Russell and Saleem, the Muslim guy, on the elevator a few minutes ago."

"Well, all I know is Ms. Dupree and that good-looking congressman met me here yesterday to pick up the suit. They said they were on their way to the airport to catch a flight to Atlanta. I wished them safe travels." Liza walked away clueless that she had just caused Gigi's blood pressure to spike.

"Hurry up with my face, Tia! I have something important to take care of before I go on the air."

*****

Jazz woke up to the sweet-smelling combination of bacon cooking and freshly brewed coffee. The soothing sound of gospel music was floating through the air, filling her heart with joy. Retired attorney, Thaddeus Day, and his lovely wife of fifty years, Carol, had a fabulous home in Ellenwood, Georgia. They were generous hosts too. Jazz couldn't remember the last time she'd eaten so much mouth-watering soul food. At dinner the previous evening, she wolfed down more fried chicken, collard greens, and potato salad than she should have. She pigged out terribly, but she couldn't help herself. Ms. Carol and her housekeeper Mabel had put their feet in the meal. Jazz had even tried chitterlings for the first time ever and enjoyed them to her surprise. She became a little bit embarrassed when Emmanuel teased her about gobbling down two pieces of his mama's famous red velvet cake. He reminded her that there was a ten to fifteen pound increase on one's body weight when they appeared on a television screen. But unfortunately, the damage was already done.

A few taps on the door startled Jazz. She sat straight up in the queen size canopy bed. She pulled the snow white duvet comforter up to her neck. "Come in," she called out.

The door opened slowly, and in walked Christina, Emmanuel's older sister, with a bright smile on her face. Her even chocolate complexion was identical to her brother's. "Good morning girl. How did you sleep?"

"I slept like a drunk man. How are you this morning?"

"I'm fine," she responded. "Manny called a short while ago."

"Did he? I hope everything is alright."

"Don't worry. All is well. He wanted to make sure you were up and getting dressed for church. Our longtime pastor, Bishop Stinson, always makes a fuss over my brother whenever he's in town. And with just two days before the election, I know he's going to go way overboard this morning. All of the Days must be present and on time at Holy Word Christian Church today. That means *you* too, honey."

41

"I'm not a member of the Day family," Jazz clarified, throwing her legs over the side of the bed. "I'll be ready for church, though. I promise."

"You're not a member of our family *yet*."

"What do you mean by that, Christina?"

"I'm Manny's big sister. I used to bathe his little ashy behind. No one knows him better than me. Baby boy has a thing for you, and you know it. I can't recall any other woman ever making him smile and unwind the way you do."

"Our relationship is strictly professional. I swear."

"Keep telling yourself that," Christina shot back with laughter in her voice. "Breakfast is almost ready. Mabel's cheese grits and buttermilk biscuits are *righteous*."

*****

"I'm not down with it, Ms. Perdue. I'm a professional photographer for Black Diamond Television. Jackson Lee is nobody's spy nor snitch. When I get to Atlanta, I'm going to take pictures of Congressman Day's final moments on the campaign trail. That's it."

Gigi stepped closer to Jackson, leaving less than an inch of space between their bodies. She had him pinned against the wall in the network's photography studio. Her perky breasts were pressed against his lower chest. "I'll compensate you beyond your wildest imagination. It'll be well worth your time and effort."

Jackson frowned and pushed Gigi backwards. "My *fiancée* compensates me properly on a regular basis. She takes care of my every need. Do yourself a favor. Get a freaking life." He brushed past her on his way to the door.

"You must be *impotent*! No real man turns me down!"

"No, sweetheart, I'm more of a man than you can handle."

Gigi was livid. All she had asked Jackson to do was keep a close eye on Jazz and the congressman and report back to her. Her regular source was on another assignment in Los Angeles. Gigi needed a fresh set of eyes and ears on the situation down in the Georgia to report every move Emmanuel and Jazz made. Jackson would've been ideal, but he had chosen to be uncooperative. Gigi would have to find someone else to do her bidding.

Chapter Eleven

"Little brother, that's a mighty fine woman you brought home with you. If I were you, we'd be doing a hell of a lot more than working on some documentary."

"Well, that's all we're doing, Tyrone. Ask your son. He can tell you that Jazz Dupree and I are only associates and nothing more."

Tyrell looked at his father and uncle and smiled. The three of them had gathered in the den after Sunday dinner to watch an Atlanta Braves' baseball game. The family patriarch had joined his sons and grandson too, but he had fallen asleep in his favorite recliner. Mrs. Day, Christina, and Tyrone's wife, Nedra, were holding their weekly gossip session in the kitchen while the younger grandchildren played outside. Jazz was with the ladies, taking it all in.

"Is it true, son? Or is my baby brother joking?"

"He ain't lying. Uncle Manny and Ms. Dupree are not smashing, Dad. I can't understand why not, though."

"I respect her," Emmanuel snapped. "Jazz Dupree is a special kind of woman. She's a lady and she doesn't mix business with pleasure. I admire her for her professionalism. She's nothing like Maya."

Tyrell and Tyrone knew better than to push Emmanuel any further on the subject. The tone of his voice had sent out a clear warning that it wouldn't be wise to do so. The nature of his relationship with Jazz was obviously a sensitive issue for him. His ex-girlfriend and former colleague, Maya Durant, was too. Everyone in the Day clan was very aware of it. That's why her name was never mentioned among them. She was a painful part of Emmanuel's past. What Maya had done to him was unforgivable. Although she had claimed to be madly in love with Emmanuel, she'd used him and his status to advance her career. As a junior litigator at the Day Law Firm, the natural beauty from Glorieta, New Mexico had wheedled her way into Emmanuel's private world and eventually into his bed. By the time he ran for congress and snagged his seat on Capitol Hill, they were an item. Maya had stomped hard on the campaign trail to help her lover of two years fulfill his dream. But behind all of her hard work was a motive. Her primary goal was to become Mrs. Emmanuel Day, the wife of a powerful and well respected congressman. Such a union would have secured Maya's presidency of the National Association of Black Female Attorneys. She wanted that position more than anything, but she also had her eyes on a partnership in the Day Law Firm. Her wish list of perks was long, but she had no worries because her man was a member of the United States House of Representatives.

So while Emmanuel was kissing up to the senior members of congress, trying very much to learn the ropes on Capitol Hill, Maya was busy dropping his name all across the country. He was oblivious until Tyrell opened a letter from the credentials committee of NABFA, thanking the congressman for referring an extraordinary candidate for their consideration. The Ebony Esquires had sent a similar email a few weeks before, but Emmanuel and Tyrell had dismissed it as spam. Little did they know that Maya wanted to be a part of the prestigious organization's executive board. She had written her own letter of recommendation to the Ebony Esquires, pretending to be Emmanuel on his congressional letterhead. Then she'd had the audacity to top it off by forging his signature. The situation wouldn't have been a big deal if Maya had not padded the letter with lies. She had misled the Ebony Esquires by falsifying the number of years she had worked at the Day Law Firm and her position. She had stretched her years of employment from four years to six as well. Also in the letter, she'd stated that she was a senior litigator on the path to a full partnership with the firm. The most scandalous lie of all had caused Emmanuel great embarrassment. Maya had listed herself as the senior research consultant on his congressional staff, which a position that was held by the husband of one of the Ebony Esquire's executive board members.

Emmanuel would never forget the day he'd received a phone call and subsequently, a copy of Maya's bogus recommendation letter via fax. His whole world shattered. The betrayal and deception of the woman he'd planned to spend the rest of his life with hurt Emmanuel deeply. He immediately sent out personal letters of apology to every member of the Ebony Esquire's executive board. Then he hopped on a plane to Atlanta and ended his relationship with Maya. In time, she accepted the fact that she would never become Mrs. Emmanuel Day after weeks of trying desperately to win him back. When all of her radical attempts at reconciliation had failed, she resigned from the Day Firm and moved back to New Mexico.

*****

Jazz sat nervously watching Emmanuel mix and mingle with his supporters. She smiled, admiring how personable he was with everyone from the babies to the silver foxes. Over two hundred people had gathered in a hotel ballroom to watch the election results roll in on huge flat screen televisions mounted on each of the four walls. There was an abundance of good food and drinks of every kind. A deejay was pumping out music from every genre in between announcements and speeches. The young folks took to the dance floor to show off their skills whenever a hip-hop song was played. Emmanuel had joined them once, and his smooth moves made the crowd roar. Jazz was impressed. She made sure the camera crew captured the moment. Natural and spontaneous actions like that were going to make Emmanuel's segment of the documentary a hit. Tonight would be the final taping of his life on the campaign trail for the project. Jazz's work with the congressman would come to an end, but they would explore new territory tomorrow. The thought of spending time with Emmanuel alone for pleasure caused her to have a hot flash. Jazz fanned her face with her hand.

"Are you having a good time, Ms. Dupree?" Tyrell took the seat next to her.

"Yes, I am. This is very exciting. Victory is just an hour away. Your Uncle is far ahead of Senator Davis. There's no way that she can catch up."

"I know. Our next step is the general election in November. Neither Uncle Manny nor his campaign manager is worried about that race. I'm confident too. A conservative could never win in our district. Our constituents are too liberal and diverse. We'll still raise lots of money and stomp hard, but we're safe."

"Your uncle is lucky to have you, Tyrell. You're a very loyal and efficient assistant."

"I try to be," he said with a humble look in his eyes. "Uncle Manny is so busy all of the time. It's my responsibility to make life easier for him, so I grind hard. But I can't do *everything*. He needs to settle down with a good woman. You know what I mean. He needs a sistah who'll make sure he eats properly and his socks match."

Jazz laughed. "I'm sure your uncle can have any woman he wants. Maybe he hasn't found the right one yet."

"Oh, he's found the right woman, alright. He just needs to make a move on her." Tyrell stood from his chair. "I better go check his email."

Chapter Twelve

Emmanuel finished his victory speech to boisterous applause and loud cheers. The deejay turned the already rowdy crowd all the way up when he started playing DJ Khaled's "All I Do is Win". Lots of people started dancing and jumping around in celebration. Emmanuel waved to them and threw up deuces before he left the stage. He walked straight over to the table where Jazz was sitting with his parents and Christina. Tyrell was right behind him with a briefcase in one hand and his iPad in the other.

"We're proud of you, son. Aren't we, Carol?"

Mrs. Day looked at her baby boy with tears in her eyes. "Of course we're proud. I would've been proud of Manny if he'd chosen to be a trash man just as long as he was a good one."

Emmanuel kissed his mother on her forehead. He looked so much like her with the exception of her fair complexion. His velvety skin had come from his father. All three of the Day siblings had inherited Mr. Day's smooth dark complexion and thick black hair.

"Maybe after I retire from congress I'll become a trash man."

Christina rolled her eyes. "No, you won't. Your staff and housekeeper have spoiled you rotten. I bet you don't even know where the trashcan is in your office. And when was the last time you cooked yourself a meal?"

Emmanuel looked Jazz square in the face. She blushed and lowered her eyes. "I made Mama's famous chili a few weeks ago, and it was delicious. Ask Ms. Dupree. She ate two bowls.

All eyes roamed over to Jazz. She wanted to jump up and run from the table. If she thought she could get away with it, she would've strangled Emmanuel for putting her in the hot seat once again. This time was worse than all the others. His family was waiting for her answer probably with millions of questions collectively swimming through their heads.

"Um…yes…um the chili was good. Congressman Day and I prepared dinner together for the documentary we're working on. The camera crew taped us. You'll be able to see it soon. The premier is scheduled to air next month."

Jazz picked up her wineglass and took a few sips. She wasn't sure if Emmanuel's family believed a word she'd just said. Most likely, they all thought there was a little hanky-panky going on between her and the congressman. For some strange reason that bothered Jazz, but it shouldn't have. They were two unattached, consenting adults. They had every right to fool around if they wanted to, and tomorrow they probably would.

Emmanuel's cell phone rang and interrupted the awkward silence. Tyrell answered it after checking the caller ID. He spoke briefly to the person on the other end before he handed the phone to his uncle.

"Senator Davis, how are you?"

Everyone at the table watched and listened as Emmanuel spoke with his defeated opponent. She'd obviously called to concede the race and congratulate him on his victory.

*****

It was well after midnight by the time Emmanuel escorted Jazz up the steps of the private plane. He, Tyrell, and the few members of his staff had a very important meeting at eight o'clock in the morning. They were exhausted from the big celebration, but politics was politics. It was a never-ending game. Emmanuel and the small group of men and women huddled at the front of the plane for a briefing. Jazz walked to the very back and took a window seat. She was tired and wanted to sleep in the worst way, but there was still a lot of exhilaration lingering in the air. Jazz kicked off her hot pink sling-back pumps and rested her head against the window. Her eyelids were getting heavier by the second. Mr. Sand Man was about to carry her away when she smelled the scent of Emmanuel's expensive cologne. She'd recognize it anywhere. It had a clean and woodsy kick to it.

"Jazz," he whispered.

The sound of his voice calling her by her first name reminded her of a jazz note being played on a five-string upright bass. It was mesmerizing and seductive as hell. Jazz lifted her head and sat up. When she looked into Emmanuel's eyes, time paused. She was lost in their deep dark orbs.

"Yes," she answered on a shaky breath.

"I hope I didn't wake you."

Jazz shook her head. "You didn't."

"I'm glad." Emmanuel smiled and sat down next to her. "I think we should talk."

The warmth of his close presence, the scent of his cologne, and the sound of his voice put Jazz on full alert. She was a sexually deprived woman, practically alone with an irresistible man in the back of a dark plane. He was a man that wanted her, and she craved him like an addictive drug. "I think it's a good idea for us to talk too," she agreed.

"What we're about to get into won't be a fling, Jazz. I know what I want and I'm too old to play games. Do you understand?"

"I understand. There's something I need you to know too. My heart has been badly broken before. I don't ever want to experience that again."

"Don't worry about that, baby. I'll take good care of your heart."

*****

Jazz looked up from the computer screen, wondering who was visiting her office so early in the morning. "Come in!" she called out.

Jackson, the photographer, walked in grinning. His well-groomed dreadlocks that were pulled back neatly in a bundle bounced as he dapped further into the room. He was carrying a fabulous gift basket full of expensive gourmet goodies.

"Some brother has excellent taste and deep pockets. If you don't want this bottle of vintage Krug 1988, I'll gladly take it off your hands, baby girl."

"Man, close my door and give me that basket."

Jackson turned around and shut the door like Jazz had asked. "I'm just saying," he joked as he approached her desk again. He sat the basket down and handed her the card. "I could help you get rid of those chocolate covered cherries and that big can of caviar too. You owe me for grabbing your bougie basket before those nosy secretaries got a hold of it. I bomb rushed the delivery man as soon as I heard him say your name."

"Thank you, buddy. Wow," Jazz whispered, examining the contents of the basket carefully. "This is nice." She opened the card and read it silently. When she lifted her eyes, Jackson was staring her down with a goofy grin still on his face. "I'm not telling you, so don't even ask."

"I already know, but don't worry. Your secret is safe with me. But please be careful, Jazz. Gigi is obsessed with the man. She wanted me to spy on the two of you at his party in Atlanta and give her the tea."

"Oh, my God, Jackson! What did you tell Gigi?"

"I told her *no*. Black Diamond doesn't pay me to spy on other employees. And I'm nobody's punk, especially not Gigi Perdue's."

"Congressman Day and I were nothing more than reporter and subject before today. We kept it very professional while we were shooting his segment of the documentary. But now that we're finished…"

"You're about to dive in head first."

"Not necessarily. Slowly, we'll build a *friendship* and see where it leads us."

*****

Gigi watched Jazz through her office window as she strutted to her car carrying the fancy gift basket. She'd heard all about her special delivery the moment she reached the office this morning. The entire secretary pool had raved over it throughout the day. Gigi was beyond sick of hearing about the damn basket, and actually *seeing* it with her own two eyes had sent her anger through the roof. Emmanuel was in too deep with Jazz for her taste, and she didn't like it one bit. He'd never bought her anything except a meal or two. Gigi wasn't going to stand by and let Jazz rub her nose in her happiness while she drowned in misery. It was humiliating. She needed to come up with the perfect plan to tear Jazz and Emmanuel apart before she left for the Kingdom of Swaziland, Africa in a few weeks. Mr. McConnell had given her the assignment to cover the coronation of the country's new king. Gigi was determined to put an end to Jazz and Emmanuel's new romance at any cost before she boarded her flight.

Chapter Thirteen

"I'm less than a minute away from your place. I hope you're ready."

Jazz checked out her reflection in the full-length cheval mirror one last time. "I'm ready. Where are we going dressed in jeans, t-shirts, and sneakers?"

"Wait and see, woman. Don't you trust me to show you a good time?"

"I trust you."

"That's what I wanted to hear. I'm almost at your front door."

Jazz rushed to the door with the phone still in her hand. She disengaged the locks and turned the door knob. What she saw standing on her stoop was too impressive for words. Her jaw dropped. No man in heaven or on earth or anywhere else in between could fill out a pair of Levi's jeans the way Emmanuel did. There should've been a law against it in the nation's capital where laws were made. The fit of his red Atlanta Braves t-shirt over his broad, muscular chest was wicked. Jazz was speechless.

"Aren't you going to invite me in?"

"Sure." Jazz stepped aside, giving Emmanuel a clear path into her condo. "Can I offer you something to drink?"

"No, thank you. I need to check in with Tyrell and Edgar, my chief of staff. I hope you don't mind. It'll only take a minute. I want to wrap up all of my business before we leave so I can give you my full attention for the rest of the evening."

"I understand. Come with me. You can make your calls from the den."

Jazz led Emmanuel to the spacious room and left him there alone for privacy. She went to her office and busied herself there editing a script for her new assignment. Business, the economy, and finance reporting wasn't very exciting, but she preferred it over traveling all the way to Africa to cover a story. Mr. McConnell had approached Jazz about flying to Swaziland in a few weeks to do a piece on the coronation of their new king. She begged him off, explaining she needed time to recover from running around with

Emmanuel for six weeks. Luckily, the old man had a soft heart and assigned the project to someone else.

*****

"I'm kicking your butt!" Jazz shot another basketball straight through the hoop. "Yes!"

Emmanuel had challenged her to a basketball shootout at a popular arcade and dining spot. Because Jazz wasn't a skilled baller like he'd claimed to be, he had shown her mercy by volunteering to shoot the ball with his left hand in the competition. His shots were going everywhere *except* through the net. Emmanuel was a true right-handed brother. Jazz was making him look pathetic.

"I quit."

"No way, buddy. You made up the rules, so I'm winning this game fair and square. Keep shooting those bricks until the buzzer sounds."

Emmanuel continued tossing the basketball toward the goal until the game was officially over. He'd hit an embarrassing total of six baskets to Jazz's eleven. He enjoyed watching her jump up and down celebrating her win. She was comfortable in his presence and having a good time. And she looked fine as wine too. Her dark denim jeans fit her perfectly, and the colorful t-shirt splattered with tiny butterflies brought out the brightness of her caramel skin.

Emmanuel pulled Jazz away from the play area and led her to a booth in the dining section. They ordered drinks and an appetizer platter. The restaurant was crowded and noisy, but Emmanuel wasn't distracted. Only one person mattered at the moment, and she was seated across the table from him.

"Are you enjoying yourself, Jazz?"

"I am. What about you?"

"I'm having more fun than I've had in a very long time."

After their drinks and appetizer platter arrived, Emmanuel asked Jazz all about her former job as a sports reporter. He was hoping his line of questioning would prompt her to talk about her engagement to Mario 'The Blaze' Thomas and why they never got married. As his luck would have it, she never mentioned her former fiancé or their breakup. Instead, she talked about some of her most memorable interviews and the many football players she'd gotten to know during her days as an NFL correspondent.

*****

Later that evening on the stoop of Jazz's condo, Emmanuel removed her keys from her hand and opened her front door. She rushed inside and turned off the security system and invited him in for coffee. But apparently, he had something else in mind. The moment Emmanuel crossed Jazz's threshold, he pulled her into his arms. Her keys slipped from his hand, crashing to the shiny hardwood floor. The heat was on. Emmanuel kissed Jazz softly at first with his lips pressed firmly against hers. When his hands slid from her small waist to her hips, pulling her body fully against his, she moaned out in pleasure. With her lips parted, Emmanuel slipped his tongue inside her mouth and started a tantalizing tango with hers. Weeks of pent-up want and need were being unleashed in the kiss. Flames of passion burned quickly and almost out of control. Emmanuel had to channel in to his Southern gentleman roots in order to save Jazz from the inferno. He wanted her at that moment more than anything he'd ever wanted in his life. But he respected her and was bound by his promise to take things between them nice and slow.

Grudgingly, Emmanuel lifted his head, breaking the kiss, but he kept Jazz possessively in his arms. He didn't want to let her go. He dreaded leaving her, but it would be improper for him to stay. *Nice and slow*, he mentally reminded himself, but his penis did not receive the memo. It was at full attention and ready for action.

"I'll see you tomorrow," he managed to say through ragged breathing as his heart pumped out of control.

"Call me when you get home."

Emmanuel inhaled a hint of chardonnay on Jazz's breath mixed with the enticing scent of her flowery perfume. The sensitivity in his erect manhood was attempting to overtake the soundness of his good sense, but he refused to succumb to the lust of his flesh. "I will. Don't fall asleep before you hear from me."

*****

Jazz closed her eyes when she heard the click of her front door closing shut. She immediately felt the chill of being left alone and sexually frustrated. She'd had to bite her tongue to keep from asking Emmanuel to stay the night. Jazz's body temperature had dropped instantly from desert heat to Antarctic chilly after he'd robbed her of his masculine warmth. It had been over seven years since she'd been with a man. Mario's betrayal had doused her passionate flame, leaving her with no desire to be intimate with anyone. But now that she'd had a little taste of Emmanuel, Jazz was ready to break her fast from sex. *Celibacy be damned* was her last thought before she hurried to the kitchen to pour herself a glass of wine. She planned to take a cold shower next because she was in for a long and restless night. Now her request to take things nice and slow with Emmanuel no longer seemed like a good idea. The tingling and throbbing between her thighs had Jazz wishing for a naughty and high speed episode of lovemaking with the man. But for tonight, a late night phone call from him would have to do.

Chapter Fourteen

"Slow down, girl! Where is the fire?"

Gigi ran and caught up with Jazz and fell in step with her. They were doing a power walk down the main hallway of the seventh floor in their office building. It was midday and many of Black Diamond's employees were out to lunch. Therefore, the hall wasn't overly crowded.

"I have a very important lunch meeting in twenty minutes and I'm running late."

"Is *Manny* still obsessed with punctuality? That was one thing I hated about him."

Jazz stopped in her red stylish stilettos and faced Gigi. "Come again."

"I assumed you were meeting the congressman for lunch. The headline around here is that the two of you are the hottest new couple on the political scene. If that's true, I understand why you're in such a hurry. That man is dictated by time."

"Stop being messy, Gigi. It's not a good look."

"Why are you so defensive? Did I push a button?"

"I don't have time or tolerance for your childish games. Take care of your business and stay the hell out of mine."

After those parting words, Jazz walked away and hurried to the elevators. Gigi smiled and watched her until she was out of sight. She felt victorious. The first punch had been thrown, and it had clearly stung. Up until a minute ago, Jazz was unaware that Gigi and Emmanuel had a past. Her hard countenance and sharp tongue couldn't hide her shock. For some mysterious reason, the congressman had failed to tell his new girlfriend that she wasn't the first reporter he'd worked his mojo on. Now that Jazz knew the truth, Gigi was sure that there would be trouble in paradise. Nothing could've pleased her more.

*****

"He said it was only one time, Jazz. And *she* seduced *him*. I believe Congressman Chocolate. Why don't you? And what difference does it make *now* anyway?"

"I do believe him, Ramone. It's just that I have to see Gigi at work just about every day unless one of is away on assignment. She'll always be able to dangle that one night in my face. I can hear her voice in my head teasing me about sleeping with Emmanuel before I did. And did I tell you he also had a fling back in college with his recent opponent, state Senator Divinity Davis? He admitted that he used to be a *playa*."

Ramone draped his long arm around Jazz's shoulders. They'd been sitting in her den sipping chardonnay for nearly an hour. Emmanuel's one night stand with Gigi had dominated their conversation, and Ramone had grown bored with it. "So that ole tramp, Gigi, sampled your man's goodies nine years ago. He was honest with you when you asked him about it. The congressman used to get around back in the day. Get over it."

"I'm trying to."

"Well, you need to try a little harder. While you're sitting here sulking over his past, you need to be preparing for your hot date tomorrow night. It could be *the night*. John Legend live in concert would definitely put me in the mood, honey."

Jazz giggled. "You're right as usual, Ramone. Gigi only had one meaningless night with Emmanuel. He has promised me *many* nights in the near future. We're just cruising along for now."

"What are you waiting for, chile?"

"My body is ready. I'm not too sure if my heart is, though. There have been nights that we've almost devoured each other, but each time we were able to pull back. A time will come when we'll let ourselves go without forethought or planning. And in that moment, my heart won't allow me to wait any longer. It's going to be a special night that I'll always remember."

*****

Jazz had insisted that she help Ms. Flora, Emmanuel's housekeeper and cook, with the food for the big viewing party. His entire congressional staff and Ramone had been invited to his home for food and drinks while they watched the premier of the documentary "Black and Powerful in American Politics". The atmosphere was festive but laid back. Emmanuel was joking and mixing it up with his staff. They seemed more like a team or even a family as opposed to a boss and his employees. Once again, Jazz had discovered yet another side of the man she was becoming more and more emotionally attached to every day. She was crazy about the casual and more personal Emmanuel. Congressman Day, the serious and in command politician, was extra hot too. Jazz was totally taken by her man no matter which element he was in.

"Six minutes!" Emmanuel yelled from the great room.

Jazz added a few more slices of roast beef and turkey to the deli platter. She grabbed a stack of napkins and left the kitchen to join the group. Tyrell removed the platter from her hands and took it into the dining room. Jazz's eyes did a quick sweep around the room. Staffers were sitting on the floor, the couches, and in folding chairs enjoying themselves. Gone were their business suits and political jargon. There were no cell phones ringing or keys clicking on tablets. Everyone was having a good time. Ramone was surrounded by a small group of ladies. He was in rare form. There was an empty space next to Emmanuel on the loveseat. Edgar, his chief of staff, and a young lady were standing above him with drinks in their hands. They were talking and laughing. Jazz walked over and sat down. Emmanuel placed his hand on her thigh and gave it a subtle squeeze. His simple gesture singed her flesh. He was clueless as he relaxed and left his hand on Jazz's lap.

A hush fell over the room when the documentary began. Tyrell increased the volume on the seventy-two-inch flat screen television. Jazz had not reviewed the finished product of her segment by choice. She'd only watched the edited version of all of Emmanuel's activities and their interviews. Narration, music, graphics, and still photographs had been added later. Jazz had opted not to watch the final production. She couldn't explain it, but for

57

some reason she wanted to wait and share the debut experience with Emmanuel.

The ninety minute premier would feature four influential African-American political figures on the rise. Jazz had been informed that Emmanuel's segment would air third in the lineup. Her nerves were all over the place as she waited impatiently to view the final results of her weeks of hard work. She couldn't keep still. Emmanuel must've sensed her anxiety. His hand left her thigh and he snaked his arm around her shoulders. The contact added a little comfort, but Jazz wouldn't be fully at ease until after she'd seen Emmanuel's portion of the documentary, and he'd given it his stamp of approval. McConnell and the other Black Diamond executives had already viewed the entire premier and congratulated her on a job well done for her part. Jazz was happy that they were pleased with her work. However, her most rewarding accolade could only come from her man *if* he was satisfied with her performance. She had done her absolute best to present a very positive image of Emmanuel Marcus Day, the congressman, the attorney, and the *man*, to the viewing audience. She hoped she wouldn't disappoint him

"Chill, baby," Emmanuel whispered in Jazz's ear. "We're going to be a hit."

"I sure hope so."

Chapter Fifteen

Jazz and Emmanuel's segment of the documentary rocked. Every social media outlet said so. Gigi had checked them all a thousand times during the show and afterwards. Viewers all across America had taken to cyber space to sound off on "Black and Powerful in American Politics". Although the entire program had received favorable reviews, Jazz's fan base hailed her queen of the night. Aside from her cool and creative approach to securing honest answers from Emmanuel, she looked fabulous doing so in every single frame. Countless female watchers went crazy over Jazz's wardrobe selections. Facebook and Twitter were clogged with compliments about various pieces of her designer wear. The orange jumpsuit she'd sported at the debate was now a coveted fashion item as well as the pink strapless chiffon gown she'd danced the night away in at the Veteran's Administration ball.

Gigi couldn't deny that Jazz's coverage of Emmanuel was exceptional. The sistah had mastered her craft. A true fashionista, Jazz's keen eye for style was no new discovery either. She used to strut her stuff up and down NFL sidelines looking like she'd just stepped off the cover of Vogue magazine. But at the moment, Gigi didn't give a damn about the chick's overpriced wardrobe or the way she carried herself in front of the camera. The thing that was messing with her head was the viewing audience's comments about how well Jazz and the congressman had connected on camera. Their unquestionable chemistry had burst through television screens all across the country and caught afire. Bloggers had lost their minds with speculation. Black Diamond fans nationwide thought Emmanuel and Jazz would make a sizzling hot couple. Thousands posted comments encouraging the cool politician to ask his interviewer out on a date. To Gigi's dismay, she knew something that Black Diamond's viewers didn't know. Emmanuel and Jazz were already involved.

One of the congressman's aides had confirmed their relationship to the speech writer of Gigi's good friend, Congresswoman Joanna Corbett from Maryland. The secret lovers had planned a watch party for the documentary at Emanuel's home. It was a home that Gigi had never been invited to before. His entire staff had gathered for refreshments and drinks while they watched the documentary featuring their beloved boss. Gigi imagined that Jazz had sashayed around Emmanuel's house, serving his guests while getting chummy with them. Regardless of whatever role she had played at the private party, Gigi would know before morning. Emmanuel's aide was sweet on Sherry, Congresswoman Corbett's speech writer. The two of them would speak soon enough, and every detail would be reported to Gigi. The information would serve no other purpose than to make her mad, but she had become obsessed with Jazz and Emmanuel. Their newfound relationship was a thorn in Gigi's flesh. That's why she was committed to sabotaging it. But time was winding up. She was scheduled to leave for Swaziland soon. Therefore, it was time for her to pull out the big guns and fire at full blast.

*****

A week after the documentary aired, Emmanuel took his whining, dining, and romancing to the maximum level. He and Jazz had accompanied Senator Isaac Blackshear from Pennsylvania and his wife to dinner and the opera. They'd walked arm in arm into a fundraiser at the Waldorf Astoria one evening where Emmanuel introduced Jazz as his date and special friend. No one in attendance had seemed the least bit surprised. The congressman and his lady had been spotted all over the District recently. They'd done everything from shutting down Pookie's Pool Hall and Grill in a wild game of spades to attending Sunday morning worship services at Metropolitan Baptist Church. Emmanuel's staff and closest colleagues accommodated Jazz during her rare visits to Capitol Hill, always respecting her and the congressman's privacy.

In between their many dates and public appearances, the delivery man from Delicieux Creations frequented Black Diamond's headquarters. The fine gift baskets, gourmet chocolates, and beautiful floral arrangements kept coming *regularly*. The secretary pool at the network had begun to look forward to Ms. Dupree's special deliveries. Had the ladies known the identity of the man behind the unique gifts, they would've been bouncing off the walls by now. But Jazz kept her relationship with Emmanuel private, never discussing it with any of her coworkers besides Jackson. Her secret was safe with him.

In fact, Jazz trusted Jackson so much, that she had secured him on Emmanuel's behalf to take pictures at a private dinner party scheduled for Friday night. The congressman and some of his colleagues would be hosting the event for the Sierra Leonean ambassador to the United States. A delegation of businessmen from the West African nation was coming to meet with American economists to discuss import and export ventures. As a gesture of goodwill, Emmanuel and five of his congressional colleagues had volunteered to throw a party for the ambassador and his countrymen.

*****

"What the hell is *she* doing here?"

Tyrell lowered the glass of brandy from his lips and followed his uncle's gaze. "I don't know. You're one of the hosts of this shindig. Didn't you check out the guest list?"

"If I had, do you really think *Gigi* would be here?"

There was no need for Tyrell to answer the question. Emmanuel wouldn't have knowingly allowed Gigi Perdue's name to remain on the guest list of any event he was hosting. Every member of his staff had been instructed to keep her as far away from him as possible at all times. She was to have absolutely no access to him whatsoever, especially when Jazz was present. Unfortunately, tonight the ball had been dropped. No one from the Day camp had checked the guest list, assuming that none of the other four hosts had invited Gigi to the event.

"I'm back." Jazz walked up to Emmanuel and Tyrell after returning from the ladies' room. "This is a nice party. I've never eaten at this restaurant before. I can't wait to taste my entrée. The hors d'oeuvres are delicious. I ate three canapés."

The men smiled at Jazz, but remained silent. Tyrell held his breath when he saw Gigi heading in their direction. Emmanuel obviously noticed her too. He grabbed Jazz's hand and pulled her closer to him. She was oblivious because her back was turned to the troublemaker making her approach.

"Good evening, everyone," Gigi greeted with way too much cheer in her voice to be genuine.

The trio was courteous and returned the greeting.

"This is an elegant affair, Manny. Thank you for inviting me. You know this is my favorite restaurant in D.C. Remember when Senator Ribeirio's wife gave him his retirement party here?"

"I may be one of the hosts of this party, but make no mistake about it. I did not invite you here."

Jackson walked up with his camera before Gigi could respond to Emmanuel. "Excuse me, everyone. May I get a shot of the congressman and Jazz alone please? I'm sure the photography department at our network would like to have it on file."

Tyrell did a cool side step away from the group when Emmanuel curved his arm around Jazz's waist. Gigi stormed off in the opposite direction no doubt crazy with jealousy. Tyrell dismissed her foolishness and gave the impromptu photo shoot his full attention. Emmanuel and Jazz looked amazing together smiling for the camera. The gold sequins in her gown sparkled against his midnight tux. His swagger and her sophistication were an appealing combination. Everything about them complemented each other, making them picture perfect for any magazine cover. Tyrell could certainly see his uncle and Jazz together on a long-term basis. They clicked in every way. Jazz was the first woman since Maya Durant who'd managed to break through Emmanuel's ironclad emotional wall. Everyone in the Day family was impressed with her, even Christina. She was a strong drink to swallow, but somehow Jazz had connected with her during her short visit to Georgia. Now that the family was on board, Tyrell was hoping that Emmanuel would waste no time establishing something permanent with Jazz. If he tarried, Gigi was bound to do something stupid to ruin whatever was developing between them.

Chapter Sixteen

"I hope you know how jealous I am."

Jazz placed some white t-shirts in her suitcase and shook her head at Ramone. "You've told me a million times already. I'm sorry, sweetie. Maybe one day you and I can go on a divas' retreat to the Hamptons and take all of the stylists from the salon with us."

"Mmm, mmm, I'm sure. What kind of *retreat* are you and the congressman going on?"

"Emmanuel said he needs a break from campaigning and politics. If he goes home to Georgia, he wouldn't get much rest once his family discovers he's in town. The firm and his field offices would track him down too. So he decided to hide out someplace where no one can find him."

"And why is he taking *you* along?" Ramone raised and lowered his perfectly arched eyebrows several times suggestively.

"He doesn't want to get lonely, I suppose."

"He could take *Tyrell*."

Jazz pursed her lips at Ramone. She was tired of playing games with him. "Tyrell has lots of work to do this weekend. Emmanuel and I need this time alone away from Washington. We're going to kick back and enjoy each other's company. He's even going to leave his cell phone here."

"What if something important comes up? How will his staff contact him?"

"Edgar and Tyrell can handle any situation in Emmanuel's absence. He has trained them well. Besides, we'll only be gone for the weekend, Ramone. Nothing out of the ordinary is going to happen."

*****

"I have run all kinds of tests on you, Ms. Perdue. You're as healthy as an ox. I don't see any reason why you can't make your flight to Swaziland Sunday afternoon."

"What about this awful rash?" Gigi scratched her thigh and wrinkled her nose. "What if I've developed some kind of incurable virus or I'm having a deadly allergic reaction to something?"

Dr. Murchison smiled at his overly concerned patient. "The rash is only a side effect from your cholera vaccine. It's perfectly normal. I'll prescribe a simple cream that will clear it up over night."

"I'll be in flight for over eighteen hours, and there're two long layovers. You'll have to give me something to make me relax. I don't want to freak out over the Atlantic Ocean."

"That's not a problem, Ms. Perdue. A mild dose of Buspar will take care of your flight anxiety. By the time you reach the Kingdom of Swaziland, you'll be refreshed and ready for the grand coronation. I must say I envy you."

"Don't," Gigi spat. "I don't give a damn about some king whose name I can barely pronounce. The trip is just a *job*. That's all. I'll be sure to bring you back a zebra bone or a tiger's tooth."

*****

Jazz shivered when the evening breeze whipped around them. She was nestled comfortably against Emmanuel's body with his arm wrapped around her waist. They were headed back to the fabulous Westhampton beach house where they were staying for the weekend after a long walk along the shore. The sun was going down, losing its brilliance to dusk. A light breeze was sweeping over the tide. Seagulls squawked in the distance, adding sound to the spectacular view of nature.

"Are you cold?"

"A little bit," Jazz answered honestly.

Emmanuel pulled her body more snuggly to his and kissed her temple. Then he stopped suddenly in his stride and released Jazz. "Hop on," he told her, bending at the waist.

"What?" Jazz giggled hysterically.

"Hop on, woman. I'm going to give you a complimentary piggyback ride the rest of the way."

Jazz couldn't stop laughing. "If you drop me Fred and Sallie Mae Anderson will hunt you down like a bloodhound and kick your butt. They don't play about their only grandchild."

"I promise not to drop you, baby. Come on now. It's getting chilly out here. I don't want you to catch a late summer cold. Hop on."

Very carefully, Jazz placed her hands on Emmanuel's back and hoisted herself up to straddle him. She tightened her thighs around his waist when he straightened his stance slightly. Her hands automatically gripped his shoulders as she balanced herself. Then she eased them around his neck. Her fingers clasped tightly together. "You better not drop me, Emmanuel. I'm warning you."

"I won't."

Seconds later he broke out into a brisk trot. Jazz's laughter and squeals rose above the crashing waves and the fading squawks of the seagulls. She threw her head back and screamed as the wind blew in her face. Up and down she bounced as Emmanuel followed the cobble stone path to the front of the beach house. Jazz's joy ride came to an end when they reached the steps leading up to the porch. Emmanuel had proven his strength and stamina. There wasn't a doubt in her mind that he could carry her up the stairs, but Jazz didn't want him to. She slid down his back and landed on her feet. Emmanuel turned around and stoked her cheek softly.

"I'm not tired. I could carry you the rest of the way, you know."

Jazz smiled and looked deeply into his eyes. "I know."

*****

"What the hell are they doing in *The Hamptons*?"

"Congressman Day and Ms. Dupree are on a weekend getaway, I guess. No one is to disturb him, not even his chief of staff. " Sherry looked around her sparsely furnished studio apartment. She was alone, but the guilt of betraying Fabian's trust again made her feel uneasy. "Look, Ms. Perdue, that's all I know. I really shouldn't be telling you anything. I feel awful enough as it is. This is the last time I'll feed you information about Congressman Day. Fabian is a sweet guy. He's the best boyfriend I've ever had. I don't want him to lose his job because of *me*."

"You will do as I tell you, little girl!" Gigi shouted into the phone. "If you try to wiggle out of our agreement now, I'll show your boyfriend all of the text messages and emails we've exchanged about his boss. What will he think of you once he learns that I've been paying you to get information from him about the congressman? If you want to continue writing those boring speeches for Joanna and if you really care about your boyfriend's job, you'll keep milking him for information. I expect a full report on Congressman Day and Jazz Dupree's *exact* whereabouts in an hour."

Sherry burst into tears when Gigi hung up the phone in her face. "Dear God, what have I gotten myself into?"

Chapter Seventeen

"I've made arrangements for us to go sailing tomorrow after breakfast. I hope that's okay with you."

Jazz leaned back into Emmanuel's solid muscular body, enjoying how good it felt to be in his arms. She kept her eyes straight ahead. There was something about the way the moon danced on the rippling water that fascinated her. It was a magnificent view from the huge picture window in the parlor. "I love sailing. It's been a while, but my grandfather used to take me all the time when I was a little girl. We've gone a few times since then, but not recently."

"So we'll set sail around nine o'clock. I ordered a picnic basket from a nearby deli to take with us for lunch. We can do whatever you want to do when we return."

"I don't know anything about this place. I'll just follow your lead. You can plan all of our activities."

"Are you sure about that?" Emmanuel placed several kisses on the back of Jazz's neck.

"Oh yeah, I'm sure."

"Tomorrow can take care of itself. Tonight I want to make love to you, Jazz."

Jazz turned around in Emmanuel's arms to face him. She initiated a fiery kiss like a woman on a mission. She wrapped her arms around Emmanuel's neck, inviting him to have his way with her. Papa Fred had told her many times as a youngster and even into womanhood that actions always speak louder than words. For weeks she had conducted herself as a prim and proper Southern belle, bound by an idea she'd proposed to protect her heart. Emmanuel, an understanding brother, had exercised great patience and restraint to honor Jazz's request to explore their attraction to each other slowly and with certain caution. Tonight, in an atmosphere saturated by passion, romance, and seduction, the primitive call of nature could no longer be denied. Jazz wanted Emmanuel. She *needed* him. The pain of the heartbreak from her past had faded away. It was time to live in the present. The special moment had presented itself at last. Fate had been kind enough to give Jazz a chance to start afresh and to make new memories with a man who had promised to take good care of her heart.

With each expert twirl of Emmanuel's tongue mating with hers, Jazz's heart fluttered with anticipation. She had denied her body's need to be loved by a man for more than seven years now. The drought was about to end in the arms of the one and only guy who had shown himself worthy. Suddenly, Emmanuel lifted Jazz into his arms, breaking the kiss. She felt like she was floating as he made his way down the hallway to the master bedroom. The soft yet firm mattress welcomed her when Emmanuel placed her in the middle of the antique sleigh bed. He stood above Jazz looking down at her. The light of the moon illuminated his handsome face through the thick darkness. In the depths of his eyes, Jazz saw his desire for her, and the bulge between his muscular thighs was evidence of his need. She reached out for Emmanuel. She wanted him in her arms.

A lazy smile crept across his face. He lifted his arms to remove his white t-shirt and flung it across the room. His hands paused at the waistband of his shorts as if to tease Jazz. She drew in a quick breath of air and held it briefly before releasing it slowly. The sight of Emmanuel's well-toned chest sprinkled with strands of fine hair added fuel to the fire. But Jazz was more interested in what was underneath the navy cotton fabric of his shorts. And as if he were a genie granting her most desired wish, Emmanuel slowly eased the shorts and his boxers down his long legs and kicked them from his feet. The brother had every reason to be proud in Jazz's opinion. His body was *exquisite*. It was heavenly designed, molded, and chiseled to masculine flawlessness. He was a beautiful creature; a magnificent descendent of African ancestry.

Jazz's legs parted instinctively when Emmanuel knelt before her at the edge of the bed. He kissed and caressed her inner thighs, causing her to squirm and struggle to breathe. Jazz's back arched high off of the bed, as she purred and whispered Emmanuel's name in appreciation of his magical touches. He made haste and removed her denim shorts and yellow lace panties and dropped them on the floor. With light flicks of his tongue intended to heighten her pleasure, Emmanuel tasted the sweet drops of Jazz's liquid heat as he licked her clit skillfully. Her wetness flowed in abundance like an infinite stream. The louder Jazz cooed and chanted Emmanuel's name, the deeper his tongue plunged into her dampness. His hands snaked up her torso and lifted her orange tank top. He then released the single front clasp on her bra, allowing her to wiggle free from it and her shirt. Emmanuel kneaded the smooth flesh of Jazz's breasts and toiled with her nipples with his fingertips. The caramel buds hardened under his masterful touch.

Bright flashes of light comparable to fireworks lit up the room as the sweetest release overtook Jazz's body. She sang Emmanuel's name in an angelic soprano pitch that filled their cozy love cocoon while she stroked the back of his head. Jazz's soul soared high above the earth and mingled with the stars. The experience was far better than her most erotic fantasy. But the magic had only just begun. Emmanuel lifted his head and kissed a path up Jazz's body. When his lips reached hers, they lingered there in a sweet and unhurried kiss. His hardness pressed and pulsated against Jazz's belly. But that was not where she wanted it to be. She was wet and beyond delirious with lust. Jazz wanted Emmanuel buried deep inside of her *now*. She thrust her hips upward several times to demonstrate exactly what she wanted. Emmanuel sat up and stretched his long arm to open the drawer on the nightstand. He grabbed a square foiled package and tore it open with his teeth. A responsible and seasoned man, he handled his business before he took Jazz into his arms again and kissed her like his life depended on it. She responded to him like a woman on fire.

Emmanuel positioned himself over Jazz, still kissing her passionately. Very gently and with perfect aim, he entered her warm and wet vagina gradually. Jazz's eyes locked with Emmanuel's when he met some resistance due to the tightness of her walls. His body stopped moving suddenly, but Jazz raised her hips, encouraging him continue giving her what she wanted. Their bodies were a perfect fit, as if they had been created purposely for each other. At last, they were one in the most intimate way known to man and woman, rocking together rhythmically to a tempo that was uniquely theirs. Smooth strokes, measured and long, took Jazz closer and closer to paradise. The journey was thrilling and seemingly timeless. Emmanuel was indeed a slow lover as he had promised he would be, pleasing Jazz thoroughly and without limits just like she deserved. As he thrust deeper and faster inside of her, he whispered words that were prettier than the finest poetry. Jazz was beautiful, desirable, and incredible.

And tonight she was completely *Emmanuel's* in every way that a man could possess a woman.

A wave of ecstasy ten times more powerful than the first one enveloped Jazz. Time, sound, and nature stood still. Her inner muscles contracted uncontrollable as continuous ripples of indescribable delight kissed every inch of her body. Jazz had lost the ability to speak, but the underlying message in her whimpers and sighs were meant to tell Emmanuel that she was completely satiated. Her sounds of fulfillment and her body's natural response to his lovemaking undoubtedly satisfied him so much that he tumbled over the edge. Jazz felt it when he climaxed. His body stiffened. Emmanuel's usually deep voice jumped octaves on the register as he repeated Jazz's name in rapid succession until his soul returned to the earth. Sweat drenched and breathless, he rolled over onto his back, cradling Jazz to his chest. She closed her eyes as she rested on top of him. Exhaustion and sexual gratification pulled the two lovers into a peaceful sleep that no longer consisted of dreams of making love. They had been replaced by the real life experience.

Chapter Eighteen

Emmanuel silently cursed himself for being greedy and inconsiderate, but he was *hooked*. He had been trying to wake Jazz for five minutes so he could make love to her again. Undoubtedly, she was tired and more than likely very sore. They had satisfied each other's physical needs to the max several times throughout the night and into the wee hours of the morning. Their sex marathon had been an adventure that had exceeded all expectations. They had made love in every position physically possible from the bed to the shower and even on the colonial rug in the middle of the floor. Now the sun had just begun to rise, and Emmanuel's appetite for Jazz had returned like a deprived man who had been separated from his lover for years. He couldn't get enough of her. Her good loving had brought out his gluttony.

Emmanuel stroked Jazz's inner thigh gently with the tip of his index finger and kissed both of her breasts. She stirred slightly and moaned, but sleep maintained its grip on her. She deserved to rest without interruption. She had shown Emmanuel great generosity, giving herself so freely and unreserved to him each time he'd asked the night before. Yet she still looked vibrant as she slept peacefully next to him. Jazz was an exceptional woman filled with passion and zest for life. Emmanuel could actually imagine waking up to her every morning for the rest of his days. No other woman, not even *Maya*, had stimulated his mind and body the way Jazz had. She was the total package, the epitome of femininity. Mario Thomas was a damn fool to have let her get away. But his loss was Emmanuel's gain, and he was nobody's fool. He prided himself on being a no nonsense brother who knew what he wanted and how to get it. And now that he had found the ideal lover who could take care of all of his needs, he intended to keep her.

The sound of Jazz's telephone ringing and vibrating on the dresser yanked Emmanuel from his thoughts. He sat up quickly, careful not to wake her, and left the bed. He ran across the room and removed the phone from its charger. Black Diamond Television appeared across the ID screen. Emmanuel hurried back to the bed and sat down next to Jazz. He hated to wake her because she looked so content, but he thought the call might be important.

"Jazz, wake up, baby." He shook her gently and nuzzled the side of her neck with his nose. "Your job is calling you."

The phone stopped ringing, but soon started again. Someone at the network was determined to reach Jazz. Emmanuel was tempted to answer the call, but he thought better and decided against it. He shook Jazz again, but with more force. Her eyes popped wide open.

She smiled at Emmanuel. "I need five more minutes please," she whispered. Her voice was hoarse and gravelly.

"Your job is blowing up your phone. I think you should answer it." Emmanuel pushed the power button and pressed the phone to Jazz's ear.

She took the phone and sat up in the bed. "Mr. McConnell? What's going on, sir?"

Emmanuel watched Jazz's facial expression change from concern to disbelief. She didn't respond to her boss with words. She simply listened and nodded her head repeatedly. Something serious was going down at BDT, and Emmanuel had a feeling that it was going to ruin his secret romantic weekend.

"Isn't there another reporter you can send, sir? I'm not in Washington right now. I'm off until Monday morning. Oh…" Jazz looked at Emmanuel with regret in her eyes. "I don't know, Mr. McConnell. Give me a few hours. I'll call you as soon as I get home." She ended the call.

"Give it to me straight, baby. I can handle it."

"I'm sorry, Emmanuel, but I have to leave right away. My boss needs me to go to the Kingdom of Swaziland to cover the coronation of their new king. It was Gigi's assignment, but she had an anxiety attack or some kind of episode. I'm not sure about the details, but she's in the hospital. I have a briefing some time later today. Then I'll need to take a series of injections at a clinic for travel immunization."

"When are you leaving for Africa?"

"My flight will take off tomorrow afternoon."

*****

Gigi was satisfied with her award-winning performance. She had convinced the attending physician at the emergency room and the team of nurses that she was in emotional crisis. All of her hysterical crying, screaming, and twitching had done the trick. She laughed when she thought about the look on the doctor's face when she lifted her dress over her head to show him her rash. He blushed with embarrassment when he realized she wasn't wearing panties. That was definitely the move of an emotionally distraught woman. The doctor diagnosed Gigi right away with acute anxiety due to stress and fear of flying. He immediately admitted her to the hospital for treatment. Now she was chilling and enjoying the comfort of her private room. She imagined that Jazz was scrambling around preparing for her unexpected trip to Swaziland. Gigi wished she could be a flea in a corner taking it all in. The thought of it tickled her to death even through sleepiness.

The strong anxiety medication and the antidepressant were kicking in, and Gigi was beginning to feel mellow. She fluffed her pillows and took a sip of water. Phase one of her mission was complete. She'd ruined Jazz and Emmanuel's weekend, and it felt pretty damn good. Next week after she had *recovered* from her anxiety attack, she would further execute her plan.

*****

"You look tired, Jazz."

"I am." She kissed Ramone's cheek. "I'll rest on the plane after I study my notes and watch all of those video clips on my portable DVD player."

"This ain't fair at all. Black Diamond could've sent one of those new reporters to get some international experience."

"Mr. McConnell wanted me on the assignment from the beginning. He only gave it to Gigi because I didn't want it. I ended up with it after all. Anyway, I love you, Ramone. Thanks for everything."

Emmanuel cleared his throat apparently to get their attention. He and Ramone had brought Jazz to the airport to see her off. Her flight would be leaving soon.

"Your man wants me to disappear. I'll be nice this time, but he better recognize who I am. You were my girl before you became his woman." Ramone squeezed Jazz tight and pecked her cheek. He walked away to give her some time alone with Emmanuel.

"You have all of my numbers. Use them, Jazz. I want to know exactly where you are over there and what you're doing at all times."

Jazz stuffed her hands inside her jeans pockets and nodded. "I'll call you when I arrive in London."

"Stay close to your chaperone, security, and the crew. Please don't venture out on your own."

"I won't."

Emmanuel enfolded Jazz in his arms and pulled her close. "The next ten days are going to be pure hell. If I didn't have such a full schedule, I would go with you. Maybe I can catch a flight out after the budget vote on Thursday."

"That would be nice," Jazz said softly.

"I have something for you." Emmanuel released Jazz and removed a square, flat jewelry box from his pants pocket. He handed it to her. "Go ahead and open it."

Jazz lifted the top and marveled at the extraordinary piece of jewelry. It was a gold diamond encrusted key shaped pendant on a petite gold rope chain. Tears welled up in her eyes. "Emmanuel, I don't know what to say."

"You don't need to say anything. Just wear it and know that it means something very significant." He removed the pendant and chain from the box. "Turn around."

Jazz did as she was told. She touched the pendant after Emmanuel secured the clasp around her neck. "Thank you."

"You're more than welcome. I'll tell you what you can unlock with that key when you come back."

Jazz reached up and touched Emmanuel's face with her palm. "I'll see you in ten days." She tiptoed and placed a soft kiss on his lips.

Fake exaggerated coughing behind them stole the moment. Jazz and Emmanuel turned around. Ramone was staring at them with both hands on his bony hips while tapping his foot. He rolled his eyes to the ceiling like a disgusted child. All Jazz and Emmanuel could do was laugh at his silliness.

Chapter Nineteen

Emmanuel buzzed Tyrell's office. "Where are the notes on the energy bill?"

"I put them on the left side of your desk with the minutes from the committee meeting."

"I don't see them. My desk is a mess! How the hell do you expect me to find anything with junk scattered everywhere?"

Within seconds, Tyrell rushed through Emmanuel's door and walked straight to his desk. He picked up the notes on the energy bill and waved them in the air. He dropped them directly in front of his uncle. The papers floated to the desk and landed in a perfect stack.

"I know you're in a sour mood because Jazz is out of the country, but you've got to stop lashing out at everybody. I'm your blood, so I can handle it, but the rest of the staff is afraid to come anywhere near you. Come on, Unc. You know better. Chill out."

Emmanuel rubbed both hands down his face and growled like a wild animal. "Have I been that mean?"

"Yeah. And it ain't cool. Your sweetheart has only been gone three days. By day seven, you may not have a staff."

"I can't eat and I'm not sleeping much at night. Thursday's budget vote may be postponed indefinitely, which makes no sense at all. Things would be bearable if *she* were here."

"Well, she's not. But politics is politics. It's a never-ending game. Isn't that what you always say?"

"Yeah, because it's true."

"In that case, grind hard while Jazz is away. The time will fly by."

*****

Jazz stuffed the bottle of insect repellent inside her tote bag and left her hotel room. The camera crew was waiting for her in the lobby. They were going sightseeing in Manzini, one of the more popular and culturally rich cities in Swaziland. Their first few days in the country had been spent in the administrative capital of Mbabane interviewing members of parliament and other government officials. Yesterday Jazz attended a luncheon held exclusively for members of the international media hosted by royal coronation planners. The event had included a tour of the grounds of Ludzidzini royal palace and the surrounding village. It was a wonderful adventure.

Jazz stepped inside the empty elevator thinking about Emmanuel. She missed him like crazy. He had called her before sunrise to tell her that he wouldn't be able to join her in Swaziland after all. The two major parties were at odds over various items in the budget. Emmanuel didn't see a vote taking place anytime soon, but he needed to be present just in case. Jazz was disappointed that he couldn't travel to Swaziland to be with her. It was a very fascinating country, and she wanted to share the experience with him. And she wanted to make love with him again. They'd only had one full night together, but it had changed her life. The magic was still very much alive in Jazz's memory. Every moment of their brief stay in the Hamptons was unforgettable.

The elevators opened, and Jazz stepped into the lobby. She immediately saw her coworkers. They were talking with Nuwan, the chaperone the Swazi government had assigned to escort them around the country. Two armed guards and a personal driver were at their disposal during their stay as well.

"Good morning, Madame Dupree," Nuwan greeted Jazz, curving his arm for her to take hold. "Are you ready to explore Manzini, my dear?"

Jazz hooked her arm through Nuwan's. "Good morning, sir. I'm ready." She looked at the camera crew. "What's up, guys?"

The four men greeted Jazz. They were all dressed casually in shorts, t-shirts, and sandals. The tour of Manzini wasn't a part of their official business in Swaziland. Therefore, they didn't have their camera or other equipment with them. The BDT team had decided to go sightseeing at their leisure. It would be their last day of down time before they started filming pre-coronation activities in Mbabane and Ludzidzini. Nuwan had promised to show them a great time on the tour.

*****

"We do not want *this* king! The man is unfit. He will thrust our beloved country deeper into poverty. It is believed that he will take on many more wives than the previous king. He will spend astronomical amounts of money to please them and his multitude of children. Our poor citizenry can no longer live under such frivolity. We must resist this new king at all cost!"

The group of men nodded their heads in silence. Obviously, they were in total agreement with their leader. Their secret meeting at his modest home in the small city of Bhunya had drawn dozens of concerned citizens who were opposed to the appointment of Swaziland's new king. As concerns were being voiced earlier by other attendees, emotions flared. It had already been decided that a rebellion would take place. The newly formed rebel group was prepared to take up arms against the monarchy and the parliament of the kingdom. Secret meetings and assault trainings had been in progress for weeks. Hundreds of men had sworn their allegiance to the rebel leader, Dogma Ludvonga. They trusted him to lead the revolt. Under his command, they would invade and overtake the American Embassy in Mbabane and hold the ambassador and his staff hostage. Their goal was to force the United States to take some form of action against the monarchy and the parliament of Swaziland on behalf of its 1.5 million impoverished citizens. Mr. Ludvonga believed that the most powerful nation in the world could appeal to the king and his government, convincing them to cease the wasteful spending of the country's dismal wealth and take better care of its people.

As it stood to date, Swaziland was one of the poorest countries in Africa. The royal family's worth was estimated at over 200 million U. S. dollars. Their outlandish spending habits had been well noted throughout the world. The new king's lifestyle was expected to be even more extravagant than the king before him. Mr. Ludvonga and his followers were adamant that he would not take the throne. And if by some unexpected flaw in their plan he did, he would not live long enough to enjoy it.

*****

"Thank you so much for an awesome day in Manzini, Nuwan. I had a wonderful time soaking up your rich culture. The food and the music were amazing, and your people are so friendly. They made us feel at home."

"I am pleased that you and your colleagues enjoyed yourselves today. I would love to show you more of my country, Madame Dupree."

"We'll be very busy tomorrow. Pre-production work starts early in the morning. We probably won't finish before late in the evening."

Nuwan cupped Jazz's elbow and held her in place. "It would be my honor for you to have dinner with me tomorrow. There is a five star restaurant near Big Bend that I'm sure you would enjoy. Nothing would please me more than to escort you there."

"I'm sorry, Nuwan. I can't have dinner with you. I'm in your country to *work*, not to socialize."

"But I will wait until you have finished your work. What would be the harm? You have no husband. Have you been promised to a man back home?"

Jazz studied Nuwan's sun-kissed face. His skin was smooth as silk. She considered him a handsome man. He was very tall and thin. His toothy grin was infectious. Jazz was quite fond of Nuwan, but only in a *friendly* way.

"I haven't been promised to any man," she finally told him. "We don't practice such traditions in America. But if you must know, there is someone special in my life. Therefore, I don't think I should go to dinner with you. It wouldn't be proper."

"I see. Well, I must bid you goodnight at this time. Enjoy your rest, Madame Dupree."

Jazz hurried to join the crew just as they reached the elevator. She was flattered that Nuwan had taken an interest in her, but she didn't feel the same way about him. There was room for only one man in her heart, and his name was Emmanuel Marcus Day. Jazz was counting down the days until she would be home and in his arms again. Time was moving much too slow for her. When they'd spoken at sunrise, she had detected longing in his voice. He missed Jazz just as much as she missed him. There was no mistake about it. Their one night together had drawn them deeper into each other. It was scary to Jazz, but she was falling in love with Emmanuel. She couldn't deny it any longer. Love was offering her another chance.

Chapter Twenty

"I get the distinct impression that you've been avoiding me, Congressman. I have called your office and left several messages over the past two days. Why haven't you returned any of my calls?"

Emmanuel stopped walking and faced Gigi. He folded his arms across his chest. "What would you like to talk about, Ms. Perdue? I have ten minutes before my next appointment. I'm listening."

"Can't we at least go upstairs to your office so I can sit down? A bottle of spring water would be nice too."

"We can sit right over there on that bench." Emmanuel nodded his head in the direction of a bench near a statue.

Gigi followed him and took a seat next to him. "How are you these days? I didn't see you at the Senator Stockton's fund raiser. He's one of your best buddies."

"I was busy. I sent him a check. I know you didn't track me down to ask me about Henry Stockton. What do you really want to discuss?"

"Why are you so distant toward me? We do have a past, or have you forgotten?"

"We had a one night stand a very long time ago." Emmanuel checked his watch. "I have to go now."

"Wait," Gigi whispered, tugging at his arm. "Meet me for a drink this evening. I'm working on an idea for a show about the mistreatment of African-Americans in the justice system. I need to pick your brain on the subject."

"Call Tyrell. He can give you copies of all my research with statistics and other details. Every speech I've ever made on the topic is on file as well as state by state legislation and all federal laws. Ask him to pull minutes from special judiciary committee meetings as far back as you care to go. I really need to get to another meeting. Take care of yourself, Ms. Perdue. I heard you've been under the weather recently. Feel better."

Gigi watched Emmanuel disappear around the corner. She had gone through hell trying to get a hold of him. Sherry had told her that he'd been working late hours since Jazz left for Africa. According to

Sherry via Fabian, the congressman was in a funk because his girlfriend was halfway around the world. Although Gigi was happy that she'd managed to put some distance between Jazz and Emmanuel temporarily, she was disturbed by his reaction to their separation. Everyone knew that absence made the heart grow fonder, which meant that once Jazz returned from her assignment, she and Emmanuel would have one explosive reunion. Gigi gagged at the very thought of it. The reconnection would only draw them closer together. If they became too close, she would never be able to tear them apart.

*****

Jazz felt like a princess rubbing elbows with African royalty. She had been fortunate to land an interview with the new king's younger brother and older sister. And she had taken pictures with two of his wives. They were very attractive and gracious women.

"This is like a dream, Nuwan. Although I didn't want to make the trip here, I'm kind of glad I did. Just think of the stories I'll be able to tell my children."

"How many children will you birth, Madame Dupree?"

Jazz rolled the question around inside her head a few times. She hadn't

entertained the idea of marriage or motherhood in years. When she was engaged to Mario, they had discussed having two or three children. She was going to work part-time in order to be a hands-on mom and a football wife. Today was a new day, and she was involved with a different type of man. Jazz wondered what kind of marriage and family Emmanuel wanted. Would he allow her to work or would he want her to stay home, raise their children, and support him in his political career?

"I want two children," she told Nuwan after a moment of pondering. "A boy and a girl would be ideal."

"Your children will be very lucky to have a beautiful, intelligent woman like you as their mother."

Drum beats alerted the crowd that the new king was about to enter the room. The official coronation would begin shortly. Jazz's pulse started to race. She searched the balcony for the camera crew. They were in place recording everything. The queen regent, who was the mother of the new king, along with other members of the royal family, marched slowly into the room dressed in colorful traditional African attire. The women wore stunning headdresses in radiant colors and fabulous gold and diamond jewelry. They glided gracefully in a straight line to the drum beats. The crowd gasped when the king made his grand entrance at the end of the procession, flanked by uniformed military guards dressed in blue. His Highness was draped in gold lace and red feathers. A unique gold necklace and medallion hung from his neck. He was a tall man with a stocky frame. His face, dark and full, was very somber and somewhat mysterious. The wooden cane he held in his hand had been carved to display faces of African warriors. The king climbed the steps that led to a high platform in the middle of the room. He stood regally to a long and energetic round of applause and chants in his native tongue.

The crowd of dignitaries and guests took their seats to witness history in the making. The head of parliament joined the king and the queen regent on the platform. The official oath and blessing began. Jazz watched in awe, committing every detail to memory.

*****

"There is no need for Ramone to meet us at the airport. You can see him later. I want you all to myself." Emmanuel rolled over from his right side and rested his back on the bed.

"We can't hurt his feelings, sweetheart. He's my best friend. He wants to see me to make sure I'm alright after my extended trip."

"You can call him from my house to tell him that you're safe with me."

"Your house?"

"Yes. As soon as you clear customs and retrieve your luggage, you're coming home with *me*. Don't argue with me, woman."

Jazz sighed in defeat. "Fine. I'll send Ramone a text message to let him know you'll be picking me up from the airport. He's going to be highly upset."

"He'll get over it eventually. What are you doing tomorrow on your last day there?"

"We're going to visit the U.S. ambassador to Swaziland at the American embassy for lunch and a tour. Later, the crew and I will join our chaperone and some of his friends for a farewell dinner."

"You'll be in my arms in forty-eight hours. I can't wait."

"Yes, you can. You don't have a choice."

*****

Jazz excused herself from the casual conversation to wash her hands. Lunch was about to be served in Ambassador Vance's office. Nuwan stopped her when she stepped out into the hall.

"Where are you going, Madam Dupree?"

"I'm going to the ladies' room. The caterers are in the ambassador's suite right now. They'll be serving lunch soon. I hope you'll join us."

Nuwan shook his head. "I can eat later. I will stay on post outside the door."

"Suit yourself, but the food smells delicious. I'll be right back," Jazz announced, walking away."

"I'm going with you."

"That's not necessary. I'm going to the *ladies' room*, Nuwan. I think I'll be okay by myself."

Jazz hurried down the hall with the heels of her sandals clicking against the marble floor. Tomorrow morning she would be on a plane en route to Nigeria, then on to London, and finally, to Washington, D.C. The thought of seeing Emmanuel brought a smile to her face. Jazz checked out her reflection in the bathroom mirror. She had a noticeable tan from the Swazi sun. Her tummy growled. Breakfast had consisted of a banana, a few slices of melon, and sweet bread. The meal was long gone now. Jazz was starving. She washed her hands quickly and walked toward the door. A huge explosion sounded and shook the building like an earthquake. Off balance, Jazz fell to the cold, hard floor in shock. Loud voices and heavy footsteps pounding against the floor below filled the air. Jazz was terrified.

"Madame Dupree, where are you? Speak to me, my dear!" Nuwan burst into the bathroom and found Jazz struggling to her feet. He picked her up and ran out the door.

Two more blasts rocked the building, causing large cracks in the ceiling. Debris and dust poured down on them like heavy rain. They both begin to cough. The shouts and footsteps seemed to be getting closer. Jazz screamed when she heard gunshots in the distance. Smoke fogged the hallway outside of Ambassador Vance's office, limiting their visibility. Nuwan turned the door knob with Jazz still in his arms. It didn't budge. The door was locked. He placed Jazz on her feet and banged on the door with his fist.

"Ambassador Vance, I am Nuwan Mdluli, chaperone for Madame Jazz Dupree. I have her with me, sir. Please allow us to come in for our safety. There is chaos in the building."

"He's telling the truth! Please help us, Ambassador!" Jazz cried. "Please help us!"

Chapter Twenty-One

Ambassador Vance hung up the phone and looked around at the troubled faces in his office. Jazz was sitting in one of the chairs near his desk. She was visibly shaken up. Nuwan was standing next to her holding her hand.

"A group of armed rebels have stormed their way into the building. They're disgruntled with the Swazi monarchy and parliament. They've taken dozens of my staff members who are housed on the first two floors hostage. Our security personnel were able to stop them before they made it any further up. For now, we're out of harm's way and so are the people on the fourth floor. The rebels said they want to indulge in peaceful negotiations."

"What demands have the bloody fools made, Mr. Ambassador?" Nuwan asked.

"They want the United States to negotiate some type of economic agreement between them and the government to help the poor people in this country. And they want the new king dethroned so his younger brother can take his place. Their leader, Dogma Ludvonga, has requested a meeting with me in two hours downstairs where they have set up a base. They have promised not to harm me or take me against my will. If I refuse to meet with them, they have promised to start torturing the hostages.

*****

"The vice president's office just called, Congressman. South African Airways flight 97483 left Swaziland over two hours ago."

"That's excellent. Thank God Jazz is safe." Emmanuel leaned back in his chair relieved.

"Yes!" Tyrell cheered and pump his fist in the air.

Edgar hung his head. "No, sir. The flight left, but *Ms. Dupree* wasn't aboard. The four men in the camera crew that accompanied her to Swaziland have all been accounted for. At this time we have no idea where Ms. Dupree is."

Emmanuel sprung to his feet. "How is that possible? Jazz was to be with them and a government chaperone at all times. There was supposed to have been two armed guards around to protect them wherever they went."

Edgar's fair complexion became fully flushed. Beads of perspiration had formed on his forehead. "At the last minute the crew decided to skip the luncheon at the American embassy. They went souvenir shopping instead. Ms. Dupree went to meet Ambassador Vance with the chaperone and one of the armed guards. The other guard accompanied the crew to a shopping center in Ezulwini Valley."

"Are you trying to tell me that Jazz is being held hostage by a group of stupid rebels?"

"Let's just wait and see, Uncle Manny. I'm sure the Pentagon will be providing frequent updates. Who knows? Maybe the chaperone and the security guard were able to get Jazz out of the embassy before the invasion."

"I'm not waiting for any updates. Edgar, get the president's office on the phone."

"Yes, sir, right away."

*****

On the flight to Jacksonville, Florida, Emmanuel had only one thought in mind: Jazz. He had prayed a thousand prayers asking God to protect her. The secretary of state had confirmed that she was indeed inside the American embassy at the time the rebels overtook it. Supposedly, she was safer than others. The rebels were holding hostages on the lower levels of the building. Ambassador Vance's office on the third floor was believed to be a secure zone for now. That's where Jazz, her chaperone, and her security guard were. They had been locked in for their safety. The rebels had been denied access to the third and fourth floors by the embassy's security team in a shootout wherein five men were killed. Reports confirmed that all five casualties were rebels.

Learning that Jazz was safe for the time being gave Emmanuel very little relief. He wanted her out of Swaziland and home where she belonged. Until that time, he believed it was his responsibility to personally inform her grandparents about her present situation. Emmanuel dreaded meeting the elderly couple under such unpleasant circumstances. He had imagined that his initial meeting with Mr. and Mrs. Anderson would be at a happy family gathering or maybe on their next visit to Washington to spend time with Jazz. They weren't supposed to meet like this. The news he was about to give them was going to upset them terribly.

Emmanuel had already experienced an emotional dramatization from Ramone when he stopped by his salon on the way to the airport to tell him what had happened to Jazz. It was like a scene out of a Broadway production. Ramone let a bloodcurdling scream and fainted at Emmanuel's feet as soon as he heard the words 'hostage' and 'armed rebels'. It took some of the stylists several minutes to wake him and calm him down once he came to.

"Unc, you've got to be strong. Jazz is going to be fine. Remember what the president and secretary of state said. If the rebels don't surrender peacefully within forty-eight hours, the U. S. will make plans to take military action against them. The marines will get Jazz and the other hostages out of the embassy safely by any means."

Emmanuel looked at his handsome nephew. He was very proud of the young man he had become. They were only twelve years apart. Tyrell was more like a little brother to him than a nephew. They shared similar physical features. Both stood over six feet tall, and their complexions were identical. They knew each other well. Emmanuel had complete trust in Tyrell because he had proven how loyal and supportive he was. If he believed that Jazz would be rescued soon, Emmanuel had to believe it too.

"I hope you're right, nephew. If something happens to her—"

"Nothing is going to happen. Jazz is an *American*. Our country takes care of its own. And besides that, she's a sistah from the south. That means she's fearless and tough. I believe she could take a rebel down if he made her mad enough."

Emmanuel laughed envisioning that scene. "Jazz once punched a big linebacker in the nose for smacking her on her ass after an interview. I'm sure she could defend herself if it came down to it. I just don't want her to get injured or raped by some overzealous idiot."

"She won't. God will protect her."

*****

Day 7- Hostage situation- American Embassy; Kingdom of Swaziland, Africa...

Jazz held her breath as her heart beat frantically. The telephone lines had finally been restored at the embassy. After waiting for hours to place a call, her turn had come. She had dialed Emmanuel's cell phone number and she was waiting for it to ring. The connection process was somewhat slow, but she was willing to wait. Tyrell answered after the third ring. Jazz breathed a sigh of relief when she heard the familiar voice.

"It's me, Tyrell...*Jazz*. How are you?"

"I'm worried to death about you. We all are. How are you, Jazz? Are you okay?"

"I want to come home. It's insane over here. I was hoping to talk to your uncle. Is he around?"

"He's in a committee meeting. I'm going to run as fast as I can to catch the elevator to the fifth floor. Can you hold on?"

Jazz looked behind her, absent-mindedly clutching the key shaped pendant lying on her chest. There was a long line of people waiting to call home to speak with their loved ones. "I don't think I can. Just tell Emmanuel that I called. Ask him to call me here at the embassy. I'm in Ambassador Joseph Vance's office. I've got to call my grandparents now, Tyrell. Goodbye."

*****

Mr. McConnell was devastated about Jazz's misfortune in Swaziland. He blamed himself for what had happened to her. He'd been maintaining constant contact with her grandparents and Emmanuel since he had learned that her name was on the list of Americans who were in the embassy at the time of the rebel invasion. The old man couldn't help but wish that it was *Gigi* over there facing rebels rather than Jazz. He wondered if she had faked an anxiety attack to avoid the assignment. If she had, there was no way he could prove it. He was going to have to keep a closer eye on Gigi from now on effective immediately. She and the rest of the senior reporters were due in his office soon for a meeting. Mr. McConnell needed someone to cover the big budget vote on Capitol Hill as soon as both parties agreed on one. He would give the assignment to anyone except Gigi.

Chapter Twenty-Two

Day 13- Hostage situation- American Embassy; Kingdom of Swaziland, Africa...

"I'm doing all I can to get you back on U. S. soil, Jazz. I need you to believe that."

"I do, Emmanuel, but the conditions in this building are deplorable. I wasn't able to call again until today because the phone lines are constantly collapsing. The running water is cold, and food is very limited. It's extremely hot here too, but we aren't allowed to open the windows. It's not safe."

"How is the ambassador treating you? I heard he was a very cool guy."

"Because I'm the only female in his suite, I receive preferential treatment. He allows me to sleep on his sofa every night, and I have the entire ladies' room to myself."

"I have a meeting with the vice president tomorrow. Hopefully, he'll have good news about a rescue operation. I'm sure the marines will be the ones to free all of you from the rebels."

"I hope it'll happen soon. I don't know how much more of this I can take. When I spoke with my grandmother earlier, she was in tears. It broke my heart."

"I will call her and your grandfather this evening."

"They like you, Emmanuel. They like you a lot."

"I like them too. I think they're a lovely couple."

"My time is up on the phone. I'll call you soon."

"Take care of yourself, Jazz. I need you to come back home to me."

"I'm praying that I will."

When Jazz hung up the phone, tears she'd been holding back spilled from her eyes. She fingered the pendant around her neck, remembering the moment Emmanuel had surprised her with it. Now she wondered if she would ever see him again.

*****

The atmosphere at Black Diamond had lost some of its flavor since the news about Jazz had circulated. Everyone was concerned about her well being. Some employees had collected nonperishable food items, clothes, and toiletries and shipped them off to the American embassy in Swaziland. Many people wrote letters and sent cards of encouragement. Jackson had spearheaded the effort with Mr. McConnell's blessing. No one knew for sure if Jazz would ever receive the box or not. The situation over there was so uncertain. Everyone hoped that the rebels would have mercy on her and give her the package.

Gigi didn't donate a single item to Jazz. She said that the U. S. government had more than likely sent aid to the embassy for the ambassador and the rest of the Americans being held there. Furthermore, she'd gotten word from Sherry that Jazz was not in any direct danger. In fact, she was receiving preferential treatment from Ambassador Vance and his staff. And sooner or later the U.S. Marine Corps was going to storm the embassy and kill all the rebels anyway. Jazz would be rescued and come home a national treasure and resume her love affair with Emmanuel. Her fame would blast to the moon as she made appearances on all of the morning and afternoon talk shows telling her story. She'd probably land a major book deal too. Gigi was pretty sure that a can of tuna or a toothbrush couldn't top that happy ending.

*****

"Mr. Vice President, sir, why can't the marines go into the embassy by night and catch the rebels off guard? Surely, they have more weapons, ammunition, and manpower than a group of thugs do. They're at a clear advantage."

"It's not that simple, Congressman. So far there have been no American casualties. The negotiators have been able to get food and supplies to all of the hostages. Those rebels don't want to kill anyone. They just want to be heard and taken seriously. We have given them reason to believe that we are interested in their concerns."

"What is our next move, sir?"

The vice president tapped his index finger casually against his jaw. "A certain amount of trust has been established between Ambassador Vance and the rebel leader. In a few days, the Swazi parliament will meet with the new king and members of the royal family. No significant changes will be made. The meeting will be nothing more than a goodwill gesture or an act of appeasement."

"The rebels aren't stupid, sir. Won't they expect to see some type of written resolution? They want to secure financial assistance and supplies for their fellow countrymen. Those men believe the only way to accomplish that is for the new king to be dethroned."

"Congressman Day, the United States does not have the right or authority to interfere with the Swazi government. Canada, Great Britain, and our country, under the leadership of the United Nations, will donate tons of rice, cooking oil, and medical supplies to Swaziland. A voucher system will be set in place to ensure that the Swazi citizens that need the most assistance will be accommodated first. It's not exactly what the rebels want, but it's the best that can be done at this time."

"Do you honestly believe the plan will work?"

"I think if the ambassador presents it as the first step of many to assist the poor people in Swaziland, it may get some of the hostages freed. If not, we'll plan a military attack against the rebels."

*****

Day 22- Hostage situation- American Embassy; Kingdom of Swaziland, Africa...

"Mr. Ludvonga, the offer we have presented to you can be very beneficial to thousands of starving people. What you are asking of my country and me can't be done overnight. There are innocent people in this building who have served the Kingdom of Swaziland diligently and unselfishly. I am one of those people."

Jazz stared at the telephone with much hope. She had been granted permission to witness the very important conference call. Voices whispering in native Swazi dialect on the other end of the line assured her that Ambassador Vance's proposal was being considered. The food and medical supplies that the United Nations and the participating countries had donated had arrived in Mbabane. Peacekeepers were ready to distribute the items to the Swazi people in need of it. However, the rebels had not agreed to the terms of the deal. Therefore, the ambassador was refusing to allow any of the supplies to be removed from the thousands of crates until after Mr. Ludvonga had released every female and elderly male hostage from the embassy unharmed immediately.

"We will release *no one* unless the leader of parliament and a member of the royal family agree to meet with me and my lieutenant. They must hear our concerns in person at once."

"So you will deny your countrymen food and supplies that are currently available for distribution, Mr. Ludvonga? That is *absurd*! I thought you wanted to help the poor in your homeland."

"I do, but on a long-term basis, not temporarily. Arrange the meeting at once or we will be forced to take drastic and very costly measures."

Chapter Twenty-Three

Emmanuel returned to his office after a meeting with the secretary of state and the secretary of defense. He was terribly disappointed. Neither gentleman thought it was expedient to send the marines into Swaziland to rescue Ambassador Vance and the other Americans at this time. As long as there were no acts of violence being reported, they wanted to wait. Emmanuel disagreed with the plan. He had spoken to Jazz late last night, and she'd sounded extremely distraught. It was the first time he had ever heard her cry. She had begged that he do whatever he could to sway the president to act immediately on the hostage's behalf. Something inside of Emmanuel snapped after hearing Jazz's tearful plea. He wanted her home and out of harm's way and he was determined to make it happen somehow.

The matter was a very personal one for Emmanuel, but he had maintained the highest level of professionalism during the course of the meeting with the two secretaries. There were moments when Edgar had to speak for him so that his emotions would not jeopardize the progress or eventual outcome of the conference. Nevertheless, nothing that he or Emmanuel said had convinced the secretaries of state and defense that a rescue attempt executed by the marines was necessary at this point. Their plan was to continue on the path of diplomacy for as long as the rebels agreed to abstain from all forms of violence against the ambassador and the rest of the Americans.

Emmanuel picked up the phone from his desk. Regrettably, it was his duty to call Jazz's grandparents to inform them that no plans for a rescue mission had been made. Unfortunately, their only grandchild would remain a hostage of Swazi rebels indefinitely.

*****

"Unc, we've received word that the deputy secretary of state is on his way to Swaziland. Edgar tried to reach you, but you were at the Black Caucus luncheon."

"Something must've happened over there. Why else would the president have sent him?"

"The rebels have turned up the heat on Ambassador Vance because the meeting with Ludvonga and the leader of parliament was unproductive. Threats have been made."

Emmanuel stopped walking. Tyrell did too. Uncle and nephew stood toe to toe in the busy and crowded capitol corridor. "What kinds of threats?"

"The rebels have promised to start torturing hostages if the new king is not dethroned within seventy-two hours. Other men have joined their cause. The president is afraid that violence will break out all over the country. Innocent Swazi citizens could be killed."

"I want to speak with the vice president before the end of the day," Emmanuel said, walking toward the elevator.

Tyrell matched his quick stride. "I'll tell Edgar to arrange the call as soon as possible. I thought you'd like to know that Fabian sent your request for a meeting with Mr. Donaldson from the CIA. He's waiting for a response."

"I'm glad to hear that. I want a full staff meeting around four o'clock. Let everyone know that they must attend without exception."

"Yes, sir."

*****

"What brings you to my office, young lady?"

Sherry stood nervously staring down at Gigi who was seated at her desk. The chilling effect of her arrogance made the room seem tiny and icy cold. Her condescending tone of voice warned the young speechwriter that she was in the lion's den. Black Diamond was Gigi's comfort zone and her territory where she had power and influence. Sherry figured that no little peon such as herself had ever dared to confront the revered and mighty reporter on her own turf. But every dog had its day, and after every game there had to be a winner. Sherry had every intention of being victorious. The first strategic step to winning any battle was to disarm and confuse the enemy. Gigi was in for a surprise attack.

"Did you not hear me?" Gigi got up from her desk chair. "What gave you the boldness to come to my place of employment unannounced?"

"I...um...I needed to speak with you, but you wouldn't take my calls. What other choice did I have but to come here?"

"Make it quick," Gigi snapped, and folded her arms across her bosom. "I'm a busy woman. I don't have time for any nonsense."

"I told Congresswoman Corbett about our little arrangement. She knows *everything*, Ms. Perdue. I confessed that I've been feeding you information that Fabian has confided in me about Congressman Day."

"Oh really? What did my dear friend, Joanna, have to say about your manipulative and deceitful behavior?"

"She fired me of course and told me I'd never work on Capitol Hill again."

Gigi threw her head back and cackled like a deranged woman. "You lost your job, and I'm willing to bet my next bonus check that your boyfriend is going to leave you too. Once he sees all of the text messages and emails we've exchanged, proving that you've been using him to help me, he'll drop you like a hot potato."

"Actually, it was *Fabian* who advised me to come clean with Congresswoman Corbett." Sherry smiled triumphantly as shock registered on Gigi's face. "Yes, I confessed to him first. Our relationship may be in limbo right now, but at least I'm free from your trap. I was stupid to get involved with you, but it was a lesson learned."

"Get out of my office! Get the hell out! You have no idea who you're messing with."

Sherry scurried to the door on shaky legs. Her hand had just touched the knob when Gigi called her name. Sherry turned around feeling dizzy with fear. She was almost in tears, her breathing choppy and labored.

"If I were you, little girl, I'd watch my back."

*****

The situation with Jazz still being held hostage in Swaziland was more than enough for Emmanuel to contend with. But after his private discussion with Fabian Battier, his senior aide, he realized he had a problem on his home front. Emmanuel, Tyrell, and Edgar had stayed behind after the other staff members left the office to sort through the mess.

"Unc, we're all guilty of mentioning minor pieces of information about you to our friends and relatives from time to time. I don't believe Fabian meant you any harm."

"I agree with Tyrell, sir. I've told my fiancée certain things about your schedule and individuals you may have had meetings with. I trust her like I'm sure Fabian trusted Sherry."

Emmanuel rocked back and forth in his chair a few times in deep thought. He stopped and looked up at his two most trusted staff members. "I'll admit that Fabian didn't divulge any top secret political information from this office. He dipped into my personal life, which is always off-limits to the public. Considering that Sherry worked for a member of congress also, I can't honestly call Fabian's trust in her naïve. Aides from different camps talk all the time, I'm sure."

"We do. I'm a little more cautious than everyone else, though, because you're my uncle."

"What are you going to do about Gigi Perdue, sir?"

"Nothing," Emmanuel answered point-blank. "I don't have time to deal with her right now, Edgar. Getting Jazz home is my top priority. Ms. Perdue will hang her own self in due time."

Chapter Twenty-Four

"Good morning, Congressman." The president stood from his desk and extended his hand. "How are you?"

Emmanuel shook the president's offered hand. "I'm as well as can be expected under the circumstances, sir. Hopefully, the outcome of this meeting will give me some optimism."

"Have a seat, Congressman. I'll cut right to the chase. The Red Scorpions, a highly trained marine special forces unit, are preparing for a rescue operation in Swaziland as we speak."

"Thank God." Emmanuel closed his eyes for a moment and exhaled. His prayers had been answered. "When will the mission take place, sir?"

"Four choppers equipped with the very latest in military technology will leave Twenty-nine Palms Marine Base in California this evening. Thirty-five of our most skillful and fearless paratroopers, marksmen, and explosive experts will be aboard the four aircrafts. Their first stop will be Arlington Air Force Base in Virginia where all equipment will undergo a final inspection. Afterwards, the choppers will fly to London first, then to Liberia and Rwanda before finally landing in Swaziland."

"How confident are you about the outcome of this mission, Mr. President?"

"I expect a successful operation. The vice president and I have been briefed by the pentagon, the CIA, and the commander of the Red Scorpions. The operation is considered dangerous but necessary. I refuse to allow innocent Americans serving in foreign countries to die at the hands of radicals. Ambassador Vance has done an excellent job meeting the needs of the Swazi people. His life is now in danger due to no fault of his own. And Ms. Dupree is an innocent journalist who was in the country covering a story. The assignment should've been one of the greatest experiences of her career. The rebels have ruined it for her, I'm certain. But she and the other's will be rescued soon, Congressman. You have my word on that."

"How long after the mission will the hostages be brought home?"

"Immediately after everyone is rescued and accounted for, they'll all be treated by U.S. military doctors and a full medical staff aboard an air force jet in waiting. If the hostages that wish to travel home are healthy enough to do so, they'll be allowed to leave Swaziland as soon as possible. God forbid that any of them are injured during the mission. If so, they'll be admitted to Mbabane Government Hospital for treatment under heavy security. Our government will be responsible for bringing them home whenever they receive medical clearance to travel."

"Mr. President, I am requesting permission to travel to Swaziland on the air force jet, sir. You have my word that I will not interfere with the military operation in any way. I just need to be there. I'm sure you understand my position, sir."

The president smiled and wagged his finger at Emmanuel. "You're a slick one, Congressman Day. You've been on top of this situation from the very beginning. I should've been prepared for your request. There're many major factors I must take into consideration before I give you an answer."

"What factors are those?"

"Setting your emotions aside, do you really think it would be wise for you to fly into a potentially uncivil country without any military training under your belt, Congressman?"

"It won't be wise at all, sir," Emmanuel admitted. "But I'm still asking for clearance to go at my own risk."

*****

Day 32- Hostage situation- American Embassy; Kingdom of Swaziland, Africa...

"Sometimes I think I'll never leave this place alive."

"No, Madame Dupree, you mustn't think like that. Hold on to your faith."

"I'm trying to, but it's hard, Nuwan. I thought for sure that the rebels would have released me and the other women in exchange for the corn meal, dried fish, and malaria medication the UN sent. It's just sitting in boxes along with the rest of the supplies going to waste. I'm beginning to believe that no matter what Ambassador Vance and the United Nations or other concerned countries offer them, the rebels will not be satisfied. They're going to let the Swazi people starve to death and then kill us."

"Again, I tell you to remain positive and stand on your faith. And please take care of yourself. I noticed that you have not eaten very much in two days. Why is that?"

"My stomach can't tolerate the food anymore. It makes me sick. And I'm afraid to drink more than two bottles of water a day because I don't know when we'll receive more. The lack of food is causing my head to hurt constantly. My body is extremely weak, Nuwan."

A cloud of impenetrable darkness had swallowed the room hours ago. Jazz was unable to see Nuwan's face. Even at midnight, the air in the embassy was hot and stale. Jazz's white t-shirt was clinging to her body drenched with sweat. The whir of the ceiling fan spinning uselessly above them was the only sound in the entire building besides Nuwan's faint breathing. The quietness made it easy to hear the dull humming sound slicing through the sky.

"Do you hear that, Nuwan? It sounds like the engine of a plane."

Jazz heard her chaperone moving from his pallet on the floor. She smelled the foul scent of his body, which was undoubtedly soaked with perspiration as he walked past her. The sound grew louder as if it were coming closer to the building.

"I think help is on the way," Ambassador Vance whispered. The sound had awakened him from his sleep.

Suddenly, a deafening thud rocked the embassy's foundation mimicking a shift in the earth's surface. The other eight men in the ambassador's suite ran into his office from the boardroom in a panic. The exterior of the building instantly became surrounded by blinding bright light. Engines—at least three—presumably from aircrafts, drowned out the screams of scared hostages all over the embassy. A series of thunderous blasts shook the building again. The sounds reminded Jazz of scenes from a military combat movie.

"I want Ms. Dupree to take cover under my desk immediately. Bring her over here, Nuwan!"

Jazz was snatched up from the sofa and carried to the other side of the room. She closed her eyes tight every time she heard an explosion. Endless rounds of gunfire and bone-chilling cries paralyzed Jazz with fear. Nuwan pushed her further under the desk when an object crashed through the window, splattering glass and concrete everywhere inside the office. A male voice barked at them from the outside. Seconds later, three men dressed in all black climbed through the window.

"Put down your weapons and show yourselves! This building and its occupants are now under the command of the United States Marines!"

Chapter Twenty-Five

"Congressman Day, you may see Ms. Dupree now, but don't stay too long, sir. It's important that she gets plenty of rest tonight. She's exhausted and very dehydrated. We had to treat her for shock too. The poor woman was terribly traumatized. The IV you will see is supplying her body with liquids and nutrients it needs to stabilize."

"I understand your concern, Dr. Simelane, but I'm not leaving Jazz alone tonight. I'll be by her side as long as she is in this hospital."

"That is against hospital rules, Congressman."

"Call the police and have me arrested. It's the only way you'll get rid of me."

Emmanuel left the doctor standing in the hall outside of Jazz's hospital room. When he entered the small sterile space, his emotions nearly unraveled. At that moment, it was clear to him that he had fallen in love with Jazz. He couldn't recall exactly when it had happened, but he knew it was true. The reality was sobering. Only love would have brought a man thousands of miles away from home to a country that was on the brink of political pandemonium to be with a woman he'd known just a short period of time. But love was timeless. Emmanuel had heard his mother say those words many times throughout his life. He now could attest to that statement. The few months he had spent with Jazz were more than enough time to connect with her in every aspect that truly mattered. They had purposely taken their time becoming acquainted, and their plan had worked. It had rewarded Emmanuel with the woman he wanted to spend the rest of his life with.

After fully embracing the truth, he approached Jazz's bed. She was thinner than before, and her hair had grown out a few inches. Regardless of her condition, she was a vision of loveliness. A sharp pain pricked Emmanuel's heart when he tried to imagine the fear and anxiety Jazz had suffered being confined in a small unfamiliar place with strangers against her will. She had endured it as only a strong and courageous woman could have. Emmanuel reached out and stroked Jazz's cheek with the back of his hand. He was tempted to wake her to let her know he was there to take care of her, but he knew that he shouldn't. He kissed her damp forehead and ran his fingers through her soft curly afro. Then he walked over to the corner of the room, picked up a chair, and placed it close to her bed. He sat down and closed his eyes and soon fell asleep.

*****

"I'm fine, Grandma. I promise you I am. Yes, ma'am, Emmanuel is here with me. I thought I was dreaming when I woke up and saw him smiling at me. All I could do was cry. It was the best surprise of my life. Yes, ma'am, I'm eating and drinking lots of juice and water. Dr. Simelane said he may discharge me the day after tomorrow if my iron and potassium levels are back to normal." Jazz frowned and removed the phone from her ear. She shoved it in Emmanuel's direction. "She wants to speak with *you*."

Emmanuel grinned and took the phone. "Mrs. Anderson, how are you, ma'am?"

Jazz stood up from her comfortable seat on the side of the bed and stared out her window. Her private room in the hospital had a nice view of a small flower garden. She rolled her eyes and sucked her teeth when Emmanuel laughed out loud. *She* was the one, who had endured a thirty-two day nightmare, so why did her grandmother insist on talking to him instead of her? Sallie Mae Anderson was usually skeptical about any man who expressed a romantic interest in Jazz. Mario's millions of dollars, fancy cars, and mansion on the hill didn't earn him any points with her. The harder he'd tried to impress her with expensive gifts and slick talk, the more suspicious she became of him. Mrs. Anderson had told Jazz from day one that she did not like Mario and she didn't trust him. But her attitude toward Emmanuel was altogether different. She thought very highly of him. He had won the older woman over the same way he had Jazz. His charm and sincerity had struck once again. Mrs. Anderson appreciated how Emmanuel had traveled to Jacksonville to personally inform her and her husband about the crisis in Swaziland. It gave her great consolation to know that someone in the United States government was working diligently to bring Jazz and the rest of the American hostages back home.

"Your grandmother is a very special lady," Jazz heard Emmanuel say. "She's funny too. We'll have to call her later this evening. She says your grandfather wants to speak to his *pumpkin*."

Jazz turned around to face Emmanuel. "Are you making fun of my nickname?"

"I wouldn't do that, baby. I think it's cute that your grandfather still thinks of you as his little girl. He loves you to no end, and so does your grandmother. They were worried sick about you."

"I know."

"Your grandmother was inconsolable after I broke the news to her about the madness going on over here. Tyrell and I didn't know what to do. Your grandfather was strong, though. He's her rock. He reminded her how brave and stubborn you could be at times. They both said you're as tough as nails. After reflecting on a few stories of how resilient and level-headed you were as a child, we all decided that you would survive and return home a stronger and more courageous woman."

"I feel like I'm mentally stronger. I'm not sure about being all that courageous. I had my moments. There were times when I couldn't stop crying. I was so afraid, Emmanuel. It was like a bad dream that I thought would never end. If it hadn't been for Nuwan, I would have lost my mind."

Emmanuel wrapped his arms around Jazz. "I owe Nuwan a lot for taking good care of you when I couldn't be here to do it myself."

"He called again while you were in the shower. He's coming to visit me later today."

"I've thanked him a thousand times already for keeping you safe. It just doesn't seem like enough, though. I'll have to think of something to give him to show my gratitude."

"Nuwan is a humble man. He will appreciate anything you give him."

"That may be true, but I'm not going to give the man just any old thing. Because of Nuwan, I'm able to hold you in my arms right now. That's priceless."

*****

"Yes ma'am. Ms. Dupree and I are very good friends and coworkers. In fact, I was the reporter from the Black Diamond network who had been assigned to cover the coronation of your country's new king initially. I became horribly ill two days before I was scheduled to leave. So, you see, I feel awful that my dear friend, Ms. Dupree, had such a devastating experience in Swaziland. I feel partially responsible."

"Because you are Ms. Dupree's friend and workmate, I will ring her room for you right away. I'm sure she will be thrilled to hear from you. Please hold while I connect you, ma'am."

Gigi smiled as the naïve switchboard operator at Mbabane Government Hospital transferred her call directly to Jazz's room. Being born with the gift of gab had its advantages. Gigi hadn't anticipated that she'd be connected to Jazz's room. She wasn't even sure if she was still in the hospital. She had made the international call fishing for information. But it must've been her lucky day. Not only had she confirmed that Jazz was indeed still in the hospital, she was moments away from hearing her voice. Gigi was smart. She would simply tell Jazz that Mr. McConnell had asked her to call on behalf of the network to find out how she was doing.

Gigi perched her backside on the edge of her desk as the phone finally begin to ring. The connection was much clearer than she'd expected. There was some humming and a slight crunching sound in the background as the phone rang, but it was bearable.

"Hello?"

Gigi's expertly arched eyebrows furrowed. The recognizable male voice that usually made her body tingle, greeted her a second time. She ended the call abruptly. Emmanuel was in Swaziland with Jazz. The implication of his actions stung like hell. He had crossed over the Atlantic Ocean and two continents to be at Jazz's bedside when he should've been back in Washington. He was in the middle of a general re-election campaign and hostile budget negotiations on Capitol Hill. *Manny loves Jazz*, an imaginary teasing voice whispered in Gigi's ear. No matter how bad she wanted it to be untrue, it was evident. Brothers loved hard, especially those from Emmanuel's generation. That was an undisputed fact. Jazz had worked her feminine super powers on the congressman, and he now belonged to her. Gigi knew in her heart that it was time to concede and accept defeat in a competition that she never stood a chance to win. But something inside of her was not ready to let it go just yet. She could never Emmanuel, but she was going to make damn sure that Jazz wouldn't either.

Chapter Twenty-Six

"Who was that on the phone, Emmanuel?"

"I have no idea," he answered honestly. "No one knows your location besides your grandparents, Tyrell, and the president's office. Maybe it was a misdirected call."

Jazz drifted back off to sleep with her head resting on Emmanuel's chest. Her hospital room had become their home away from home. Emmanuel was eager for Dr. Simelane to discharge Jazz so they could return to Washington. While it appeared that the rebels had been disarmed and the threat of violence no longer existed, he still wanted them to leave Swaziland as soon as possible. An air force jet would be sent under a direct presidential order to transport Jazz and the eleven Americans that were either injured during the rescue operation or took ill while being held hostage at the embassy back to the States. The four women and seven men were also patients at Mbabane Government Hospital. Emmanuel wasn't sure about the details of their injuries or illnesses, but he'd been told they all were stable.

Jazz's condition had improved a great deal. She was much stronger and had more energy than she did when she was first admitted for treatment. Hopefully, she would be released the day after tomorrow. Emmanuel had his fingers crossed. He thought it would be wise to alert the president's office that she may be able to travel before the end of the week. He didn't want to delay the air force jet's return for one second, especially after the strange phone call to Jazz's room. Something about it made Emmanuel uncomfortable. He had heard someone breathing on the other end through the hissing and buzzing before the call dropped. It may have been a bad case of paranoia, but he didn't want to take any chances. The sooner Dr. Simelane discharged Jazz from the hospital the better. An extended stay in Swaziland was not an option. If at all possible, Emmanuel wanted the air force jet to be waiting at the airport the moment he, Jazz, and the other hostages left the hospital.

*****

"Carol, Manny is on the phone!" Mr. Day walked through the house in the direction of the kitchen with the cordless phone in his hand. "He's still in Africa, so you can't talk all day, sweetheart."

Mrs. Day took the phone. "Manny, how are you, baby?"

"I'm fine, Mama."

"How is Jazz?"

"She's as good as new. We're just waiting on the results from a few more tests. If everything looks good, the doctor will discharge her in a few days. I hope to have her on a plane en route to the States soon afterwards."

"I'm happy to hear that Jazz is okay. My women's group has been praying for her. We didn't forget about you. You were in our thoughts and prayers too."

"Thank you, Mama. Give all of the women my love. Tell them Jazz thanks them for thinking about her."

"I certainly will. Now tell me something, Manny. What are your intentions for Jazz? You must be awfully serious about her to have taken a leave of absence from work in the middle of a campaign and budget talks."

"I'm in love with Jazz, Mama."

"I figured as much, baby, but does *she* know it?"

"I haven't told Jazz yet, but she should know by now."

"Tell her, Manny. Tell her right away. It's good to take your time about certain things, but when you truly love someone, there's no reason to delay. Let Jazz know exactly how you feel about her soon."

"I will. I promise."

*****

"No Emmanuel," Jazz pleaded. "I want to go home. Please don't make me stay here a minute longer. You heard Dr. Simelane. He's going to discharge me the day after tomorrow. I want to get out of this country the moment I leave the hospital."

109

"There's nothing I can do, Jazz. The Swazi government promised to provide us with twenty-four-hour security at secret accommodations until the others are stable enough to leave the hospital. An air force jet will be ordered to return to Swaziland, but it'll only make *one trip*. You'll have to wait until the rest of the hostages are released by the doctors."

Jazz wiped a fresh flow of tears from her eyes and sniffed. "I can't stay here. I'm afraid. I want to leave Swaziland and never come back again. Take me home *please*, Emmanuel. I'm begging you. I can't stay here!" She ran into the bathroom, slamming the door behind her.

"Jazz, please open the door, baby." Emmanuel knocked softly. "Let's talk about this rationally. I know you're afraid to be in this country. I won't lie to you. I have no idea how you felt all those days. It must've been scary as hell being trapped in that building for a month not knowing if you'd live or die. But it's over now. I'm here. I won't let anything happen to you. I promise. Open the door please."

"I want to go home, Emmanuel! I just want to go home," Jazz cried from the other side of the door.

*****

Tyrell closed the door to the conference room after the rest of the staff left. He and Edgar had just finished co chairing an emergency meeting to brief everyone on Emmanuel's position in the latest polls and to inform them about the attack ads his very wealthy opponent was running on television throughout his congressional district. Rex Westmore, a third generation millionaire whose family had amassed its fortune in construction and real estate, had launched a nasty smear campaign against Emmanuel. Mr. Westmore had spent millions on television ads, accusing his incumbent opponent of being a career politician who was out of touch with his constituents. He'd labeled Emmanuel a supporter of liberal wasteful spending and socialism. He questioned his patriotism because of his opposition to the war in Iraq and his adamancy about bringing U.S. troops home from Afghanistan as soon as possible. Worst of all, the Westmore camp had managed to get its hands on information about Emmanuel's private life. They were aware that he and Jazz were involved and that he had flown to Swaziland to be with her after the rescue operation. None of the information about Emmanuel's personal affairs had been included in Mr. Westmore's television ads, but he and his staffers never failed to mention it secretively wherever they went on the campaign trail. Political spies from the Day camp had reported the gossip to Edgar on more than one occasion. He believed the Westmore team would eventually go public with the information before the November election. The possibility caused him great concern, but Tyrell wasn't worried the slightest bit.

"Relax, Edgar and think about it. Uncle Manny hasn't done anything wrong. He's entitled to a personal life. The man is single. Just because he went to Swaziland to take care of his woman doesn't mean he's neglecting his duties on Capitol Hill. Women voters will find his actions honorable. Happily married men will understand why he did what he did without a doubt. Let Mr. Westmore and his folks spread all the rumors they want. We're still ahead in every single poll, so there is nothing to worry about."

"You're right. I guess I'm tripping over nothing, huh?"

Tyrell nodded his head and studied his worried friend's face from across the conference table. "Uncle Manny and Jazz will be back in the country tomorrow. Thank God he hasn't missed much on the Hill. They're still fighting over several items in the budget. After he gets Jazz settled, he'll row right back into the flow of things."

"I'm glad Congressman Day and Ms. Dupree didn't have to stay in Swaziland longer than they needed to. Mr. Mortimer didn't hesitate to send his pilot and plane over there when I called and asked on your uncle's behalf. He was happy to do it. Having rich friends isn't a bad thing at all."

＊＊＊＊＊

"Ms. Flora, I'm Ramone Sanchez, Jazz Dupree's best friend."

The housekeeper opened the door wider. "Come on in, chile. I've been expecting you." She stepped aside, so Ramone could enter the congressman's house. "You can put the suitcase and tote bag right here by the door."

"I thought I would unpack for Jazz. I know how she likes her things arranged, ma'am. Just show me to the room she'll be sleeping in, and I'll get started."

"It won't make much sense to set up anything in this house. They ain't staying here when they get back to the States."

Ramone eyed the petite older woman skeptically. He and Jazz had spoken at length before she left Swaziland. She had given him very specific instructions that he'd promise to follow down to the tiniest detail. Ramone had gone to Jazz's condo with her spare key that had been dangling from his ring for years. He packed every clothing item and toiletry on the list. Now he was at Emmanuel's house where he'd been instructed to deliver her suitcase and tote bag to his housekeeper. But the elderly woman didn't want him to unpack Jazz's things. It didn't add up.

"If Congressman Day isn't bringing Jazz *here* to stay, where is he taking her?"

Ms. Flora planted her fists on her slender hips and penetrated Ramone with her gaze. "You're gonna have to ask *Manny* that question. I reckon he didn't want me in his business because he didn't mention it. Nobody even knows they're on their way back from Africa except us important folks." Flora laughed at her own humor. "Like I said, you can put Jazz's luggage by the door and be on your way."

Chapter Twenty-Seven

The captain of Mr. Mortimer's private plane announced that he had run into turbulence over the country of Morocco in northwest Africa. He assured everyone aboard that there was nothing to fear. The crew of six took seats and fastened their seatbelts. The three other hostages from the American embassy in Swaziland—two men and a woman—did the same. All of the other hostages had been left behind in the hospital. Against safety rules, Emmanuel stood up and walked to the private cabin in the back of the plane to check on Jazz. She had slept from Swaziland to Nigeria where the pilot had stopped to refuel. An airplane attendant served her a light lunch of soup and salad at that time, and Emmanuel reminded her to take her medication. Shortly afterwards, Jazz returned to the private cabin to rest and had remained there.

Emmanuel opened the door and was surprised to find her awake. She was sitting up in bed against a pair of pillows watching a movie from Mr. Mortimer's Blu-Ray collection. "I came to make sure you were okay. We ran into some turbulence. I guess you felt it." He sat down on the bed.

"I'm not afraid of turbulence. I can handle that. Angry rebels with guns and explosives terrify me."

"There aren't any on this plane. I can guarantee you that, so please stop worrying."

Emmanuel took off his shoes and stretched out on the bed next to Jazz. She automatically rolled over into his arms. It was the place he wished she could always be. From now on, he intended to keep her as close to him as possible, starting with their visit to Jacksonville. Neither Jazz nor her grandparents knew that Emmanuel had planned a small surprise family reunion for them. He thought it would be a good idea for Jazz to see her folks after her horrendous experience in Swaziland. Tyrell had arranged for a driver to collect the luggage that Ramone had packed for Jazz from Emmanuel's home and deliver it to Mr. Mortimer's private airstrip at his Virginia estate. After a safety inspection of the plane and refueling its engine, a new pilot would fly the congressman and Jazz to Jacksonville where they would spend quality time with Mr. and Mrs. Anderson. There was nothing more comforting than the love and affection of one's family. Emmanuel was looking forward to seeing the expression on Jazz's face once he told her about his secret plans.

As much as he would've preferred spending every second of the day with Jazz, especially at night, he'd asked Tyrell to reserve a suite for him at the Crowne Plaza hotel on Jacksonville's riverfront. Unselfish sacrifice for the woman he'd fallen madly in love with would reward Emmanuel in due time. But for now, all he wanted was for Jazz to feel safe and secure around the two people she loved more than life. There would be plenty of days ahead of them when they could hide away from the rest of the world without interruption. He would have to be patient until then.

Jazz shrieked and put a death hold on Emmanuel when the plane suddenly dropped a few feet in altitude. He rubbed her back to soothe her. The turbulence continued rocking and jerking the plane up and down. The captain's calm voice floated throughout the cabin, informing the passengers and crew that if the turbulence continued, he would make an emergency landing in Madrid, Spain. He encouraged everyone to remain seated and restrained by their seatbelts. Jazz buried her face in the crook of Emmanuel's neck. Her warm breath fanning across his sensitive skin awakened a certain part of his anatomy that he had purposely laid to rest for the time being. The plane bobbed up and down again, causing their bodies to roll and shift. Emmanuel landed on his back with Jazz's left leg curled over his lower torso. Now face to face with her lips only a fraction of an inch away from his, their eyes met. Emmanuel swallowed hard trying to relieve his thirst for Jazz. An entire month had passed since the one and only time he had ever made love to her. It would be close to another week before he would have her totally to himself again.

Emmanuel pressed his lips to Jazz's open mouth. She responded the way he had hoped she would by wrapping her arms around his neck. Jazz returned his warm and soft kiss with hunger, but slowly. Emmanuel pulled her fully on top of his body. The kiss deepened just as the plane rocked and flopped.

"Emmanuel, we can't," Jazz whispered against his moist lips.

"Oh, yes, we can and we *will*."

Before Jazz could protest again, Emmanuel's lips regained control of hers. This kiss was hungrier and more urgent than the one before it. His hands cupped her butt and caressed it gently, pulling her softness closer to his hardness. More turbulence tossed their bodies into a position of advantage for Emmanuel. Jazz was underneath him gazing into his eyes. She looked sexy yet vulnerable. He sensed her apprehension, but the twinkle in her eyes revealed that her body longed to be loved by him. Emmanuel chose to seize the moment. He sat up and undressed with lightning speed as Jazz watched him in silence. Then he stumbled to the door through more turbulence and locked it before he returned to the bed. The plane rocked back and forth as he reached down and untied the tiny bows in the straps of Jazz's bright red sundress. The diamonds in her pendant sparkled against her smooth caramel skin. Emmanuel pulled the top of the dress down, exposing Jazz's bare breasts. He leaned over and circled each nipple with the tip of his tongue, causing them to stand at attention. With each downward tug on the red fabric, more of Jazz's flesh was revealed. Emmanuel's tongue burned a hot, wet path down her belly and lingered at her navel. Jazz elevated her hips to help him ease the dress lower. Emmanuel froze when he reached the red lacy triangular barrier covering her vagina. He inhaled her potent feminine scent and closed his eyes. It was intoxicating. He wanted Jazz desperately, but he was determined to take his time and relish the experience thoroughly. Again, she raised her hips, allowing Emmanuel to remove her panties.

When his two long fingers entered Jazz's wetness she parted her legs wider to give him better access. Emmanuel stroked her stiff wet clit gently with the perfect amount of pressure to give her the pleasure she deserved. The instant his lips found hers again, Jazz moaned her response and received his tongue in a sizzling kiss. She hummed, and Emmanuel answered with deep moans. His lips left hers and traveled down her body again, searing her flesh with hot moist kisses. His tongue dipped lower to the wet and hairy spot between her thighs. He twirled and flicked his tongue against drenched hardened bud. The plane dipped and Jazz whimpered and jerked. She rubbed the back of Emmanuel's head in rhythm with the continuous flicks of his tongue to her clit.

"Oh, Emmanuel…" Jazz whispered on a faint breath as her body bucked and trembled under his oral pleasure.

Emmanuel drank in the sweet nectar of her release like a thirsty man in need of a cool drink of water. When the waves had fully subsided, Emmanuel stretched across the bed and grabbed his khaki pants from the floor. He found the protection he needed inside his wallet. Emmanuel opened the foiled packet with his teeth and slid the shield onto his hardened penis. Jazz reached out her arms to him, silently inviting him to take her at his will. And he did. He started with a slow and careful entry and transitioned into an even and measured ride. In a moderate tempo as steady as the ticks of a timepiece, Emmanuel and Jazz's bodies worked in perfect coordination giving one another as good they got. Her hips rolled and thrust, meeting him halfway on each long stroke. Emmanuel began to pump deeper, faster, and more energetically inside of Jazz as they climbed higher and higher toward the mountaintop. He kissed her to muffle her chants of his name, which grew louder as he repeatedly touched that part of her soul that had been deprived of him for too many days.

Simultaneously, Jazz's body spiraled toward euphoria just as the plane dipped and rocked. It could've been the turbulence. Emmanuel didn't know for sure, but strong sensations gradually gripped his body from head to toe, nearly sending his heart rate dangerously over the max. A climax of the greatest magnitude he'd ever felt swept him up. Every muscle in his body yielded to its vibrations. Emmanuel was weakened by his love for Jazz and the way she made him feel inside and out. He kissed her softly and closed his eyes. Rolling onto his side with her in his arms, he stared at her face. She was peaceful and comfortable with her eyes closed. Her soft and mild expression was that of a sexually satisfied woman.

Chapter Twenty-Eight

"Fabian composed a list of hot issue questions that he believes will be asked in the debate. Do you think your uncle will take the time to at least look over them while he's away? I could email them to him."

Tyrell took the red binder and walked out of the elevator with Edgar right behind him. "He doesn't want to be disturbed unless it's an emergency that only *he* can handle. The debate is two weeks away. Unc is superior in standoffs. He'll be ready."

"I'm sure he will be, but I'm a little concerned, Tyrell."

"About what?" he asked, slowing his pace on his walk down the busy corridor.

"We've slipped in the polls slightly. The numbers aren't significantly different, but…" Edgar shrugged both shoulders.

"Uncle Manny is in the loop, Edgar. We talk every day. He wouldn't have taken this much time off if it wasn't important. You're in love. If it had been Nadia being held hostage in Swaziland, you would've done the same thing. I would've helped you too."

"Yeah, I can see me now parachuting from a chopper dressed in all black like Rambo, man. I would've been throwing grenades and firing off rounds from an AK-47, trying to rescue my woman."

Tyrell laughed. "You're crazy, but I believe you. Any man in love can understand exactly where you're coming from. Uncle Manny ain't exactly Rambo, but he did use his influence to get to Jazz and the others rescued as fast as he could. I don't blame him."

"I don't either." Edgar checked out their surroundings as they made a turn headed down the corridor leading to the private congressional offices. He leaned in and lowered his voice. "Someone from Black Diamond has been calling every day asking when the congressman is expected to return from his trip."

"Did the person leave a message or a callback number?"

"Nope. But it's a *woman*. Garcelle said so."

"It's probably Gigi Perdue or one of her cronies. Mr. McConnell knows Uncle Manny and Jazz's schedule and their whereabouts. He's the only person at Black Diamond who needs to know anything about those two. The female who's calling our office digging for dirt is up to no good. I'll speak with Garcelle about how she should handle our mystery caller from now on."

*****

The co captain's voice over the communication system awakened Jazz. She sat up in the bed and looked around. One glimpse outside the plane's window confirmed that they had landed in Virginia. She could hear the crew and other passengers stirring outside in the main cabin. She imagined they were gathering their belongings, preparing to exit the plane. Emmanuel was still sleeping and snoring lightly. Jazz smiled. He had every reason to be tired. The brother had put in an abundance of time and plenty of energy making love to her high above the clouds. They had been officially inducted into the infamous mile-high club. After their first session of lovemaking, they napped until the pilot stopped in London for an hour. Emmanuel had then dressed and left the private cabin briefly and returned with a tray of food. An attendant had been kind enough to keep their dinner warm for them after she had attempted to wake them while she and the crew were serving the other passengers. Her thoughtfulness was greatly appreciated because both Emmanuel and Jazz were famished when they woke from their post sex nap.

The chicken Marsala, wild rice, and mixed, steamed vegetables they'd shared was a tasty and filling meal. Jazz kicked back after dinner and prepared to watch another movie. But Emmanuel seemed to have gotten a burst of new energy from the food. He wasn't starving anymore. His belly was full. The hunger he was experiencing wasn't for food. It was for *Jazz*. By the time the captain made his ascent into the starlit sky over London, flying westward, Emmanuel was in full seduction mode. His blazing kisses and caresses caused another episode of turbulence on the plane. But it was confined to the private cabin that he and Jazz occupied. There was more motion over the Atlantic Ocean in the small space than an entire unit of turbo jets could've ever caused. A hot flash hit Jazz as she closed her eyes and relived the episode in her mind.

"Congressman Day," a female attendant called. She tapped on the door.

Jazz jumped and pulled the bed sheets up to her chin. The door was locked, and no one could enter the cabin. But she and Emmanuel were naked and in bed together. Jazz felt extremely vulnerable. "We'll be out shortly. The congressman is a little jet lagged." She got up and searched for her panties and sundress. She put them on quickly and sat down on the bed. "Emmanuel," she whispered, shaking him with all her might. "Wake up. We're in Virginia. The captain and crew are waiting for us to exit the plane. The other hostages are already on the strip greeting their families and loved ones. Wake up."

"I'm awake." Emmanuel rolled over and peered at Jazz through sleepy eyes. "It'll take me five minutes to get dressed. Wait for me. I don't want you to go out there alone."

*****

One of Gigi's worst nightmares was about to become a dreaded reality. Mr. McConnell's memo with the words 'Jazz Dupree' typed boldly on the subject line had summonsed her and the rest of the reporting staff to a special meeting. The level of excitement in the boardroom was sickening. Everybody seemed happy. As expected, Mr. McConnell wanted to make a big deal out of Jazz's saga in Swaziland. He claimed that Black Diamond's website had almost crashed twice over the past few days because of the overwhelming influx of inquiries and well wishes. The viewing audience was demanding an update on their much beloved reporter after surviving her thirty-two-day hostage situation in Africa. The marine's successful rescue mission had made international news, so Jazz's fans knew she was alive, but they were begging for more details. Thousands had flooded Black Diamond's website, asking when she would return to work. They missed her presence on the air and they were eager to hear her story about being a hostage of political rebels from her lips.

Apparently, the demanding requests from Black Diamond's viewers had put pressure on Mr. McConnell. He wasn't hailed a media mogul without merit. The wise and seasoned CEO always had a plan to keep his network miles ahead of his competitors. It was simple. Mr. McConnell consistently gave the viewers whatever they wanted. This time it would be no different. He had already selected a writer, producer, director, and camera crew to create an hour-long special featuring Jazz. All he needed was the perfect reporter from the Black Diamond team to conduct the interview to get the project underway. A new guy by the name of Dale O'Neal was the likely choice.

In her own words, Jazz would give her exclusive account from beginning to end about her horror in Swaziland. The piece on the king's coronation would be included also. Mr. McConnell had called the meeting to inform the reporting staff of his brilliant plan. He was soliciting ideas for the project from everyone in the room. He needed a few Black Diamond employees to make brief appearances throughout the special to describe the activity around the network when they first learned that Jazz was a hostage in Swaziland. Jackson was on the top of the list of volunteers. McConnell had asked Shay, Jazz's makeup artist, to talk about the mood in the image and wardrobe department for those thirty-two days. Other employees had been approached as well.

Gigi had sat like a statue throughout the entire meeting. She tuned Mr. McConnell out as soon as he leveled his pitch. Nothing about the project interested her. Gigi had no intention whatsoever of spending her precious time or energy boosting Jazz Dupree's career. She would become America's next black media princess without any assistance from her. In fact, Gigi hoped the special would be a total flop. More than likely it wouldn't be, but a sistah could dream.

Chapter Twenty-Nine

"Emmanuel, you're going to start a fire on my carpet if you keep walking back and forth to that room to check on Jazz. That girl is fine. You brought her to the safest place in the world. Sit down and relax, honey."

"I can't believe how long Jazz has been asleep. It's been eight hours. She missed lunch and her midday medication. Maybe I should wake her." Emmanuel turned around and started down the hallway again.

"Come back here," Mrs. Anderson snapped. "Do I need to take a switch to you? Leave that child alone. You can serve her lunch, dinner, and a snack too whenever she wakes up. And she will take her medicine. I'm sure if she refuses to, you'll hogtie her and shove it down her throat. Until then, I want you to sit down and talk to me."

Emmanuel sat in a recliner right next to the sofa where Mrs. Anderson was sitting. She was busy folding a basket of freshly laundered towels. Emmanuel picked up a bright green one and folded it neatly. He placed it on top of a tall stack of other ones in another basket. He couldn't recall the last time he had done any kind of housework. He grabbed another towel and started folding it.

"Where is Mr. Anderson?"

"He went to the barber shop."

"But his head is completely bald," Emmanuel said, cocking his head to the side.

"Oh, Fred doesn't go to the barber shop to get a haircut. All of his hair fell out twenty years ago. He goes over to Melvin's shop to play checkers, eat junk food, and gossip. He'll be home soon, though. It's almost dinner time. I cook smothered pork chops and black-eyed peas every Thursday. Fred has never been late for dinner."

Emmanuel smiled and picked up another towel. "Mr. Anderson is a lucky man. He has a wife who cooks like a gourmet chef. And you're very beautiful too. Jazz looks a lot like you as did her mother. I saw the pictures in the living room."

"Yes, Jazz is the spitting image of Inez, and everybody said Inez looked like *me*. I only wish her outlook on life had been more like mine or even Jazz's for that matter."

Choosing his words carefully, Emmanuel rushed to offer some consolation. "I'm sorry about your daughter. Losing her had to be devastating. I'm grateful that you and Jazz had each other and Mr. Anderson to help you pick up the pieces. You're a strong woman, and you're a smart too. I saw your degrees and all of your teaching awards on the wall in your study. How long did you teach?"

"I taught forty-three years. I could've become a principal in my early thirties, but my place was in the classroom with the children teaching English. I also helped with the chorus. Music is very important in this family. We all sing. Jazz has a beautiful soprano voice, but she never wanted to perform. I guess her mama and daddy ruined the idea for her."

"Yes, ma'am, Jazz told me all about her parents. It's a shame how they both died as a result of drug addiction. They were very talented people. Their gift was passed along to their daughter. I've heard Jazz sing before. She does have a nice voice."

"When did you hear my baby sing?"

Emmanuel had heard Jazz singing in the shower at the beach house in the Hamptons the morning they had to leave suddenly. But he couldn't tell her grandmother that. She would go get that switch she'd threatened him with earlier for certain if he did. "Um…Jazz sings every now and then along with the radio when we're driving. And I heard her sing once when we shared a hymnal at church."

"Well, would you look at that?" Mr. Anderson walked into the den smiling. "I better take a picture. Nobody will ever believe that a powerful member of the U.S. Congress came to my house to do my laundry."

"Hush your mouth and go wash up for dinner, Fred." Mrs. Anderson stood from the sofa and kissed her husband on the cheek. She left the men in the den while she went into the kitchen.

Mr. Anderson stood above Emmanuel with a cold, hard look on his face. His smile had completely vanished. "Now that I have you alone I need to ask you something."

"You can ask me anything, sir."

"What are your intentions for my pumpkin? She already had one fancy pants hustler break her heart. He fooled me with all of his fast talking and big spending. Sallie Mae didn't like him from the moment she laid eyes on him. I should've listened to her, but I didn't.

I won't be tricked again. So I need you to tell me right now what your plans are for Jazz."

"Mr. Anderson, I'm not Mario Thomas. There is no other woman in my life besides Jazz. I don't want anyone else. I promise you that I would never do anything to hurt her—*ever*."

"You better not. "

"Papa, are you threatening Emmanuel?"

Jazz walked into the den eyeing both men with a hint of suspicion in her eyes. Mr. Anderson hugged her and held her to his side. Emmanuel saw nervousness in Jazz's features. He didn't want her to be alarmed. Her grandfather had had every right to confront him about the nature of their relationship. It was his duty to protect Jazz from men with bad intentions. Emmanuel was proud that he was not in that category. He loved Jazz, and hurting her was not on his agenda.

"Your grandfather wasn't threatening me at all. We were having a man-to-man talk about something very important." Emmanuel stood and reached out his hand to Jazz. "I know you're hungry. Let's go to the kitchen so I can feed you. You need to take your medication too."

*****

Gigi approached the table in the back of the restaurant when she noticed Tyrell sitting there. He was talking with a large group of people. She assumed they were members of Emmanuel's staff. "Hello Tyrell."

"Ms. Perdue, how are you?"

"I'm quite well. How is Congressman Day? Has he made it back to the States yet?"

"Didn't you or your assistant ask Garcelle, our secretary, that same question this afternoon?"

Tyrell's defensive attitude took Gigi by surprise. He was usually mild and pleasant. "I have no idea what you're talking about. If someone from Black Diamond called the congressman's office today, it wasn't me."

"It's weird because no one from your network should be calling our office asking questions *period*. Mr. McConnell is up to speed on everything concerning my uncle, and he certainly knows what's going on with Ms. Dupree in her absence. If he needed additional information from us, he would've contacted *me* directly. So who do you suppose is making those pesky phone calls to our office every day, Ms. Perdue?"

"I can't answer that question. I'll do some snooping around and find out who's trying to get a sneak scoop on the congressman and Jazz."

"Yes, ma'am, please do that. I spoke with Mr. McConnell about it a few hours ago, and he promised to look into the matter as well. With both of you on the case, I'm sure we'll soon find out who our phone pest is."

*****

Emmanuel kissed Jazz one last time and swatted her playfully on her ass. "I better get out of here before your grandfather wakes up and shoots me. I feel like a sixteen-year-old kid making out with you on your grandparents' front porch. I'm a grown ass man. I'm too old for this."

"My grandmother invited you to stay in the guest room. She even refreshed it for you after dinner."

Emmanuel shook his head. "There would be too much temptation if I stayed across the hall from you. You wouldn't be able to fight the urge to sneak into my room. Admit it. I make you hot and weak."

"I would be cool sleeping across the hall from you. You don't trust *yourself*. You wouldn't be able to control your body parts, Mr. Mile High."

"You're right. That's why I'm going to my suite. Your grandmother threatened to get a switch and whip my butt twice already. She would beat me good if she caught me in your bedroom. I'm out."

After a chaste kiss on the cheek, Emmanuel turned and left Jazz standing on the front porch of her childhood home. She watched him walk down the steps toward his rented Cadillac Escalade. He turned and smiled before he opened the door. Jazz blew him a kiss and went back into the house, locking the door behind her.

"You're in love with that fine man."

"*Grandma*!" Jazz shrieked. She turned around with her palm pressed to her chest and leaned forward. "You almost gave me a heart attack. Were you spying on us?"

"I wasn't spying on you. You know I would never do anything like that. I was thirsty, so I got up to get a bottle of water. I saw the front door open with you standing on the porch looking like a woman in love."

"I think I love Emmanuel. My heart tells me I do, but my head is warning me to slow down. It's too late, though. We're over the speed limit now. If I could be with Emmanuel every second of every day, I would, Grandma."

"My, my, my, baby, what did he do to you?" Mrs. Anderson closed her eyes and threw up both hands, waving them in front of her face. "Never mind. Don't tell me. Dr. Waller has finally gotten my blood pressure under control. I don't want you to cause me to stroke out by telling me the juicy details of your love life."

Jazz was shocked with embarrassment. "I would never do that anyway, Grandma. I'm going to bed now. This conversation is too awkward for me. Good night."

Chapter Thirty

"Welcome back, Congressman Day."

"Thank you, Garcelle. It's good to be back."

"Everyone is in the conference room waiting for you. I'll hold all calls until after the meeting, sir."

"That sounds like a plan. But you know if—"

"Yes, sir," Garcelle said, smiling with a gleam in her eyes. "If *Ms. Dupree* calls, I'll put her through immediately."

Emmanuel walked down the hall swinging the briefcase in his hand back and forth. For the first time since he'd been elected to congress, he didn't feel the enthusiasm he once had for politics and making laws. Time away from the Hill had given him the opportunity to do some soul searching. Two things were certain: he loved Jazz and wanted her to be a permanent part of his life. At the mature age of forty-two, he had started hearing wedding bells and babies crying. He could actually envision his life as a husband to Jazz and the proud father of two or three little ones with her good looks. Both thoughts had caught him by surprise, but he'd accepted them as a normal part of being in love. Emmanuel's love affairs with the law and politics were still very much alive, but neither could compare with what he now felt for Jazz. She was his number one priority. He wanted to make sure that she was safe, happy, and healthy at all times.

Emmanuel had left Jazz in his bed sleeping peacefully when he left for work. She wasn't due back at her office for another two days. He had insisted that she spend her final days off at his house so Ms. Flora could keep an eye on her. The thought of Jazz returning to her condo soon, leaving him lonely and bored, punched Emmanuel in the gut. Some type of arrangement would have to be made between them. He would suggest that on his long days at the capitol, he'd spend the night with Jazz at her place. It was closer to D.C. than his house, so it would be more convenient. All other nights, they would share his space out in the suburbs away from the hustle and bustle of the city. Sleeping apart was no longer acceptable.

Emmanuel paused outside the closed conference room door. It had been two weeks since he'd seen Tyrell, Edgar, Fabian, and the rest of his staff. His return to reality was bittersweet. He hated to be away from Jazz, but he was mandated to get back to work on behalf of his constituents. The oath he had taken to represent them and their interests in congress was a serious one that he had every intention of fulfilling for as long as he was in office. Emmanuel turned the knob and pushed the door. The smiles and hand claps that greeted him reminded him why he loved his job so much.

*****

"You didn't have to drive all the way out here to do my hair, Ramone. I could've waited until Saturday. I wanted to drop by the salon so I could see the gang."

"Oh, no, sugar, these split ends are scary." Ramone clipped the small section of Jazz's hair secured between his two fingers. "You needed that deep conditioner I gave you too. I will not have you returning to work after all this time looking like Ronald McDonald."

"I guess my hair was pretty damaged, huh?"

"Hell yeah! Anyway, where is the congressman?"

"Emmanuel called before you got here. He'll be home soon. Today was his first day back at the capitol. There was a stack of work on his desk waiting for him, and he was in and out of meetings all day long. Plus he's preparing for a debate in Atlanta coming up Tuesday evening. I sure hope he'll perform well. If he doesn't, it'll be my fault."

"The man took a leave of absence from his job and campaign to play hero to you by choice. The marines didn't need his help, honey. If that rich conservative unseats Congressman Day, it will be *his* fault and not yours."

"I love him, Ramone. I don't want to hinder his career."

"I know you love him. And you're not a hindrance to him. He loves you too, Jazz. Why do you think he dropped all of his business to fly to Africa?"

"I don't know," Jazz answered softly. She fingered the pendant resting on her chest subconsciously. "Maybe he likes me a lot."

"That's your head making you talk crazy. Your *heart* knows the truth."

127

"Jazz!" Emmanuel called from the front of the house. "Jazz, I'm home. You wouldn't believe how backed up the traffic was." He stopped talking when he found Jazz with Ramone in the den.

"Hello, Congressman Day."

Emmanuel extended his hand for a shake. "It's good to see you, Ramone. I had Tyrell order some food from Symphony's before we left the office. The delivery guy should be here shortly. Why don't you stay and have dinner with us?"

"I would love to, but I have a hot date. I'll be leaving as soon as I finish taming this bush."

Emmanuel bent down low and kissed Jazz's lips. "How was your day?" he asked, standing to his full height.

"It was productive. Mr. McConnell has me working with two of our staff writers to come up with the script for my special. I had an amazing conversation with Dale O'Neal. He's the reporter on the project. I can't wait to get back to the office. I'm so excited."

"I'm happy for you, baby. Well, I'm going to get out of this suit. Let me know when dinner arrives. I'm glad you came for a visit, Ramone. I know you and Jazz have plenty to catch up on."

"Does he need you to help him get out of that expensive beige suit?" Ramone whispered when Emmanuel left the room. "I could come back tomorrow and finish your hair, boo."

"No. Why would you ask me that silly question?"

"Didn't you see the fire in his eyes and the way he was breathing when you were telling him about your project? He was looking at you like you were smothered in gravy. He is hungry for you, girl. I can still smell the scent of lust in the air."

"Stop it, Ramone. Your overactive imagination is out of control as usual."

"No, it's not. I'm warning you, sweetie. That hunk of a man has one thing on his mind, and it ain't takeout food from Symphony's."

*****

"Emmanuel seems distracted, Tyrell. Look at him. He's not focused. I wish you were there with him."

"Uncle Manny is doing okay. It's not his best debate performance, but he's holding his weight. Edgar flew to Atlanta with him this time because he needed to meet with each field office director. I had no other choice but to stay here and manage our staff. My parents and Auntie Christina are in the audience. Grandma and Granddaddy are watching the debate at the church with Bishop and some of the other members."

"I should've gone with Emmanuel for support, but it wasn't possible. My schedule wouldn't allow me to. The special project is consuming me. I'm putting in ten hours a day at the office, but I still have to bring work home with me in order to stay afloat."

Tyrell placed a comforting arm around Jazz's shoulders. "Don't worry. You're there in spirit."

Jazz's heart was in Atlanta with Emmanuel, but she preferred to be there with him in the flesh. There were too many miles between them. It was impossible to encourage him with a wink or a smile through a computer screen. Jazz had spoken to Emmanuel an hour before he took the stage for the one and only debate against his super conservative opponent. His confidence seemed to be intact, and he'd assured her that he was well prepared for any question he had coming his way. But since his opening statement, he had lost some of his usual swagger. All of the questions about social entitlements, healthcare, and tax loopholes had stolen some of Emmanuel's steam. Rex Westmore was on the attack, making himself appear fiscally responsible, while Emmanuel was looking like Santa Claus giving away free gifts and benefits to the undeserving. That wasn't a part of his platform. Emmanuel was an advocate for the poor and working class Americans. Fortunately, his constituents knew him well. Their cheers and positive responses to his answers could be heard over the internet. The people in Emmanuel's district were aware of his compassion for the less fortunate and his strong work ethic. No matter how rude and sarcastic Mr. Westmore behaved during the debate, Emmanuel remained the shining star to the majority of the audience. Jazz found great relief in that.

Chapter Thirty-One

"Thank you very much, ma'am. I'll be in touch."

Trey Jamison ended his phone call and smiled like he had just won a grand sweepstake. He leaned back on the soft leather seat in the back of his boss' limousine as the driver zipped through the busy streets of downtown Atlanta. The conversation he'd just had wasn't about money, but to him, the information was just as valuable. Trey hoped the news would cheer his boss up. According to the bloggers, political pundits, and the social media outlets, Rex Westmore had lost the debate against Emmanuel Day. The audience didn't appreciate his blunt responses to certain questions or the jabs he'd taken at his opponent. They had even booed him a couple of times during a rebuttal. Trey wondered how the congressman's loyal supporters would feel about him if they were privy to the information he had just learned. His ears were still ringing from the tip he'd received. He looked over at Mr. Westmore who was on a conference call with key members of his campaign staff. Trey was eager to spill the goods on Congressman Day, but he would be patient. The limousine stopped at a traffic light. Seconds later, Mr. Westmore ended his phone conversation.

"Who were you talking to?"

Trey smiled. "I just had the most interesting conversation with someone who knows Congressman Day quite well. It seems like your opponent pals around with shady characters. Does the name Zeus Mortimer ring a bell, sir?"

Trey watched Mr. Westmore rack his brain with the name for a moment. The multimillionaire's club in America had an elite membership roster. Most of its wealthy members knew of each other in some remote way. They usually traveled around the same circles. Trey had heard of Zeus Mortimer, the international investment tycoon originally from Atlanta. The man was a walking bank. He owned stocks of all kinds in every type of industry across the seven seas. He was an extremely successful business mogul and entrepreneur. Mortimer had accumulated wealth that Mr. Westmore was yet striving for. There was no comparison between the two men's net worth. Mr. Westmore was rich, but Zeus Mortimer was *filthy* rich.

But according to Gigi Perdue, the two prosperous gentlemen had earned their fortunes in very different ways. Mr. Westmore had inherited his empire from his father via his great-grandfather and grandfather. And since he had taken over the family business, he had expanded it and increased its value three times more than its original profit margin. Mr. Mortimer, on the other hand, had a reputation of acquiring his riches through criminal activity. He was nothing more than a modern day mobster in the eyes of many businessmen. They didn't respect him because of his questionable dealings with disreputable members of the underworld in the States and abroad. Supposedly, Mr. Mortimer was involved in everything from racketeering, international drug and weapons smuggling, as well as fraudulent investment schemes.

"Yeah, I've heard of Zeus Mortimer," Mr. Westmore answered Trey after some time. "I can't honestly say I know much about him. He's a *billionaire*, or so I've heard. I think he invested globs of money in oil reserves in Saudi Arabia, Venezuela, and Libya. They say his business practices are a little dark. What else should I know?"

"There's a female reporter from some black television network in Washington. Her name is Gigi Perdue, and she is a looker. Apparently, she's one of Congressman Day's past lovers. He's left a string of broken hearts from Atlanta to D.C. since he was elected to congress. This Perdue woman is bitter, and she knows things."

"Do tell."

"Mortimer is one of Day's most loyal supporters. He happens to be his biggest financial contributor too. There's extensive history between the two families. Over a decade ago, the congressman and his father's law firm down in Georgia helped Mortimer avoid a life sentence. He'd been indicted on multiple counts of cheating hundreds of innocent people out of their lives' savings."

"I remember reading about that trial a while back. It was a nasty one if my memory serves me correctly."

"It was *huge*. The scumbag walked away without even a simple slap on the wrist, and he's been faithful to the Day family ever since. In fact, it was Mortimer's pilot and private plane that flew down to the jungle to bring the congressman and his lady friend back to the States. Apparently, Day has a thing for female journalists. His new love interest works at the same network with the Perdue woman."

"Well, well, well, my day didn't turn out so bad after all. Let's come up with a plan to leak this information to the public, shall we?"

"I'm way ahead of you, sir."

*****

Emmanuel tiptoed into his house around two o'clock in the morning. Exhausted and in need of a hot shower to relax his aching muscles, he followed the familiar path from the front foyer to the den. It was pitch dark, but he knew the way. He dropped his briefcase and overnight bag on the floor in the great room. It landed with a thud.

"What's up, Unc? We weren't expecting you until after sunrise."

Emmanuel turned on the lamp on the end table. Tyrell sat up on the leather sectional sofa. His uncle sat down next to him and snatched the tail of his tailor-made shirt from inside his pants. He leaned back and stretched his long legs in front of him.

"I wanted to get back here so I could get to the office early. Thanks for holding it down for Edgar and me while we were away. I missed having you there to keep me organized and on track, but I didn't want Jazz to be here alone. Her friend, Ramone, is in New York."

"Well, the next time you contract me for babysitting services, make sure your *baby* is cool with it. The situation almost got violent up in here."

"What happened?"

"Your woman threatened me. She didn't appreciate me hanging around here after we watched the debate. Jazz is a grown woman, Unc. You need to stop treating her like a helpless little girl. Because of you, I almost got my lights punched out."

"I'm sorry about that." Emmanuel released air from his cheeks and propped his legs on the coffee table. "I guess I have been acting a little paranoid since we got back from Swaziland."

"You think?"

"Tyrell, please try to understand. When Jazz is with me, I know she's safe. And there's sufficient security at her job, so nothing will happen to her there. It's during those short periods of time when she's alone that I tend to worry about her."

"That's crazy because there're no threats of a rebellion here in America. Name one anti-government group that would be bold enough or stupid enough to attempt a takeover of a federal building. What went down in Swaziland was a case of Jazz being in the wrong place at the wrong time. Those rebels weren't after her. Their problem wasn't with Ambassador Vance, either. Ludvonga and company were disgruntled with the Swazi government and the monarchy." Tyrell stood and picked up his jacket from the sofa. "Think about it."

"Who died and crowned you the king of reason?"

"I'm not the smartest cat on the block. It's just rational thinking based on facts. You taught me well, Unc. Anyway, I'm going home. I want to hit the gym before our eight o'clock meeting."

Emmanuel walked Tyrell to the door, secured the locks, and activated the alarm system. He dismissed all thoughts of danger, his debate performance, and politics from his mind. The woman he loved was in his bed, and he wanted to join her. Visions of Jazz put a bounce in Emmanuel's step. By the time he reached his bedroom, his pulse was thumping fast. He had no plans to wake Jazz. He was more considerate than that. Her presence alone was enough to please him. Any man could appreciate coming home to find the love of his life resting in his bed with the heavenly scent of her skin weaving its way through the room. Emmanuel couldn't resist kissing Jazz's lips. She was lying flat on her back with the bronze duvet comforter and sheets covering her body from the waist down. Her firm set of breasts rose and fell in slow motion each time she drew in and released a breath. The silky lavender fabric of her chemise was thin. Emmanuel's sharp vision caught the outline of her nipples teasing him underneath. The sight nearly caused him to salivate as his taste buds suddenly became overly sensitive.

Exercising more sexual restraint than King David or Sampson had, Emmanuel stripped naked, leaving his clothes in a pile on the floor. He went into the master bathroom. The hot shower he needed to relax the muscles in his legs, shoulders, and back had been canceled. Instead, he turned on the cold water at full blast to relieve the throbbing of the manly muscle between his thighs.

Chapter Thirty-Two

"Look at you, baby girl. You're glowing like a light bulb. What's going on?"

Jazz ignored Jackson's question and followed him toward the elevator bank. She was balancing a decorative edible arrangement made up of an assortment of fruit and candies in her hands. It was almost too pretty to eat. Emmanuel was still spoiling her with expensive treats. He was back down in Georgia crisscrossing his district, making speeches, kissing babies, and shaking hands. The general election was three weeks away, and he was on a quest to solidify a victory. He'd invited Jazz to tag along with him, but she was too busy wrapping up her special project. A premier date had been set, and it was right around the corner. She couldn't possibly break away to stomp on the campaign trail.

Jazz pinched Jackson on his shoulder as soon as the elevator doors closed, giving them privacy.

"Ouch! What did you do that for?"

"You know it's against the friend code to tease me about my love life in the halls of this building."

"I whispered, didn't I? At least I thought I did."

"We have to be careful, Jackson."

"Why? Everybody knows you and the congressman are an item."

"Do you really think so?"

"You two made the front page of "Urban Politics Today". It was a nice shot too, although I could've captured you guys much better than their photographer did."

"I'm sure you could have. Emmanuel framed two copies of the picture you took of us at the dinner party for the Sierra Leonean ambassador. He put one on his desk at the capitol. The other one is in his office at his law firm in Atlanta."

"He probably has a humongous wall portrait of you at his house outside the District."

Jazz shook her head as the bell chimed signaling that they'd reached the seventh floor. She followed Jackson out into the hallway.

"He doesn't need any pictures of me at his house here. He has the *real thing*," she teased in a hushed tone.

"Good morning. What a lovely arrangement, Jazz." Gigi walked up to them smiling. "Manny is feeding you too much chocolate, darling. You better be careful. A moment on the tongue could make you burst out of your thong." She let out an annoying laugh and sashayed down the hall in the direction of her office.

"Don't pay her any attention, Jazz. She's jealous. If the congressman sent her a box of chocolate covered roaches she would eat every one of them."

*****

"So, what do you think, sir?"

"It's kind of mild. I think it lacks an edge. Where is the lethal blow? I couldn't feel the sharp stab. It needs to go in for the kill. The voters must know that Congressman Day defends the rich and corrupt in court, but preaches about equal justice for the less fortunate on Capitol Hill."

Trey forwarded the disc to display a collage of still photographs. There were dozens of them showing Congressman Day and Zeus Mortimer in various settings. A picture of them sipping cocktails on the upper deck of a yacht caught Mr. Westmore's eye. Trey picked up on his boss' curiosity instantly.

"That is a shot of the devious duo off of the coast of Saint-Tropez a few years ago." Trey pressed the control button to show another picture. "Look at them at a fundraiser on St. Simons Island. Mortimer raised over a million dollars for his buddy that night."

"Pictures and snippets are fine," Mr. Westmore grumbled, leaning back in his chair. He rubbed his pot belly. "We need to rattle the rafters."

"What you want is an outright attack ad accusing the congressman of defending a wealthy criminal in court."

"That's exactly what I *need*. Tie Day and Mortimer together like Siamese twins. Let the voters know how that thug is bank rolling the congressman's campaign and flying him all around the world in his fancy private plane. Expose *everything*."

"Yes, sir. By Election Day Congressman Day's squeaky clean, heroic image will be destroyed. Voters will know him for the scandalous, lowlife liar he truly is."

"And we'll owe it all to the lovely Gigi Perdue." Mr. Westmore lifted his glass of expensive scotch from his desk and extended his chubby arm.

Trey picked up his half filled glass and touched his boss' drink. The two glasses chimed on contact. "To Ms. Perdue."

* * * * *

Emmanuel took the seat he'd been offered by the friendly production assistant and thanked the young man.

"Can I get you something to drink, sir?"

"No, thank you. I'm fine."

Emmanuel sat quietly in awe watching Jazz do her thing in front of the camera. She was in the middle of taping an interview with Dale O'Neal about the marine's rescue operation in Swaziland. Hearing her share the intricate details about that night with raw emotion in her voice gave Emmanuel chills. Her eyes were glossy with unshed tears, and there was a distinct tremble in her usual golden voice. Emmanuel was in a trance, taking it all in as if hearing it for the first time. Sure, he knew the story. He had heard Jazz's account of her hostage experience the morning after she and the other Americans had been brought to safety. In her hospital room, she had cried in his arms, reliving every frightening moment of the thirty-two days she'd spent in Ambassador Vance's office. The terror would forever be engraved in Jazz's memory.

A strong hand clapped Emmanuel's shoulder. He looked up and saw Mr. McConnell and Jackson standing above him. The two men had slipped into the production room undetected.

"Congressman Day, it was very nice of you to stop by, sir." Mr. McConnell extended his free hand.

Emmanuel stood quickly and gave the older gentleman a firm handshake. "Thank you, Mr. McConnell. I had an unexpected break in my schedule and I decided to stop by to surprise Jazz. I hope you don't mind."

"Nonsense. You're always welcome here at the Black Diamond network. As a matter of fact, Jackson and I were just doing a little brainstorming about you. Imagine how high the ratings on Jazz's special would be if *you* made an appearance."

"Excuse me?" Emmanuel's eyes darted back and forth between Jackson and Mr. McConnell.

"Yeah, my boss and I thought it would be a good idea if you were to tell your side of the story. You can give our viewers the scoop about what went down behind closed doors on the Hill and at the Whitehouse. Describe the process. We know a whole lot of strategizing took place before the marines were sent in for the rescue."

"Do us the honor, Congressman Day," Mr. McConnell encouraged.

"It's an amazing idea, and I would love to, but Jazz and I have a very strict policy about our careers. We've made a vow to never let our professional paths cross."

Mr. McConnell belted out a hearty laugh. "So you met my star reporter while the two of you were working on the political documentary together. You fell in love with her, and now that she's your *companion*, you refuse to collaborate with her on a professional assignment?"

"That's a pretty accurate summary, sir."

"That's very selfish and unfair of you, but I like it. I admire you, Congressman." The old man patted Emmanuel's shoulder. "You're one smart and lucky man."

*****

Emmanuel's devoted congressional staff members entered the conference room one by one in complete silence. Casually dressed early on a regular Saturday morning, they took their seats and waited as others rushed in. Edgar sat visibly restless in his spot left of the empty seat at the head of the table. Tyrell paced back and forth in front of the window.

A buzz from the intercom sounded, and Garcelle's voice followed. "He's coming down the hall."

Tyrell rushed to his seat. He and Edgar stared at each other. An uncomfortable quietness and a sense of shock intensified the anticipation in the room. Fabian looked down at his legal pad covered with notes. Some were highlighted in blue and others were written in red. Everyone at the table had brought their electronic tablets to do whatever was necessary in the emergency meeting. The entire team had been informed by its dutiful chief of staff via text message or phone call that they were in crisis resolving mode.

"Good morning, everyone." Emmanuel hurried through the door dressed in a black and white jogging suit and a matching pair of running shoes.

His greeting was returned in unison by his staff in a very somber tone.

"Let me see it," he ordered and dropped down into his chair at the head of the table.

With the simple click of a button, Tyrell revealed the source of panic for Emmanuel and his staff. The latest television ad released by Mr. Westmore was a *killer*. The bold and harsh words accusing Emmanuel of defending a known mobster against innocent, hardworking citizens were chilling. There were pictures and rolling video footage of the congressman and Mr. Mortimer sharing happy moments all across the globe. Newspaper articles, outlining the crimes that the Day Firm had helped their wealthy client escape conviction from flashed across the projector screen throughout the ninety second attack ad. The accusations rendered the entire room speechless.

*****

"We don't have to go out tonight, sweetie. There are plenty of leftovers from the food Ramone cooked yesterday, and I bought a new bottle of wine. Let's stay in and watch a movie." Jazz rubbed Emmanuel's shoulder as he stood in the mirror tying his necktie.

"I'm not going to hide out because of a bunch of lies, Jazz. If you want to stay home, you can. I'll see you when I get back if you're still awake."

"I'm not suggesting that you hide out. I just think it's a good idea to address the public about the accusations on your own terms and not be forced into answering questions at the gala. I'm a journalist, Emmanuel. I know about these types of situations. Overly aggressive reporters will be everywhere tonight. You haven't even prepared a statement yet. Please let's stay in."

Emmanuel left the mirror and went inside Jazz's walk-in closet to get his tuxedo jacket. Brushing past her, he returned to the mirror to finish dressing. Jazz sat down on the bed fully dressed in a mint green strapless gown. Her eyes met Emmanuel's in his reflection in the mirror. She looked away, unable to bear the disappointment in his face. He turned around and approached the bed.

"Do you believe I represented Zeus Mortimer, knowing he was a criminal, huh?"

"No."

"Am I the type of man who would ignore hard core evidence implicating a hoodlum and still help him get exonerated?"

Jazz shook her head.

Emmanuel cupped her chin and lifted her face to look into her eyes. "Then why are you ashamed to go to the Prism Gala with me?"

"I'm not ashamed to go anywhere with you, Emmanuel. I'm *afraid* for you. I don't want the media to fuel the fire and keep the story alive. It can be vicious out there. They will draw blood if you show your face tonight."

"You shouldn't be afraid for me. I'm a man and I know the game of politics well. I can handle the media, the political pundits, and my opponent. Come out with me. Your man needs you by his side tonight as always."

Chapter Thirty-Three

Just as Gigi had expected, Emmanuel showed up for the Prism Gala with Jazz on his arm. *Wow! He is one brave dude*, she had to concede to herself if to no one else. His confidence only added to his sex appeal and good looks. Gigi studied Emmanuel as he graced the red carpet. As usual, he was impeccably dressed in a classic black tux. The man was Hollywood fine. There was nothing in his stance, smile, or mannerisms that indicated he was the subject of a political scandal. But he was. A pack of tenacious reporters was waiting to pounce on him the moment he stepped off the red carpet. Gigi wondered how the cool and courageous congressman would handle the press. More importantly, she was eager to see Jazz's reaction to microphones and cameras being thrust in her face. The table would be turned on her this evening. She wouldn't be the one digging aggressively for a hot scoop. *She* would be a major part of the scoop.

"Congressman Day! Congressman Day, can I have a minute of your time, sir?"

Emmanuel smiled and walked past the blonde female reporter, pulling Jazz by the hand along with him. The young woman followed them with a microphone in her hand. A husky cameraman gave chase too. Several other reporters made fast steps behind Emmanuel and Jazz as well. Cameras were flashing and humming all around them. Gigi followed the crowd inconspicuously, keeping a safe distance.

"Did you know Zeus Mortimer was guilty, but decided to represent him regardless for the money all those years ago?"

"Is Zeus Mortimer bank rolling your campaign with the millions he conned innocent people out of, Congressman?" A tall male reporter screamed over the others.

"Why are you friends with a criminal? Is he still your client too, Congressman Day?"

The reporters continued firing questions at Emmanuel as he and Jazz walked down the long breezeway leading to the entrance of the auditorium. Bright lights from cameras blinded them, but they kept moving. Gigi couldn't believe how calm and composed Emmanuel was. He was surrounded by reporters questioning his integrity, but they couldn't break him.

"Ms. Dupree," a young male reporter yelled above the mayhem. "Aren't you afraid that your relationship with a congressman involved with a notorious criminal will tarnish your image as a credible journalist?"

Emmanuel spun around briskly to face the reporter. "You can ask me any damn thing you want to, but don't you ever address Ms. Dupree! Do you understand?" He wrapped his arm protectively around Jazz's waist and entered the auditorium.

*****

"I will tell Emmanuel that you called. He'll be glad to know you're enjoying your mountain bike and computer. Please say hello to Ambassador Vance for me. Take care of yourself, Nuwan. We'll talk again soon."

Jazz was grateful for a surprise phone call from Nuwan. The sound of his cheerful voice had given her a brief break from the madness going on in her life. For days she and Emmanuel had been avoiding phone calls and unexpected visits from the press at both of their jobs. Their world was no longer private. It had been turned into a circus minus the fun. Nuwan couldn't have chosen a better time to call Jazz. She was reading Emmanuel's short speech for his press conference when the phone rang. He had decided to address the accusations regarding Mr. Mortimer tomorrow at noon. His father was flying to Washington in the morning to be with him. He was Emmanuel's co counsel throughout the trial over a decade ago. Together, they had successfully represented Zeus Mortimer against a long list of charges he'd been indicted for. Without Emmanuel and Thaddeus Day, he would've possibly spent the rest of his life in prison for crimes that his older brother had committed.

It was *Caesar* Mortimer who had single-handedly cheated investors all over the world out of millions of dollars. His underhanded dealings with well known criminals had nearly cost Zeus his freedom and all he had worked hard for. By the time he realized Caesar had used the family's investment securities firm to swindle decent people out of their hard earned money, it was too late. All of the transactions appeared to have been approved by both brothers, but only *Caesar* had profited from the shady investments. And he had long since vanished with every dime of his ill-gotten fortune. No one knew where Caesar had fled to in exile—not even his wife and eight children. Offshore accounts in the Cayman Islands, Switzerland, and the Dominican Republic were discovered in his absence, but the man who was linked to the millions remained a ghost.

Meanwhile, angry investors began to file charges against Mortimer's Investment Securities and its only partner left at the firm. Zeus was in a serious jam to say the least. His reputation as a businessman and his freedom were at stake. His wife of fifteen years left him and took their four children with her. Threats against his life started pouring in, and eventually he got indicted on a boatload of charges. But Zeus knew he was innocent just like the people Caesar had deceived. His problem was that he couldn't find a lawyer who was willing to take a chance on him. By divine intervention, Zeus stumbled upon a young, hotshot, African-American attorney who had recently represented a rapper in a rape case. All of the evidence presented by the state of Georgia in the cocky entertainer's trial appeared to substantiate the woman's claim that she had been raped multiple times over a period of three days in his suburban mansion. But the brilliant Emmanuel Marcus Day was able to shatter the aspiring model's tall tale in the eyes of the jurors. She and the rapper had been tucked away in his home for a wild weekend of sex, drugs, and alcohol, but a rape had not occurred. The woman's concocted account was reported to the authorities only after the rapper had refused to give her one hundred thousand dollars for her time and services. In a nutshell, the young woman felt she had earned financial compensation for the eventful weekend, but the rapper disagreed.

At the end of defense summations, the jury was fully convinced that the alleged victim was a disgruntled opportunist who had willingly accompanied a rap star to his home after meeting him for the first time at his concert. Her intentions had been to show him a weekend so far beyond his wildest sexual fantasy that he would shower her with money and gifts. But when he refused to do so, she cried rape. Oddly, she did not seek medical treatment after the alleged sexual assault nor did she contact the police immediately. There was no physical evidence of an attack or false imprisonment. But there was a long line of witnesses placing the young woman at the rapper's dressing room door before and after his performance. Her friends and associates took the stand and described her as a groupie on a mission to hook an entertainer. Ultimately, a not guilty verdict came just two hours after deliberations.

Zeus Mortimer had been so impressed that Emmanuel had won the case that the media and the court of public opinion had deemed a slam dunk in favor of the state, that he tracked him down at a restaurant having lunch. It was an awkward chance meeting, but it proved to be the moment that saved another innocent man's life. It took Emmanuel only a few days to poke holes through the prosecutor's weak case against Zeus. Nothing had linked him to any of the fraudulent activities that had taken place in the business he'd once shared with his brother and other members of their family. The state had made no attempts to find Caesar for questioning. Their entire focus from day one had been on Zeus. Investigators from the Day Firm quickly traced a trail of money to a small city at the southern tip of Greece. They found Caesar living a stress-free, lavish lifestyle while his brother awaited trial for crimes he hadn't committed. He confessed everything to the investigators and agreed to return to the States with them to turn himself in and vindicate Zeus.

On the morning that Caesar and the two investigators were to board a flight to Atlanta, he was found dead from multiple gunshot wounds inside his extravagant oceanfront home. His death was ruled a homicide, and it is yet to be solved. The investigators returned to the States with a brief recorded confession from Caesar with very few details about his fraudulent activities. The prosecution dismissed the tape as garbage and proceeded with their case against Zeus. It was all up to Emmanuel and his father to save their client by planting the seed of reasonable doubt in the minds of the jurors. Their phenomenal legal expertise trumped the prosecution's case, and Zeus Mortimer walked out of the Fulton County Federal Courthouse a free man at the end of a three week trial. He didn't care that some people would go to their graves believing he was guilty. His conscience was clear. Zeus was only concerned about getting his life back on track.

As an act of gratitude, he invested in Emmanuel's future political career. In time, the two men became good friends. Zeus worked hard to rebuild his reputation and his business. A stream of luck came his way and he overcame the scrutiny and skepticism of his past. To his dismay, someone had dug up his unpleasant history and misrepresented what had actually happened all those years ago. The anonymous person had opened a very painful wound with distorted facts. And now Emmanuel was on trial in the court of political opinion for his involvement.

Chapter Thirty-Four

"Many people who have reviewed Mr. Mortimer's case find it hard to believe that he had no idea what his brother was doing. With all due respect, I happen to be one of those individuals, sir. Can you shed some light on how Zeus Mortimer missed Caesar Mortimer's illegitimate dealings?"

"It's simple. In a firm each partner or associate is responsible for the clients he or she has been assigned. They work independently on each investment. All profits brought in are recorded separately, but are deposited into the firm's central primary account. Caesar Mortimer had countless secret accounts in the United States and abroad hiding the millions of dollars that he had been awarded illegally."

Ramone reached over and grabbed Jazz's hand. She was a bundle of scrambled nerves. The press conference was taking much longer than she had expected. So far, Emmanuel and his father had handled themselves like upstanding, professional, Southern gentleman. Their knowledge of the law, past and present, combined with their in-depth familiarity of the case they'd tried over a decade ago was unbelievable. They had recalled small but pertinent details about the trial and were able to pinpoint major pieces of evidence or lack thereof that had led to Mr. Mortimer's acquittal. At the age of seventy-five and eight years into retirement, Thaddeus Day's memory was extraordinary. His mind was sharper than men's half his age.

"So there is no doubt in your mind that Zeus Mortimer was and still is guilt free of the crimes he was accused of?"

Jazz knew her friend and coworker, Tyra, was only doing her job. Black Diamond had given her the assignment to cover Emmanuel's press conference. She was very fair and professional. Jazz looked toward the podium and locked eyes with the man she loved more than she could put into words. Even under enormous pressure, he had the ability to make her heart skip a beat.

"Zeus Mortimer is no criminal, nor has he ever been one, Ms. Tisdale. He's a man of outstanding character and integrity. He's honest, generous, and hard-working. I would never have defended him if he were anything less. He is still a client at the Day Firm, although I don't represent him personally. Our current relationship is more of a private one than anything else. I'm proud to call Mr. Zeus Mortimer my good friend despite what is being reported about him by my opponent and many of your colleagues. The transcripts of his trial are on record. The evidence or absence thereof is included. I suggest that you and other members of the media do your homework."

Emmanuel left the podium to the sound of shouts for his attention and cameras buzzing. His father followed him. Edgar took over the microphone, reciting the case number of Mr. Mortimer's trial transcript for those who wanted the information. He also announced Emmanuel's position in the polls where he remained several points ahead of Mr. Westmore.

"Go and catch up with your man, sweetie. He needs you." Ramone patted Jazz on the back of her hand. "Go on now. I'll check on you and the congressman later. I may even drop by for dinner."

Jazz left Ramone sitting on the third row of chairs facing the podium. The crowd of onlookers was beginning to disperse. Fabian was busy talking to a cute female reporter from a local television station on camera. The scene was pretty chaotic with reporters pushing toward Emmanuel and his father while Tyrell and another staffer kept them away. Jazz wiggled her way through the press pool. She came to face to face with her friend and coworker, Tyra Tisdale. Gigi was with her.

"I'm sorry, Jazz. I had no other choice but to ask Congressman Day that question. You know how it is."

"Of course I do. I'm a reporter too. We have to do our job."

"You believe him, don't you?" Gigi jumped in, obviously with no regard for Jazz's feelings. "You're going to stand by him in spite of the facts. Isn't that right?"

Jazz found new and unbelievable strength on the spot. She could attribute it to why she didn't slap Gigi across her face and serve her the tongue lashing she owed her. "Emmanuel is telling the truth. Why wouldn't I stand by him? Excuse me, Tyra. I'll talk to you later. Thank you for being fair and reasonable. You're the ultimate professional."

Jazz's heart was hurting for Emmanuel, but her blood had begun to simmer because of Gigi's implication that he had been less than honest. Holding back tears and a few spicy words, she hurried through the throng of lingering reporters. A capitol security guard

146

attempted to block her from her target. Tyrell ordered the man to allow her to pass through. Emmanuel and his father were giving a joint statement to a small group of print journalists. Jazz intentionally stopped several feet behind them, not wanting to be a distraction. Emmanuel must've sensed her presence. He turned around in the middle of his sentence. He faced the reporters again.

"Excuse me. My father can finish up here. His memory is much better than mine." Emmanuel walked over to Jazz who was shivering as if she were freezing. "Are you alright?"

She nodded her head and rubbed both hands up and down her arms. "I'm just tired. I didn't sleep that much last night."

"I know. You tossed and turned a lot. I hate how this bullshit is affecting you. There's no need for you to worry about me, baby. This too shall pass. Come on. One of my staff members is going to drive you and Daddy home. I'll be there in time for dinner. Ms. Flora likes to show off whenever my parents are in town. I'm sure she's preparing a feast."

Jazz smiled. "I know she is. Maybe I can give her a hand."

"No. I want you to take a long nap. You need to rest, Jazz. Will you do that for me?"

Jazz nodded her head. She would do anything for Emmanuel because she loved him. "I promise."

"Go with Tyrell. He'll walk you and Daddy to the car. I'll see you later."

*****

Trey flipped through all of the major news channels, catching bits and pieces of the today's top stories. Most commentators were talking about Congressman Day and his involvement in the old Zeus Mortimer trial. Trey was in a bad mood because the attack ad and the leaks to the press had not landed the devastating blow to the congressman's re-election campaign that he and Mr. Westmore had hoped. To the contrary, their entire plan had backfired. Gigi Perdue had failed to complete a thorough investigation into the case. And Trey and his boss had been stupid to take her word without confirming it because she was a reporter. They assumed she had accurate information. All of her so-called evidence that the congressman and Zeus Mortimer had made a mockery of the judicial system and became wealthy as a result of it had turned out to be false. The prosecution had tried the investor on a dozen counts of fraud based on circumstantial evidence. Gigi's tip had turned out to be nothing more than garbage. She had given the Westmore campaign false hope on insufficient evidence. It had not helped them in the polls or with the media at all. The only thing anyone in the Westmore camp had gained from its association with Gigi was three nights of sexual pleasure in her bed. Trey was the lucky guy on the receiving end of that deal.

*****

"I am stuffed. Flora, the meal was mighty fine as usual. Thank you very much."

The housekeeper removed Mr. Day's empty plate and utensils from the table and smiled. "I hope you saved some room in your belly for my pecan pie and French vanilla ice cream."

"Maybe I'll have a slice later. Right now, I'd like my son to share a glass of that expensive brandy I like so much. I can't afford to buy it myself. I only get to enjoy a taste of it when I visit Manny."

Jazz left the dining room table and went to the bar to pour Mr. Day the drink he'd requested. "Here you are, sir." She handed him the crystal glass.

"Thank you, Jazz. You're too kind. Manny is lucky to have found you. Carol and I are waiting patiently for an engagement announcement. Don't make us wait too long. I'd like to meet my new grandchildren before I die."

Tyrell went into a coughing fit in the middle of chewing his food all of a sudden. Flora patted his back. Jazz reclaimed her seat next to Emmanuel, totally embarrassed. He wrapped his arm around her shoulders.

"Flora, I'd like a slice of pie with two scoops of ice cream please. Jazz and I will share it."

Later that evening, as the group sat talking in Emmanuel's great room, Jazz stifled a yawn with the back of her hand. After such a filling meal, she was tired again.

Emmanuel leaned over and kissed her temple. "Why don't you go ahead and turn in for the night? I'll join you later. I want to hang out with Daddy and Tyrell for a little while longer."

"I think I would feel more comfortable sleeping at my condo tonight. Tyrell can drop me off on his way to his apartment," Jazz whispered in Emmanuel's ear.

"That's not going to happen, sweetheart. If you don't want to stay here with me because of my father, we can stay at your place. I'll take you home as soon as Daddy hits the sack."

"Emmanuel, you don't have to do that."

"Yes, I do, baby. Don't you know how miserable I'll be without you? I love you, Jazzlyn Dupree and I need you with me tonight."

The three words she had longed to hear swaddled Jazz like a warm blanket. Her heart had told her that Emmanuel loved her. His actions had confirmed it, but there was nothing more meaningful to her than to hear his declaration from his lips. Jazz held back her tears and rested her head on Emmanuel's shoulder.

"What's all the whispering about, son? Tyrell and I are over here. Don't forget about us."

"I'm sorry, Daddy. Jazz and I were having a private discussion about something important. We're finished now. The matter has been settled."

Chapter Thirty-Five

"You nailed it, Jazz! The special is your best work to date."

"Thank you, Mr. McConnell. I'm glad you approve, but I can't take all of the credit. It was a team effort. Jake, Dale, Saleem, and the whole crew put a lot of work into the production."

"I know they did, but it was *your* story to tell, and you took us directly to the scene. I felt your fear, uncertainty, and agony. Our viewers will feel all of those emotions too. What are your plans for the premier?"

"Actually, I haven't given it much thought."

"Let me know what you'd like to do. We could have a viewing party for you right here or at my home. It's up to you."

"I'll keep both offers in mind and let you know as soon as possible, sir."

Jazz exited Black Diamond's in-house theater and went directly to the elevator. It was very gracious of Mr. McConnell to offer his home for a viewing party in her honor. Jazz was truly flattered. But she had pictured something small and intimate at Emmanuel's home with Tyrell, Edgar, and Ramone. It wasn't her intention to be ungrateful, but since the scandal had finally lost some of its wind, she and Emmanuel preferred spending all of their spare time alone. They welcomed occasional visits from Tyrell and Ramone, but they appreciated their privacy. Their relationship had taken on new meaning since they'd confessed their love for each other.

Later that evening after Emmanuel had revealed his feelings for Jazz, she'd opened up her heart to him. The words had flowed freely from her soul after he kissed her and told her again how much he loved her. Jazz's heart had been on fire since that night. She couldn't imagine her life without Emmanuel. She was hooked and ready for the long haul. On the elevator ride up to the seventh floor, visions of what her life would be like as Emmanuel's wife and the mother of his children popped inside her head. His father's request that they not keep the family waiting too long for an engagement made Jazz smile. Mr. Day wanted grandchildren from his baby boy soon. According to Emmanuel, his mother and Christina had dropped hints about a summer wedding. And Mrs. Anderson was just as anxious for Jazz and Emmanuel to start a life together. She had dreams of teaching her great-grandchildren how to sing and play the piano. The Days and the Andersons were ready to unite their families. The idea excited Jazz too. Just this morning over one of Ms. Flora's big country breakfasts, Emmanuel announced that as soon as his election was over, they were going away for the weekend to make some decisions about their future. Jazz didn't know exactly what he had in mind, but she was eager to find out.

*****

Emmanuel had purposely saved the master suite for the last stop on the tour of his ranch style home in Georgia. He opened the door wide and stepped aside. "And this is my bedroom."

Jazz entered the enormous space slowly and looked around. She sat down on the bed and crossed her legs. With a smile on her face that caused Emmanuel's pulse to increase to turbo speed, she asked, "Where am *I* going to sleep?"

"You know I'm a generous man and a courteous host. I'm willing to share my bedroom with you."

"Thank you. You're too good to me. Tell me about the victory party Tuesday night."

Emmanuel sat next to Jazz on the king size scroll back bed. "It'll be here with only a few guests. I decided to have something private with just the family, our closest friends, and my campaign staff. I'm sure Bishop Stinson and the first lady will join us too. I hope you don't mind."

"It sounds perfect to me."

"Mama, Mabel, and Christina have volunteered to prepare all of the food. Tyrone hired a bartender. I didn't really want to, but I agreed to allow the media to bring their cameras in for a little while. Edgar and Tyrell insisted that I grant them access because the voters have a right to see what's going on in my world that night."

"They were right, sweetheart. After all of the craziness over your relationship with Mr. Mortimer, it'll be great for your supporters to see that you're still standing strong."

"Zeus will be here, so everyone can see us celebrating together. He's flying down with my congressional staff on his plane and he's putting them all up at the Ritz Carlton Atlanta for the night."

"Mr. Mortimer is a good friend, Emmanuel. I'm glad you stood up for him."

"After what he did for you, I had to have his back. And he has supported me over the years. He promised to never forget what my father and I did for him, and he's kept his word."

"Emmanuel, have you given any thought to who may have dug up that old case and leaked it to Mr. Wetmore and the media?"

He shook his head. "I haven't made many enemies or burned any bridges over the years to my knowledge. I can't imagine who would've done it."

"Someone wanted the public to lose its confidence in you. They intended to destroy your career, except they didn't take the time to get all of their facts straight."

"I'm sure the Westmore camp investigated my personal life and my career prior to my election to congress and stumbled on Zeus' case. To the legally untrained eye, he appeared guilty as sin. So they took it and ran with it. It's too bad for them that their legal team failed to sort through the prosecution's shoddy evidence. They spent a grip on that ad and centered the final weeks of their campaign on Zeus' trial."

"It makes me wonder why a man as wealthy and resourceful as Rex Westmore took such a risk. Someone must've convinced him that they knew more about Mr. Mortimer's case than everyone else. Maybe he hired a private investigator, and the person screwed him over for the money."

"Or maybe I really do have a secret enemy somewhere out there that fed Westmore false information on purpose because they knew he was desperate."

"And instead of verifying the contents, the Westmore camp used the misinformation in the attack ad. I bet they're a bunch of very angry people right now, especially Mr. Westmore."

*****

When Gigi turned around and saw Trey sitting on her sofa, the grocery bags she was holding slipped from her hands. All of the food and cleaning items crashed to the floor. "How the hell did you get in my house?"

"I know people, babe. And it doesn't hurt to have a pocket full of money. It's amazing what a poor fellow hard on his luck will do for two hundred dollars." Trey jumped up from the couch and lunged at Gigi.

The flash in his steel gray eyes and the menacing sneer on his beet red face frightened her. She turned and ran toward the front door, but she was too slow and clumsy. Trey grabbed Gigi from behind and slammed her body against the cold hard wood of the closed door. She screamed in horror, but he reached around and clamped his hand tightly over her mouth.

"You think you're pretty damn smart, don't you?" he growled in her ear. "You knew the details of Mortimer's case. He wasn't convicted because he didn't do anything wrong. I trusted you, and you made a fool of me."

Gigi shook her head frantically as warm tears rolled down her face and fell onto Trey's hand. She tried to speak, but she couldn't. Trey pressed his body forcefully against hers, pinning her flatly to the door. Her breasts and stomach ached. His hot, foul breath made Gigi nauseous. She felt weak with fear. Her heart was beating violently. A vision of Trey slashing her throat and leaving her to die alone in a pool of her own blood flashed before her eyes. Gigi didn't want to die because of the cruel trick she had played on him. Maybe she hadn't told him the full story about Mr. Mortimer's trial and Emmanuel's involvement. She had deliberately misled Trey, but she didn't deserve to be butchered for it. Gigi suddenly realized the plan she had executed out of jealousy to destroy Emmanuel hadn't been worth it. She was about to lose her life over a stupid political prank.

"I could snap your neck right now and leave you here to rot. No one would discover your body for days. Not many people like you, Gigi. They don't think you're a very nice gal. Men only like you for one thing, and most women find it despicable the way you hunt down men like a desperate dog in heat."

Gigi's pleading cries were absorbed by Trey's hand squeezing her lips and face with his full strength. It was very painful, but he didn't seem to care. He was enraged. There was anger in his voice, and it scared Gigi to death. She squirmed and moaned, but it didn't do any good. Trey was too strong, and he was mad as hell.

"If you ever think about me or Mr. Westmore again, I'll expose you for the vicious tramp you are. I *know* you. Remember that."

Trey released Gigi and left her condo. She collapsed to her knees on the carpet and sobbed rocking back and forth. There was no need to call the police. It would only complicate matters, and she didn't need that kind of drama in her life. Her ego had been bruised, and Trey had scared her out of her mind. But at least she was still alive.

Chapter Thirty-Six

Jazz stepped out of the master bathroom wrapped in a towel and discovered the most pleasant surprise. There was an incredibly gorgeous dress lying on Emmanuel's bed. It was bright turquoise with long bell sleeves and a tapered waist line. The trapeze bottom was mini in length, guaranteed to show off a generous portion of Jazz's legs. She blushed knowing all too well that Emmanuel had selected the dress for that reason. He often told her that God had blessed her with the most beautiful pair of legs he'd ever seen. Jazz sat down on the bed and picked up the dress to check the size tag. It was a six.

"Aw, he got it right." She closed her eyes and rubbed the fabric of the designer dress against her bare shoulder.

"Of course I did." Emmanuel entered his bedroom grinning and carrying a shoe box in his hands. He closed the door behind him. "Your man is very observant. Plus I get to see you in your *barest* form every day. It wasn't hard to figure out your size."

Jazz noticed the shoebox in his hand. "Are those for me too?"

"Yeah, I couldn't let you greet our guests barefoot. I hope you like them." He handed Jazz the shoebox.

"Thank you. I'm sure I will. Why did you decide to dress me this evening? Don't you appreciate my sense of style?"

"You're a fashionista on and off camera. I just wanted to do something special for you today. This is the first time in many years that I'll have a woman that I love by my side on an election night. Thank you for supporting me through the scandal with the press and Zeus and the campaign. Most women would've left the scene forever and never looked back."

Jazz carefully placed the dress and shoebox on the bed and stood up. She reached up and rubbed Emmanuel's cheek. "I believed you from the start. It'll take more than a political attack ad to run me away from you."

"You know we have about forty-five minutes before our guests start trickling in." He tugged at the knot in the towel secured above Jazz's breasts.

"Get out of here, Emmanuel. I need to get dressed and I can't do it with you in here tempting me to do naughty things. Besides, your mother and your sister are downstairs. Ms. Mabel is with them."

"They're cooking in the kitchen. We can do a little cooking up here."

Jazz put her hands on her hips. "If you don't leave so I can get dressed *now*, I won't let you stick around and watch me undress *later*."

"I'll be downstairs with Tyrone and my dad."

*****

"Bartender, I...I n-need another one." Trey slammed his empty glass on the bar counter. He glanced at the television mounted high on the wall above the bar and frowned. "Bartender, I need another gin and tonic!"

The tall thin guy stuck out his chest. "Hey buddy, I heard you already. Wait your turn."

Mr. Westmore wasn't just losing the election; he was getting slaughtered in the process. His opponent was ahead by twenty-one percentage points and by several thousand votes. More than three quarters of the precincts in the district had already reported their results. It was not a good night for Trey. He hadn't received an invitation to Mr. Westmore's party at the Venetian Ballroom. He had fired him days ago from the campaign. He had gotten the boot because he had trusted a good-looking woman with a sassy tongue. Gigi Perdue had tracked down Trey and offered him information that she'd promised would be the silver bullet in Congressman Day's political career. But instead, it was his profession as a conservative political consultant that was now on life support. Trey didn't stand a chance of securing any more contracts in the state of Georgia. Mr. Westmore had guaranteed him that. He'd vowed to blackball him for his incompetence. Trey's flight back to Utah would leave very early in the morning. He would return home to reevaluate and regroup. Never again would he trust a pair of dancer's legs or a big round ass when it came to politics. Gigi Perdue had taught him a valuable lesson.

*****

"Mr. Bartender, please make sure that everyone has a drink in their hand. Of course make sure the bishop and his wife have something mild."

Everyone in the room laughed at Tyrone. Even Bishop Stinson seemed appreciated his sense of humor. The atmosphere was cheerful. Delicious Southern comfort food and strong drinks were in abundance. Emmanuel's house was overflowing with energetic laughter and chatter. It was indeed a night of celebration.

Once everyone had been served their beverage of choice, Tyrone cleared his throat to regain their attention. "I'd like to propose a toast to the man of the hour, my baby brother, Emmanuel Day."

The small gathering of family and friends cheered and raised their glasses. They all looked around for Emmanuel, but he was nowhere to be found. Jazz excused herself from the room to search for him. As she neared his home office, she heard his deep voice. It was loud and animated. Jazz peeped through the crack in the slightly open door. She was surprised to see the love of her life sitting in the middle of the floor surrounded by two of his nieces and his youngest nephew. His other niece, five-year-old Satin, was sitting on his lap with her thumb in her mouth. The television was on showing the results of elections all around the state and the country, but not a soul was watching it. They were too indulged in a competitive game of Uno.

"Rhema is *cheating*, Uncle Manny! She always does."

"I am not!"

"You are too! Isn't she, Croix?"

The only male cousin in the group looked away. "I don't know."

Emmanuel intervened to settle the dispute. "Gem says you're cheating, Rhema. Is that true, sweetie?"

"Not really."

Gem picked up a stack of cards that was supposed to have been hidden under her cousin's thigh. She held them up for everyone to see. "See? I told you. Rhema is a *cheater*!"

Jazz giggled from her hide-out spot behind the door. All heads turned in her direction. She was embarrassed. Emmanuel signaled for her to come into the room with a curl of his index finger.

"I'm sorry. I didn't mean to interrupt."

"It's fine, Jazz."

"I came to tell you that Tyrone and the others need you back in the family room for a toast."

"Come on kids. It's time for some strawberry soda. Let's go with Ms. Jazz to the family room."

*****

"Hold on, Emmanuel. Fred wants to congratulate you too." Mrs. Anderson handed her husband the phone and left the den.

"I'm mighty proud of you, son. You did well. Now that you've earned yourself another term in congress, what are your plans for your *personal* life?"

"I'd planned to have this conversation with you when I got back to Washington, but I might as well do it now. Jazz is in the family room entertaining our guests, so she won't be able to hear what I'm about to say. Your granddaughter has brought so much joy into my life since we've been together. I'm a better man because of her. I have every intention of marrying Jazz, sir. That is, if you and Mrs. Anderson will give me your blessing to do so."

"Nothing would make us happier. Sallie Mae has been praying for the day when you would ask Jazz to marry you. I'll admit I was a bit doubtful about you at first, but you proved yourself to me. You have my blessing to marry my pumpkin."

"Thank you, sir."

Chapter Thirty-Seven

"Yo, Blaze, ain't this your girl on TV? Come check her out looking like a caramel sundae. I would love to spread some whipped cream all over her."

"I would too, man. I'd lick her from head to toe," a Dallas' Stars wide receiver yelled back.

The entire room exploded with laughter and high fives. Mario slammed his locker shut loud over the outburst. He walked toward the television. A group of his teammates were huddled around it. They reminded him of a pack of wolves salivating over a piece of raw meat. His eyes stretched wide at the sight of Jazz. She *did* look amazing. She was even more beautiful than she was in his dreams.

"Turn it up. I want to hear what she's talking about."

One of Mario's teammates turned away from the television and looked at him. "She's probably talking about *you* and how you fooled around on her with a dumb cheerleader and knocked her up."

Like a brother on the edge, Mario snapped. He rushed toward the stocky nose guard in a brisk sprint and pushed him against the wall. "Watch your mouth, punk!"

It started off as a shoving match, but within seconds, Mario swung and landed a hard punch to his teammate's jaw. The guy responded with a combination of quick jabs to Mario's chest and lower body. They knocked over tables, chairs, and a few of their teammates as they wrestled and eventually, fell to the floor. Each screamed vulgar expletives and insults at the other as a group of players struggled to separate them. Each man was determined to kill the other. The brawl quickly began to spiral out of control. Three uniformed members of the stadium's security team burst into the locker room. With the help of two burly football players, the security guards were able tear Mario and his teammate apart.

"Don't get mad at me because you messed up, you pimp!"

"At least I can get a woman! That anorexic pop star you're hanging out with only wants your money! You better hope the owner offers you a new contract. You can't keep that honey without a fat bank account!"

"You had plenty of money, but you still lost that fine reporter!"

Mario tried to break away from the security guards, but his teammates helped the men restrain him. The other officer escorted his trash talking rival out of the room. The dude cursed, ridiculed, and threatened Mario all the way down the hall. The other football players packed their bags and left the locker room without saying a word. Mario sat down and rubbed his jaw. He had taken a few bruising punches. The hardest one hadn't landed anywhere on his body, though. His heart had taken the worst hit.

Mario knew Jazz had moved on. He didn't expect her to spend the rest of her life waddling in sorrow over their breakup. Almost eight years had passed since she had called off their wedding, but the wound in Mario's heart was still fresh. He didn't think it would ever heal. Losing a woman like Jazz had hurt him more than losing the Super Bowl three years ago. There would be future opportunities in his football career to win another championship, but Jazz was out of his life forever. Mario would never forgive himself for his stupidity. God had blessed him with the woman of his dreams, and he lost her because he was too weak to remain faithful to her.

The almighty macho male ego had led him down the wrong path and into the arms of another woman. But it was just sex. There had been no intimacy whatsoever between Mario and Kerri, the cheerleader with whom he now shared a daughter with. Seven and a half-year-old Marissa was his pride and joy. Mario loved her to pieces, and he had never considered her a mistake. However, the circumstance by which she was conceived was a definite error in judgment. Mario had acknowledged that many times over the years. Cheating on Jazz was the biggest regret of his life, but he would never make any apologies for taking responsibility for his daughter. He had refused to do so no matter how she was conceived.

Mario had attempted to reach out to Jazz a few times to apologize to her after she had left Dallas. Her grandmother and her friends at Sports World International made sure it never happened. They'd blocked him by any means, intercepting his calls, letters, and any other form of communication. Soon he gave up and accepted the fact that his actions had cost him his one and only true love. Mario then invested his time and energy into fatherhood. He poured all the love he'd had for Jazz onto Marissa. She became the center of his world. His baby girl helped him heal from the pain of losing the woman he loved.

Mario shook his thoughts away from his memories and looked around the room. Besides the magical tone of Jazz's voice telling the world about her misfortune in Swaziland, it was quiet and empty. It was kind of like his life outside of his daughter and football. He hoped that one day fate would grant him another chance at love. But above that, he wished for the opportunity to ask Jazz for her forgiveness for breaking her heart.

Chapter Thirty-Eight

"Girl, you were *fierce*! Steven Spielberg and Tyler Perry will be calling you soon, honey. Let them duke it out over the movie rights. I can see it now. "Suffrage in Swaziland: The Jazz Dupree Story" will be a box office hit."

"You have lost your natural mind, Ramone. Thanks for coming, sweetie. I'll see you at the salon early Saturday morning. Call me tomorrow."

Jazz kissed her friend on the cheek and watched him strut down the walkway toward his red BMW convertible. Ramone had tarried behind after the other guests left to help her clean up after the watch party. Tyrell and Edgar had said their goodbyes over an hour ago. They both had brought dates to the gathering. Jazz and Emmanuel weren't surprised that Edgar showed up with his fiancée, Nadia, but Tyrell had shocked everybody. He had strolled into the house coolly and introduced Iris, a museum curator, as a close friend. She was a very attractive young lady with a curvaceous, full figure.

Jazz locked the door and activated the security system. When she turned around, Emmanuel was standing a few feet behind her looking like he had just finished a photo shoot for GQ magazine. Everything about his casual attire pushed all of Jazz's hot buttons. The sight of him in blue jeans made her woozy every time he wore a pair. As long as she lived and breathed, Jazz would never get enough of him. Her thirst for Emmanuel was unquenchable.

"You were awesome. I'm very proud of you, baby. All of the long hours and hard work you poured into your special project paid off. Come here." He opened his arms.

Without hesitation, Jazz walked into an embrace so warm and inviting that her body seemed to melt into Emmanuel's. They were a perfect fit in every way. No other man on the planet could make Jazz feel the way Emmanuel did. She felt like the luckiest woman alive. The love of a good man was what she had been missing over the last several years. Emmanuel released Jazz and looked down at the key shaped pendant lying on her chest. He lifted it.

"You never told me what I could unlock with it."

"You unlocked my heart months ago and you didn't need a key to do it. The first day you walked into my office I wanted you. You played hard to get, but I'm a tenacious brother. I had to have you."

"Now that you have me, what do plan to do with me, sir?"

"Just like I told you last weekend on final night in the Appalachian Mountains, you're stuck with me, baby. I'm not going anywhere and I'll never let you get away."

Jazz believed Emmanuel was in love with her and that he was committed to their relationship, but she wanted *more*. And she wanted it soon. Every time she spoke with her grandmother, she received the ageless lecture about the man, a cow, and free milk. On those days, Jazz wanted to grab Emmanuel by the collar, shake him a few times, and ask him where her ring was. But tonight wasn't the time for that conversation. It was a night to celebrate the success of her special project. Jazz shoved all concerns about rings, proposals, and marriage to the back of mind for the time being. She relaxed in Emmanuel's arms when he lifted her off her feet and carried her to his bedroom. He had promised to make love to her all night long. Jazz wanted him to make good on his word.

*****

"Nah, Unc, put it back." Tyrell shook his head and frowned. "That ring costs more than I make in six months. Find a cheaper block of ice. I saw a couple of nice ones over there for a fourth of the price."

"This is the one. It's the kind of ring Jazz deserves."

Tyrell could tell from the look in Emmanuel's eyes as he examined the ring more closely that his protesting was in vain. He was already in love with the high-priced piece of jewelry. Akbar, his uncle's personal jeweler, had told them that he'd deliberately saved the best for last. The instant he removed the seven carat emerald cut diamond ring from the display case, Emmanuel became hooked like a mouse on cheese.

Tyrell sat down on the stool next to his uncle. "The price tag is high up in the five-figure range. You could feed an entire village of starving children with that amount of cash."

"I feed hungry children every day in the U.S. and in Somalia. I'm only proposing *once*, and everything has to be perfect, especially the ring. Jazz is a classy woman, and she's worthy of the very best that I can afford."

"I feel you. I just don't want you to spend a grip on an engagement ring for the wrong reason."

Emmanuel looked up from the ring and studied his nephew's face. "What are you talking about?"

"I'm talking about the article I read on the internet about Mario Thomas. I told you all about the fat slice of ice he gave Jazz when he proposed to her back in the day. I hope you're not about to drop a lot of dough on a ring to compete with your woman's ex."

"Man, I thought you knew your uncle better than that. I don't have to compete with Mario Thomas unless he challenges me for my congressional seat. The size of this diamond and its price has nothing to do with the ring he gave Jazz. I'm going to buy this ring for the woman I love because she's worth every damn dollar and then some. You, more than anyone, know how much I love Jazz, Tyrell."

"Yeah, I do."

"She is everything I've ever wanted in a wife and more. When have you ever seen me happier than I am today?"

"Never."

Emmanuel clapped his hand firmly on Tyrell's shoulder. "A happy man makes his woman happy." He held up the black velvet ring box and inspected its exquisite contents again. "I'm going to blow Jazz's mind when I slide this on her finger."

"So when is the big day? Christmas or New Year's Eve?"

"Neither. Holiday proposals are too typical. Emmanuel Day is not a typical brother. I'm taking Jazz home with me for the Black Belles and Beaus' holiday ball in a few weeks. I'll pop the question some time that weekend. I don't need an audience. It'll only be Jazz and me in some romantic setting. By Christmas, she'll be shopping for a wedding gown and naming her bridesmaids."

*****

Jazz screamed and did an energetic happy dance around Ramone's styling station. Her curvy hips swayed left to right and back and forth as she snapped her fingers to music inside her head. Then she went into a slow version of the snake with her head and neck leading the way.

"Who was that on the phone, honey? Santa Claus? Is he bringing you a little red Corvette for Christmas?" Ramone rolled his eyes and popped his lips.

"That was one of the producers of "What's Happening USA". He wants me to make an appearance on the show to talk about my nightmare in Swaziland. They're going to fly me to New York the week after Thanksgiving for an interview with *Sage Normandy*!"

"Girl, you know I love Ms. Sage. I want an autographed picture."

"That shouldn't be a problem. I wish you could go with me to hook up my hair and makeup. I need to get my wardrobe options together," Jazz said, rubbing her hands together. "We'll have to go shopping next week. My appearance has to be popping from head to toe. Oh, I have to tell Emmanuel. I'll surprise him tonight after dinner."

"I'm sure he'll be happy for you."

Chapter Thirty-Nine

Jazz's interview in New York on "What's Happening USA" had screwed up Emmanuel's proposal plans. It had also forced him to attend the Black Belles and Beaus' annual holiday ball without a date. Before he'd turned in his player's card, he seldom attended high society functions without eye candy on his arm. An attractive date would usually keep the undesirable female hunters off of his tail. Since he was officially off the market, Jazz was his constant companion wherever he went, until tonight. She was in New York on a mini media blitz, and he was sitting in a corner alone at the ball nursing a glass of brandy.

The Black Belles and Beaus Historical Society, an Atlanta-based civic organization for the African-American affluent and elite, hosted extravagant events. Their annual holiday ball was always second to none. Every year they would secure a national recording artist to grace the stage for a performance. The finest caterer, the best local R&B band, and Atlanta's most highly sought after decorator were always contracted to create a spectacular affair suited for royalty. The chef had outdone himself with a delectable spread of down home Southern cuisine. Thousands of white cascading lights, gold bows, and red linens had transformed the ballroom into a scene from a holiday fairytale. The only thing missing was Emmanuel's queen.

He did a quick scan of the crowded ballroom and noticed several women, who like him, had arrived solo. When he'd first reached the Georgia World Conference Center, he was greeted by some of them and was asked to dance. A respectable guy, Emmanuel flashed his signature smile and declined all offers to cut a rug, but he did take the time to chat with a few of the women. They'd mostly discussed his recent election victory as well as their individual plans for Christmas and New Years. After that, Emmanuel had enjoyed the meal and a couple of drinks. Many attendees had approached him to talk politics. He wasn't in the mood to discuss work or much of anything else, so he'd retreated to his quiet little corner in the back of the room. From his vantage point he was able to observe all of the guests and their activities. Emmanuel had a clear view of the bar, the bandstand, and the dance floor. One person he was unpleasantly surprised to see in the midst of the crowd was *Gigi*. She wasn't from Atlanta, so Emmanuel hadn't expected her to be there. The Black Belles and Beaus organization wasn't exclusive to his hometown, but he had a hunch that there wasn't a chapter in New Iberia, Louisiana. Gigi was a native and still reigning queen of the small town near the Gulf Coast. She didn't speak very much about her humble beginnings, but she used it to her advantage from time to time to boost her career. Her poverty to prominence story had earned her lots of respect in the world of journalism. Emmanuel didn't know how or why Gigi had ended up at the holiday ball and he didn't care. He was just grateful that he had managed to avoid her all evening while she pranced around the room flirting with unattached men.

Other than a mediocre performance by neo soul songstress, Black Berry, nothing had brought the event to life. The band was decent enough to keep the dance floor full, and it was good to see old friends and acquaintances. But Emmanuel was ready to bid his fellow belles and beaus farewell until the next major gathering. He drained his drink and headed over to a table occupied by a few attorneys from his law firm and their spouses. Since Jazz was missing in action, he was going to swing by the office in the morning to check on things. He wanted to invite his colleagues to join him if they had nothing better to do on a Saturday.

"I'm about to get out of here, my good people. Who wants to meet me at the firm tomorrow after my early morning run around my neighborhood? I want to check out a few cases some of the junior associates are working on and go over the accounting books."

"I'll swing by around eleven o'clock," Ishmael Mustapha, a senior litigator announced.

"Count me in," Aisha Collins, the youngest lawyer at the firm said. "I don't have anything else to do. I might as well work. My big murder case is coming up."

Willis Cunningham shook his head covered with snow white hair. "I can't. My grandson has a football game. His pee-wee team is in the playoffs."

"I understand, Willis. Ishmael and Aisha, I'll see you two tomorrow. Good night, everyone."

Emmanuel left the ballroom and made his way down the corridor to valet services. He gave the attendant two tickets. One was for her to retrieve his overcoat, and the other one was for her to send for his vehicle from the parking deck. Emmanuel thanked the young lady for his coat and threw it over his arm. She assured him that his SUV would be in front of the building by the time he got outside. Emmanuel turned around and nearly collided with a couple behind him, but he managed to stop in the nick of time.

"Whoa! Hold on, sweet thing. Let me help you."

"Oops, I...I... can't find m-my...my...ticket," the woman slurred to her partner. Her silver beaded evening bag fell to the floor, spilling all of its contents.

"I got it, baby."

The intoxicated woman giggled and leaned forward. She lost her balance and almost fell flat on her face. She threw her head back and giggled when Emmanuel grabbed her seconds before she hit the floor and helped her stand upright.

"*Gigi*, are you alright?" he asked out of genuine concern.

"She's fine, man. I'm about to take her home."

Gigi rubbed the guy's chest. "Manny, this is my new friend...um...um...What's your name, handsome?"

"I'm Lawrence. Come on. Let's get your coat so I can take you home, baby."

All kinds of warning signals shot through Emmanuel's head. Gigi was drunk as hell and she was about to get in the car with some strange stocky dude whose name she didn't even know. He wasn't going to take her home because she didn't live in the city. And if she had been from the Atlanta area, she was in no condition to give the guy her address or directions. Emmanuel's ego told him to let Gigi go and do her own thing. She was a big girl and she was accustomed to playing adult games with members of the opposite sex. But even though she was a pain in the ass, his conscience wouldn't let him turn his back on a woman who was about to be taken advantage of. Emmanuel closed his eyes and counted to ten. He hated involving himself in other people's affairs, but he didn't have a choice. His father had taught him to respect all women and protect them whenever he could. In her state, Gigi didn't deserve much respect, but she needed his protection. The Lawrence character was obviously up to no good.

Emmanuel pulled Gigi toward him so he could whisper in her ear. Lawrence held on tightly to her other arm, apparently, making sure that she didn't get away. "I'm going to take you to your hotel room or wherever you're staying. I don't think it's a good idea for you to get in the car with a man you just met. You've been drinking, Gigi. It smells like you've been drinking *a lot*."

"Manny?" She looked at Emmanuel's concerned face. "W-what are you...you talking about? Lonnie likes me."

"I'm *Lawrence*, baby. But you're right. I really do like you. We've been hanging out all evening, and I was nice enough to offer you a ride home."

"She's not going anywhere with you. Are you some kind of sexual predator that lurks around looking for vulnerable women? Ms. Perdue is heavily intoxicated, and I will *not* allow her to leave here with you."

"Wait a minute, man." Lawrence stepped closer to Emmanuel. "Look, I found her first, and she's going with *me*."

"I'm not going to argue with you. I don't have time. We'll let the police decide. I don't think it'll be a hard play to call. Maybe they'll let Ms. Perdue go with you, a man she doesn't know who got her drunk so he could take advantage of her. Or they will allow me, a member of the U.S. Congress, whom she has known for almost ten years, to escort her to her hotel."

"Hotel?"

"That's right. Ms. Perdue is visiting Atlanta from Washington, D.C. She doesn't have a home here. So tell me...where had you really planned on taking her?"

Lawrence threw up both beefy arms and shook his head. "Take her. She ain't worth the hassle. I'm going home to my wife and kids."

Chapter Forty

"What do you mean that you don't have any more flights leaving from New York to Atlanta tonight? That can't be possible. Could you please check again, ma'am?"

Jazz chewed on her thumb nail while she waited for the airline's customer service representative to find a flight from NYC to the ATL. The last event of her media run in the Big Apple had ended earlier than the host had expected. Jazz had intentionally written a short speech for her appearance at the facility for homeless teenage mothers, hoping that she could get out of the city ahead of schedule. Her plan was to catch a flight to Atlanta to surprise Emmanuel. When he'd dropped her off at Reagan International Airport earlier that week, he was one ticked off brother. He supported her career and he'd told her how proud he was of all of the appearances she was scheduled to make in New York. But it wasn't a secret that he preferred that Jazz travel home with him for the holiday ball. She wanted to be with him as well, but the conflict in their agendas was out of her control. An opportunity to be interviewed on the number one morning news show in America did not fall in one's lap every day. And it was with the lovely and sassy Sage Normandy. She was a household name all across the country. The other events had been arranged by Black Diamond. Mr. McConnell believed that it was a good idea to book Jazz to appear at other venues in New York to tell her story and promote the network. Her business in the city was now over, and she wanted to reunite with her man. Phone calls, text messages, and video chats were convenient forms of technology that had kept them connected while they were apart. But Jazz missed Emmanuel so much that her heart was aching. She needed to be with him as soon as possible.

When the customer service rep returned to the line after placing Jazz on hold for three minutes, she didn't have good news. She confirmed the postponement of all flights from New York City to Atlanta until tomorrow morning.

"No, no, no, ma'am, I need to leave New York for Atlanta *tonight*. It doesn't matter which airport. I can get to La Guardia or JFK. I just need a flight, lady. It's an emergency."

Jazz massaged her temples as the woman repeated her options. Due to heavy rainfall and gusty winds in Atlanta and surrounding areas, every flight to Hartsfield-Jackson International Airport from all New York City airports had been delayed until early tomorrow morning. The news disappointed Jazz. Fresh tears pooled in her eyes. Her plan to surprise Emmanuel at his home in the middle of the night was ruined. Instead, she would appear on his doorstep just before sunrise. The setback in time was only a few hours, but to Jazz it seemed like a lifetime. She had no other option than to settle for a six o'clock flight for tomorrow morning.

*****

"Gigi, wake up and tell me the name of the hotel where you're staying." Emmanuel reached over and nudged her shoulder several times trying to shake her from her sleep. She didn't budge. "Wake up now. I need to know where I should take you."

Emmanuel was frustrated and running out of patience. If it hadn't been for the parking attendant, he wouldn't have been able to get Gigi into his SUV. Her floppy body and wobbly legs had made the simple task of walking straight impossible. And she'd behaved like an animated, mouthy, and resistant child the entire time the two men tugged and pushed her to the vehicle. At one point, Emmanuel had felt tempted to stuff his handkerchief inside of Gigi's mouth because of her excessive laughter and rambling. The scene was an ugly one as he and the attendant had struggled to drag her a few feet before eventually picking her up together and carrying her to the SUV. Now that she was safe and secure in Emmanuel's Jeep Cherokee, she was asleep and snoring like a bear. Her mouth was wide open, filling the air inside the vehicle with the bitter odor of her breath. It reeked of garlic and strong alcohol. Emmanuel wanted to crack his window to allow some fresh air to flow in and circulate, but it had started raining heavily again. It was not the weekend he had planned for.

Emmanuel looked in his rearview mirror before he carefully pulled over to the side of the road and stopped. He picked up Gigi's evening bag from her lap and searched through it. He was hoping to find a hotel key card or maybe a receipt or brochure. Unfortunately, there was nothing in the cluttered purse to indicate where she was staying or why she was even in town. He found her cell phone and was relieved, but only for a moment. As luck would have it, he wasn't able to scroll through it because the battery had died. Calling the last person in Gigi's phone log could've possibly given him the information he needed about her lodging accommodations in Atlanta. Emmanuel leaned back in his seat and rested his head to contemplate his next move.

*****

Iris sat down on the couch next to Tyrell. "Were you able to reach him?"

"No. Maybe he's still at the holiday ball. But that's so unlike Unc. He didn't even want to attend the affair without Jazz. The only reason he went alone was because the organization made a sweet donation to his re-election campaign, and he's been a member since he was a senior in undergraduate school. He told me he would only hang out for a couple of hours."

"I bet the congressman ran into some old friends and started having a good time. They're probably throwing back drinks and telling plenty of lies right about now. Stop worrying about your uncle. You should be concentrating on *me*."

Tyrell pulled Iris into his arms and gave her chaste kiss on the lips. It was the first weekend in a very long time that he didn't have to work or be on call for his uncle. He was supposed to be enjoying his time off with Iris, but there was an unsettling feeling in the pit his stomach that would not allow him to relax. Emmanuel was missing in action down in Atlanta. Tyrell and Fabian could not reach him to give him an update on one of his colleague's legal status. It wasn't an urgent matter, but they were sure he would want to know the outcome of his friend's trial. Congressman Harold Matthews from California had escaped bribery charges and other allegations of misuse of his office. Emmanuel had consulted with the congressmen's defense attorneys several times on the case and he'd expressed confidence that he would be found innocent.

Fabian had attempted to reach his boss with the good news about his friend, but he'd been unsuccessful. That's when he called

Tyrell and learned that he hadn't spoken with his uncle either. Both men had dismissed the matter, assuming that Emmanuel was unable to hear his phone over the loud music at the event. But when Jazz called Tyrell complaining that she too could not connect with his uncle by phone, he became alarmed. Something wasn't quite right. Emmanuel would answer his phone in the middle of a snowstorm in Siberia for Jazz. Occasionally, he would ignore his staffers, but never his woman. If Jazz was having difficulty getting a hold of Emmanuel, there was something terribly wrong going on in the ATL. Thoughts of a car accident, a chance mugging, or sudden illness hit Tyrell. He stood abruptly from his seat.

"Let me try to reach Uncle Manny one more time. I'll check in with my parents and grandparents too. Somebody in the family down there has to know where he is."

Iris sighed, obviously annoyed. "I'm going to bed. Don't bother waking me up when you're finished playing hide and seek your uncle."

Tyrell watched the ample hips he had grown fond of sway from left to right heading in the opposite direction. He'd much rather follow Iris to his bedroom, but he couldn't shake the weird feeling that had him on edge. He had to follow his instincts. In his world, politics always came before passion or pleasure. It was how the ball rolled in his line of business. The day he and Iris met, he'd warned her that his job was very demanding and required his attention more than eighteen hours a day sometimes. Politics was politics. It was a never-ending game. If Jazz could deal with it, Iris would have to get with the program as well. If she couldn't handle it, Tyrell would have to let her go.

Chapter Forty-One

"I'm too damn old for this crap!"

Emmanuel sprinted through the cold and hammering downpour for the second time. He slid and nearly fell in a shallow puddle of water at the end of his walkway. Angry, he barked a few curse words at the top of his lungs and continued his run to the vehicle. The rain was so relentless that every article of clothing on his body was drenched. Emmanuel's tuxedo shirt and jacket were pasted to his chest and back by the cold moisture. An inebriated Gigi was protected from the harsh elements of the weather by his overcoat.

Emmanuel pulled the front passenger's door open and found her sprawled out comfortably in the seat and still snoring loudly. The sight of a drunken woman had always disgusted him no matter how pretty she was. He bent down and released Gigi's seatbelt. Then without much effort at all, he scooped her up into his arms and hoisted her over his shoulder in a caveman-like gesture. After a sharp side kick to the door, securing it shut, Emmanuel took off toward his house again. He'd left his front door wide open and turned on the lights on his first trip so that he could carry Gigi into the house without mishap. Her flaccid body bounced up and down as Emmanuel trotted through the rain. She coughed a few times and mumbled incoherently when chilly drops of rain pounded the side of her face and hair. Emmanuel stumbled into the house cold, tired, and fuming. He drew in a long, deep breath before he braved the staircase. His bedroom door was slightly ajar. He pushed it open further with the toe of his wingtip shoe and entered. Carelessly, he dropped Gigi on the bed. She landed on her back like a ragdoll, without stirring.

Emmanuel tiptoed around his bedroom, gathering a few personal items and his overnight bag. A long hot shower in the guest suite down the hall would be his first order of business. Then he would call Jazz and tell her all about his evening from hell. Nothing else mattered much after that. In the morning after his jog, he would deliver his unwelcome houseguest to wherever she was supposed to be. One thing he knew for sure was that she did not belong in his house or in his bed.

*****

Jazz smiled when she realized Emmanuel had called her a total of nine times last night and throughout the early hours of the morning. There was urgency in his voice in each message he'd left. Apparently, she wasn't the only person in the relationship having love withdrawals. Emmanuel was missing her too. Jazz was happy to learn that she wasn't suffering alone. It had taken three glasses of chardonnay and a long article about Morris Chestnut to calm her nerves the night before. The white wine buzz and Ebony magazine's feature article had put Jazz to sleep. She had rested so well that she missed Emmanuel's phone calls. But she would make it up to him, and they would catch up on all of the time they'd spent apart in a few hours. Jazz's little surprise visit to Atlanta was going to be a very rewarding one. It was the most brilliant idea she'd ever had.

"I'm on my way, baby," she whispered before she turned off her cell phone and shifted in her seat.

A handsome airline attendant appeared at her side. "Good morning, Ms. Dupree. Before we take off, may I get you a cup of our premium brewed coffee or would you prefer tea?'

"Tea would be fine. Thank you."

The tall young man leaned down. "I'm a huge fan, ma'am. May I please have your autograph and a picture with you at some point during the flight?"

"I can make that happen. After I've had my tea, I'll be ready."

Truthfully, Jazz was ready for anything with or without a cup of tea. She was on a natural high, knowing that in a few hours she would be in Emmanuel's arms. An autograph and few pictures could not steal her joy. Nothing could.

*****

Emmanuel placed a note on the pillow next to Gigi who was still asleep before he left the house for an early morning run. In Washington, he hit the gym three times a week to maintain a healthy body weight, but he enjoyed breathing in the fresh Georgia air whenever he was home. He also appreciated the sight of grass and tree lined streets in his neighborhood. Friendly morning greetings from other joggers, walkers, and cyclists added to his appreciation for Southern living. Everyone was usually pleasant. That wasn't the case on the streets of D.C. The hustle and bustle of life in the nation's capital had the tendency to make its residents somewhat grumpy.

Emmanuel waved to a group of older women walking at a carefree snail's pace on the opposite side of the street. They all waved back and addressed him by name. As usual, being recognized at home brought a smile to Emmanuel's face. Thinking about heading back to Washington Tuesday morning to reunite with Jazz broadened that smile. Six days apart seemed like a prison sentence. They wouldn't be separated again anytime soon if Emmanuel had his way. He was ready to propose to Jazz and make her his wife. On his first evening back in Washington, he was going to pop the question over a bottle of wine and a pot of spicy homemade chili at his house.

*****

The sound of Jazz's voice calling Emmanuel woke Gigi to a splitting headache. She thought she was dreaming at first, but as the familiar voice grew louder and closer, she realized her nemesis was actually in the house. Gigi noticed the note lying on the pillow next to her. She read it quickly, crumpled it, and threw it under the bed. Emmanuel was out jogging through the neighborhood. He wanted her up and ready to leave his house by the time he returned. Gigi jumped up from the bed and stripped out of her clothes, allowing each piece to fall to the floor. She spotted Emmanuel's black bathrobe hanging from a hook in his open walk-in closet. As the wicked idea continued to unfold inside her head, she smiled, imagining how it would all play out. She hurried to the closet and put Emmanuel's robe on her naked body. At the spur of the moment, she dashed into the master bathroom to turn on the shower to add a little steam to the scene. Then she waited for the doorknob to turn as adrenaline swooshed through her veins. As if on cue, Jazz opened the bedroom door.

"Manny," Gigi purred. "Are you back home already, baby?" She walked out of the bathroom with the front of Emanuel's robe open, exposing her naked body.

"Gigi! What the hell are *you* doing here?"

"Manny brought me here last night after the Black Belles and Beaus' holiday event. *We* thought you were still in New York doing your thing. Should I call Manny and tell him that you're here? I'm sure you two have a lot to talk about."

"No, I don't need you to do a damn thing for me! I knew you were desperate and needy, Gigi, but this is pathetic."

"Don't be naïve, darling. I had Manny *first*. Remember? I guess he decided to come on back home to Mama."

Jazz took a few steps to close the distance between them. "If I didn't know for a fact that I was a better woman, friend, and journalist than you are, I wouldn't mind choking you to death and spending fifty years of my life in prison because of it. But because I know beyond a shadow of a doubt that I am *everything* you wish you could be, I'll pass on the opportunity and go on with my fabulous life instead."

Jazz retraced her steps and ran back down the stairs.

*****

A steady drizzle and moderate wind cut Emmanuel's run short. He did a brisk turn and headed for his house. As he rounded the corner leading to his street a few minutes later, he immediately noticed Jazz standing on his stoop talking on her cell phone. Fear and disbelief grabbed him. A tightening sensation in his chest made it hard for him to breathe. Suddenly, Emmanuel's legs grew heavy as iron, but he pumped them as fast as he could, running like his life depended on it. Jazz ended her call and looked up in his direction. Their eyes met and locked. Emmanuel cringed when he saw pure distress in her face. She was crying through bloodshot eyes. He could see her tears even through the raindrops.

"Don't come near me, Emmanuel," she warned. "Stay away from me or I will scream. My cab is on its way. I don't have anything to say to you."

Emmanuel had no intention of staying away from Jazz. He loved her too much to do that. She needed to hear his explanation. Finding Gigi in his house had definitely confused her, and he wanted to set the record straight. He ran up his walkway and stopped in front of Jazz. He reached a hand out to her.

"I tried to call you a thousand times last night and this morning to tell you. Why didn't you answer your phone?"

Jazz reached way back and swung. Her open hand landed hard on the left side of Emmanuel's face. "What did you want to tell me? Were you going to explain that you missed me so much that you needed a substitute in my absence? How could you, Emmanuel? You promised that you would never hurt me! Why did you sleep with *Gigi* of all females? Just tell me why?"

"I didn't touch her, baby. Is that what you think happened? Is your faith in me so small that you would jump to that insane conclusion?"

"I saw her wearing your bathrobe in your bedroom," Jazz whispered, easing away from Emmanuel. "You brought her here. She told me. That tramp was about to take a shower in the master bathroom where some of my personal items are stored. I'm not stupid, Emmanuel!"

"Jazz, baby, listen to me."

Jazz shook her head and ran down the walkway with Emmanuel right behind her. He watched her struggle with the handle on her rolling suitcase. Then her cab arrived and stopped directly in front of Emmanuel's home. He motioned with his hand for the driver to leave.

"Wait!" Jazz shouted and waved her hand in the air.

The driver rolled down his window. "Make up your mind, lady. Are you leaving or staying?"

"I'm definitely leaving. Can you please help me with my suitcase, sir?"

The driver exited the car, but left the motor running. He lifted Jazz's suitcase and placed it in his trunk. She escaped to the back seat of the yellow midsize sedan and slammed the door.

Emmanuel knocked on her window. "Jazz, nothing happened between Gigi and me. I know how it may have looked to you, but you *have to believe me*. I love you."

The cab driver pulled away from the house slowly. Emmanuel jogged alongside the car until it picked up speed and drove out of his reach. He yelled Jazz's name loudly into the rain filled air. He looked up into the sky as if he were pleading with God for help. The low-hanging clouds were dark, robbing the new morning of sunlight. Emmanuel shivered in the cold rain. He looked up at his bedroom window and saw Gigi standing there with an emotionless expression on her face.

Chapter Forty-Two

"Emmanuel doesn't know where you live, Ramone. No one does. Please let me stay here a few more days until I can figure out what I'm going to do about my job."

Ramone sat down on the bed and pulled the covers up to Jazz's chin. "Of course you can crash here with me for as long as you need to, but you are *not* going to quit your job, boo."

"I can't work at Black Diamond anymore. I refuse to torture myself. Gigi will make my life a living hell. She won, Ramone. I've accepted it. She waited patiently for the perfect opportunity and dug her claws deep into my man. Gigi stole Emmanuel from me."

"I don't believe it. I will not render a verdict until after I've heard the congressman's side of the story. This is America, sweetie. You ain't in Swaziland anymore. Over here we have a judicial system that declares all suspects innocent until proven guilty."

Jazz threw the covers from her body and sat up. "I saw Gigi parading around Emmanuel's bedroom in his robe. She was butt naked underneath it. Did I mention that?"

"I've heard the story too many times over the last forty-eight hours, darling. I know what you saw. But let me break down what your eyes did not see. You didn't catch the congressman and the harlot in the act. Nor did you find any evidence whatsoever of a rodeo in the sack. You said the bed was a *little bit* rumpled. How does his bed look after you and him have spent the night feeding each other's passions?"

"You don't want to know."

"Has your man ever had the energy to go jogging the morning after a wild night with *you*?"

Jazz shook her head and sighed. "He told me that he can't, so he waits until the afternoon to work out at the gym. He started drinking energy drinks after we hooked up. Tyrell teases him about it all the time. He told Emmanuel that I'm going to give him a heart attack one day. We're ten years apart, you know."

"I know, Jazz. If you give that chocolate congressman a heart attack he'll die a happy man. He loves you, and you love him. This whole situation is messy. You need to talk to him."

"Why are you taking Emmanuel's side, Ramone? Gigi had no business in his house under any circumstances. They have a past. I was *supposed* to have been his present and future." Jazz burst into tears.

"Listen to me, honey," Ramone demanded, holding Jazz's tear stained face between his palms. "Talk to the man. You owe it to yourself to hear whatever he has to say. You will never know the whole truth until you get your man's side of the story."

"I'm not ready to talk to Emmanuel right now. It hurts too much. Every time I close my eyes and see Gigi in his bedroom, my heart aches. She shouldn't have been there, Ramone."

"You're right. That hooker had no business all up in your future home. But you don't know why she was there, darling. Gigi told you *her* version of how she got to the congressman's house. I don't believe anything that hussy says. You know she's jealous of you and she has been chasing after the congressman for a long time. Don't take Gigi's word. Talk to the man who promised to take good care of your heart. I need you to promise me that you'll have a conversation with him soon."

"I will talk to Emmanuel. You have my word, but give me a little time."

"You better hurry up because the next time he dials my number, I'm going to answer and listen to him."

*****

Emmanuel closed the ring box and tossed it on the coffee table. He raised the bottle of beer to his lips and took a long swig. He leaned back in the recliner and propped his legs on the coffee table.

"What are you going to do, Unc?"

"What the hell can I do? Jazz won't take my calls. She hasn't been to work since she got back from New York, and I have no idea where she's staying."

"You do know where she's staying. Jazz is with Ramone. You just don't know the exact location. Go by his salon tomorrow. He likes you. Maybe he'll give you his address so you can visit Jazz at his place."

"They're close. Ramone wouldn't betray Jazz's trust, and I don't want him to. Mario Thomas has scarred her for life with his cheating. That's why trust is so important to her. She obviously doesn't trust me anymore. I don't want her to lose faith in Ramone too."

"But you didn't do anything."

"I know that, but *Jazz* doesn't. And that makes me angry. She was supposed to trust me. I've never given her one reason not to. Because she loves me, she should've listened to my explanation and believed every word."

"I agree. But can you imagine how the scene must've looked in her eyes?"

"It appeared that Gigi and I had slept together."

"Exactly. Now it's up to you to find a way to talk to Jazz without any interruptions. Make her listen to you. And if you have to, force Gigi to tell the truth."

*****

Jazz walked into her office and was greeted by an array of gifts covering her desk. Flowers, gift baskets, balloons, and presents wrapped in beautiful colors of paper occupied every inch of space. She was sure Emmanuel had sent the gifts, hoping to get some type of positive reaction from her, but the display only made Jazz sad. She sensed someone standing behind her, so she turned around quickly. It was Jackson.

"Welcome back, baby girl."

"Thank you," Jazz responded with tears in her eyes.

Jackson immediately closed the door and hugged her. "I knew something was wrong. I couldn't put my finger on it, though. Gigi has been way too cheerful around here lately. And I couldn't figure out why Congressman Day kept sending gifts even though you weren't at work. Is the cupid trying to snatch his arrow back?"

Jazz nodded and her tears begin to flow freely. She went and sat down behind her desk and motioned for Jackson to sit as well. Then through a series of sobs and sniffles she told him everything about her surprise heartbreaking trip to Atlanta.

*****

After a long grueling week of politics as usual without a word from Jazz, Emmanuel finally got a breakthrough. For the first time since their breakup, he felt hopeful. He now knew for sure that Jazz was staying with Ramone temporarily, but he had no idea where the house was located. To his surprise, Emmanuel had also learned that Gigi was keeping a tight lip about the incident in Atlanta. As a matter of fact, she was staying clear of Jazz altogether. For some strange reason, she was spending the majority of her time at work locked up in her office. All of this information had found its way to Emmanuel from a very reliable source. Jackson had contacted him out of concern for his distraught friend and coworker. He sincerely cared about Jazz, and he liked Gigi about as much as he liked hemorrhoids.

Emmanuel had agreed to meet Jackson for lunch Friday afternoon to help him come up with a plan to win Jazz back. The two men spoke extensively about the disaster in Atlanta. Emmanuel confided in Jackson in detail about how he had rescued an intoxicated Gigi from getting into the car with a complete stranger on that rainy night. He regretted taking her to his home, but at the time it was his only alternative. Emmanuel concluded that his actions, although well-intended, had backfired on him, causing him to lose Jazz. In hindsight, Emmanuel wished he had ditched Gigi's troublesome ass at the nearest Motel 6. That's what most brothers in his situation would've done. The woman had acted inappropriately too many times toward him. Gigi's past mission to keep tabs on him by paying Sherry, the young speechwriter, to use Fabian was not cool. And Emmanuel had not forgotten about it either. The only reason why he'd never made a big fuss over her irrational behavior was because no damage had ever been done. So he had let it all roll off of his back.

The men mutually agreed that Gigi's ruse in Atlanta had been a calculated scheme concocted on a whim to hurt Jazz. It was the final straw for Emmanuel. Her antics had destroyed a meaningful relationship just for the hell of it. Emmanuel had no intention of letting Gigi off the hook this time. He planned to make her pay for her evil deeds. But first he had to get his woman back. And Jackson had volunteered to help him.

"So it was all a big stupid misunderstanding just like I thought."

Emmanuel nodded and took a sip of his drink. "I messed up, man. My intentions were honorable, but I ended up hurting Jazz. But she should've trusted me, Jackson. I tried to reach her the night before to tell her what was up. Then after she showed up at my house unexpected and found Gigi naked in my bedroom, I did my best to assure her that nothing had happened. Jazz refused to listen to anything I had to say."

"You're right. A woman should always trust her man no matter how bad it may look." Jackson checked out the scenery around their table in the swanky restaurant before he continued. He cocked his head to the side. "How much do you know about Jazz's broken engagement with The Blaze?"

"Everything. Jazz and I have been totally transparent about our past relationships. We didn't see the need to hold anything back. Mario Thomas is a loser. Any man who would cheat on Jazz and get another woman pregnant on top of it is a damn fool."

"I know you didn't sleep with Gigi that night, so she can't be pregnant with your child. But I'm sure the appearance of her prancing around in your bedroom, wearing her birthday suit was pretty incriminating in Jazz's opinion. If Gigi had a single ounce of decency in her character, she would've come forth with the truth by now. You should waterboard that psychotic witch and make her tell Jazz what really went down."

"I don't want Gigi to do me any favors. She'll think I owe her something. That's how distorted her mind is. It's my mess, and I'm going to fix it if I have to die trying. I'm not living without Jazz, Jackson. Trust and believe that."

Chapter Forty-Three

Jazz turned off the television and slid the remote control onto the end table discreetly when Ramone walked into the room. He was carrying a tray covered with delicious smelling food.

"Why are you sitting their tormenting yourself, honey?" Ramone rolled his eyes dramatically and placed the tray of goodies on the coffee table.

"I'm not tormenting myself. What are you talking about?"

"I heard his voice from the kitchen. You were watching the DVD of the political documentary *again*. You're still in love with him. Admit it. The man is stuck in your head and your heart. He's all in your soul, girl. Why don't you call him, Jazz?"

"Emmanuel should be calling *me*. He's the one who cheated." Jazz raised her chin and sliced her finger through the air. "I don't see any reason why I should dial his number."

"You gave me your word that you would. Have we started lying to each other after eight years of friendship?"

"I've changed my mind. That's my God-given right. Emmanuel stopped calling, and he hasn't sent me one apology gift this week. I guess he's moved on, and so have I."

"You're acting like a child. I hate to say it, but it's true. When you're done playing games, you need to call the congressman so the two of you can clear the air. Now eat." Ramone waved his hand over the tray of food. "I'm about to take a shower and get dressed. It's disco night at Cash 21."

*****

"If you get to the restaurant around two o'clock, your timing will be perfect. The luncheon should be wrapping up by then."

"Are you sure?"

"I'm sure. Just wait for the other journalists to clear out, and then corner Jazz. She misses you, man. She admitted it to me yesterday when I stopped by her office. However, she's still hurt and very angry, but I think she'll talk to you. Jazz is too much of a lady to act a fool in public."

Emmanuel checked his watch. He had another hour to wait. "My driver will have me there on time. Thanks for everything, Jackson. I appreciate your concern."

"I know you do. Just don't screw up again. I may not be willing to dig you out of another hole."

"I won't. Thanks again."

Emmanuel hung up the phone and picked up the bouquet of red roses from his desk. There were three dozen in all. The red rose was Jazz's favorite flower. Pralines were her preferred gourmet snack. He'd thought about buying her a box, but she would probably be stuffed after the Christmas luncheon at Brevard's Grill. Jackson had informed him about the Truth Finders Society of Journalism's noon get together at the popular downtown restaurant. Jazz had been inducted in the elite organization four years ago. This year she would be receiving an award for her hour-long special about her crisis in Swaziland. Emmanuel had made reservations at the restaurant with hopes of having Jazz join him afterwards so they could talk. He was tired of existing day after day without her. His life just wasn't the same since their breakup. Before the end of the day, Emmanuel expected reconciliation so they could start planning their future. He believed that once Jazz heard the truth about what had actually taken place in Atlanta, their lives would return to normal.

*****

"Oh, my God, you're Mario 'The Blaze' Thomas!"

"I am, but could you please lower your voice, sweetheart? I'm only in town until tomorrow, and I'd like to keep it low-key if I can."

"What brings you to the District?" The waitress flung her strawberry blonde hair over her shoulders and batted her bright green eyes."

"I'll be speaking at a boys' detention center in the morning. I try to inspire the youth as often as possible."

"That's wonderful. What can I get you to eat and drink today?"

"I haven't decided on a meal yet, but I could use a glass of water with a few lemon wedges on the side for now. Hold the ice."

"Sure. I'll be right back with your water."

Mario turned his attention to a group of people cheering and applauding in a private dining room on the other side of the restaurant. There was a program or some type of meeting going on. He looked more intensely at the group. A gorgeous woman sporting a stylish burgundy pantsuit was standing at a podium speaking over the microphone. There was some kind of award in her hands. Mario couldn't quite make out her words, but the voice gave him goose bumps. It was the same voice that used to sing his name many years ago while they were in the throes of passion. Sometimes it haunted him in his dreams even until this day. He couldn't believe his luck. As populated and busy a city as Washington was, he had never imagined he would cross paths with Jazz of all people.

"Here is your water, sir. Are you ready to order an appetizer or would you rather skip to your entrée?"

"Um, give me a few more minutes please. I still haven't decided yet."

"Take your time. I'll come back later."

Mario watched Jazz until she finished speaking. Then the group of people gathered around her for a photo session. She looked fabulous. No woman alive had the right to be so irresistibly good-looking. Mario was in a daze, unable to move or speak. He took pleasure in watching Jazz laugh and talk with her friends. Some of the attendees left the private dining area with their coats and scarves in their hands. Mario assumed the event was over. As the group dwindled down, Jazz and a few others stayed behind talking. Mario had prayed many times since their breakup for an opportunity to talk with Jazz face-to-face. He refused to let this chance slip through his finger tips. He left his table and walked directly to the room where she stood talking with three other women. Determined, Mario entered the room.

"Excuse me, ladies."

The women turned toward the door. They all smiled, except Jazz. She just stood there speechless, obviously shocked to see Mario.

"Jazz, I hope all is well with you. I'm sure you're surprised to see me, but I'd like to speak to you for a few minutes please when you're done."

*****

Emmanuel arrived at Brevard's Grill a few minutes before two o'clock. He was full of hope, confidence, and determination. Leaving the restaurant without making up with Jazz was not an option. He was innocent of what she *thought* he had done, and somehow he was going to convince her to believe him. Emmanuel made his way to the hostess' stand. There were a few people ahead of him. He scanned the dining area in the front of the restaurant. The place was busy. Sudden movement at a table facing the front window grabbed Emmanuel's attention. A tall and muscular brother dressed in a sharp charcoal gray suit stood up and offered his date his hand. He pulled her to her feet and took her in his arms for a long embrace. Even with the woman's back turned to Emmanuel, he recognized her right away. How could he not? Every inch of Jazz's anatomy was familiar to his sight, sense of smell, taste, and touch. He could decipher her voice through the most distorted and highest decibel of sound too. Emmanuel knew his woman from any angle or distance. And at the moment she was standing a few feet away from him in the arms of her ex-lover.

Emmanuel exited the restaurant angry and confused. He tossed the roses in a nearby trashcan and hailed a cab. Once inside the car, he called his driver to let him know that he wouldn't need a ride back to the office because his lunch date had ended early unexpectedly. Nothing had gone according to plan. While he had been preparing to win Jazz back after a misunderstanding, she was backtracking to a dude who had actually done her wrong. It was the worst possible predicament any man could find himself in.

Chapter Forty-Four

Jackson opened Jazz's office door and poked his head inside. "Knock, knock. May come in?"

"Sure. What's up?" Jazz asked, looking up from her computer screen. She lifted her arms high above her head and stretched her back.

Jackson closed the door behind him and stood in the middle of the floor. "So how did it go?"

"How did *what* go?"

"How did the little Christmas luncheon and the award presentation turn out?"

"It was nice. I was happy to spend time with the other members. The food was magnificent. I wanted to show you the award, but I accidentally left it in my car."

"Is that all? Did anything else happen?"

"Okay, Jackson, I get the feeling that you're fishing for something. What's going on with you? Why are you so interested in the Truth Finders Society's Christmas luncheon all of a sudden?"

"I'm not really interested. I was hoping...you know...I thought maybe—"

"Spit it out." Jazz stood up and planted her fists on her hips.

"Alright, you got me. I told the congressman that you would be at Brevard's Grill today. He was supposed to have surprised you. You really need to talk to him, Jazz. That's why I set the whole thing up. He didn't sleep with Gigi that night. I know what happened. If you'll listen to him, he would tell you too."

"You set me up?"

"Yes. The congressman needed a little help, so I threw him a bone. Did you see him? Please don't tell me that you blew him off again."

"I didn't see Emmanuel at the restaurant, but I ran into *Mario*."

"Your ex is in Washington?"

Jazz nodded her head. "He's here on business. I was shocked to see him. He approached me after the luncheon and asked me to sit and talk with him."

"Did you?"

"At first, I was a bit thrown off, but Mario assured me he wouldn't take up very much of my time. So *yes*, I sat and spoke with him briefly."

"Aw Jazz, if you were talking to Mario, then Congressman Day must've seen the two of you together. Like you, when you found Gigi at his house in Atlanta, he got the wrong impression and—"

"Emmanuel assumed the worst. Oh, Jackson, why is this happening? Why didn't he say something? Emmanuel should've come over to our table. He would've realized that nothing was going on. Mario was just apologizing for cheating on me when we were together. I told him all about Emmanuel and our current situation. He encouraged me to call him so we could talk and work things out."

Jackson rushed over to Jazz's desk and picked up her phone. He offered it to her. "Call him *now*, damn it! This situation has gotten way beyond complicated. It's time to fix it, Jazz."

✳✳✳✳✳

"Unc, she just called again. That's the *fourth* time. How long are you going to play this stupid childish game?"

"I'm too old to play games, Tyrell. Don't you see me working? It's what taxpayers pay me to do. Politics is politics. It's a never-ending game. I thought you knew that."

Tyrell walked fully into Emmanuel's office and took a seat. "I also know that you love Jazz, and she loves you. I think the two of you need to sit down and hash it out once and for all. Put your ego in check and swallow your pride, Unc. Talk to your woman."

"I had every intention of speaking to Jazz today." Emmanuel slammed the folder he'd been reading from on the top of his desk. "When I got to the restaurant, she was entertaining her ex. Apparently, they had some unfinished business, and it involved more than just talking. They were quite affectionate toward each other."

"You're joking, right?"

Emmanuel's eyes shot lethal bullets at Tyrell. His silence and unpleasant glare were scary, but Tyrell was adamant about having his say.

"You were ticked off with Jazz because she assumed you had slept with Gigi after she found her nude in your bedroom. Most women would've reacted the same way she did. You looked guilty, Unc. Accept it."

"But I wasn't."

"Jazz may not be either. You don't know what she and Mario Thomas were discussing at the restaurant or why. So he hugged her. It couldn't have been that big a deal. They were in a *public place* surrounded by other people. That's not very romantic to me. I seriously doubt the dude was trying to seduce Jazz."

"Jazz should not have been with him anywhere at any time. Case closed."

"That's true. Can we agree that Gigi had no business at your house or in your bedroom either?"

"You know why she was there."

"Return Jazz's phone call and explain to *her* why Gigi was in your bedroom. Maybe she'll tell you why she was with her ex at the restaurant today."

*****

Jazz had been given permission to work from home for two days because she couldn't handle being in the same building with Gigi. Constant visions of strangling the evil bitch with her bare hands and burning her lifeless body at the stake constantly clouded her mind. After Jackson had filled her in on the details about what had really gone down in Atlanta, he'd had to physically restrain her. Jazz had stormed toward her office door mad as hell with every intention of confronting Gigi wherever she found her. She was fuming, to put it mildly. Jackson later told Jazz after she had calmed down that she was stronger than a man three times her weight and size. He swore she was more vicious than a professional killer too.

Gigi wasn't the only source of Jazz's fury. Just thinking about how wrong she had been about the entire situation in Atlanta caused her to be angry with herself. How could she have been brainless enough to accept Gigi's word for the truth? Emmanuel was her man. He had never lied to her before. What they had built together with love and trust was supposed to have been stronger than anything or

191

anyone that threatened to come between them. Jazz had screwed up big time. And to make matters worse, her innocent conversation with Mario might have given Emmanuel a reason to believe that she had moved on. No wonder he wasn't taking her calls. He hadn't responded to the many messages she'd left on his voicemail or with Garcelle and Tyrell either.

Jazz grabbed her cell phone from the credenza and dialed Emmanuel's private line at his congressional office. She had no idea what she was going to say to him. The words would come from her heart once she'd heard Emmanuel's voice. The two things Jazz could always depend on were her abilities to think smart and speak fast. It's what she needed to do to let Emmanuel know how sorry she was for refusing to listen to him in Atlanta. She owed him an apology. Then she would have to explain why she'd spent time with Mario at Brevard's Grill. There was so much that needed to be said, and Jazz was prepared to say it all.

Chapter Forty-Five

"Damn it!" Emmanuel yelled. He stumbled past the umbrella stand into the dark house and rubbed his shin.

It had been the day from hell. Emmanel had rushed from meeting to meeting all day and well into the evening. Afterwards, he'd hurried to a Christmas party hosted by one of his colleagues. It was a very festive affair with wonderful food, drinks, and music. Emmanuel could've actually enjoyed himself if it hadn't been for the continuous annoying questions about Jazz. Everyone he had run into wanted to know where she was. Apparently, they'd all grown accustomed to seeing them together. Since the day he and Jazz had officially became a couple, Emmanuel had never ventured out socially without her on his arm. This evening her absence had felt weird. He wasn't going to get used to being a single man again anytime soon. That lifestyle no longer suited him. Coming home to an empty house and an empty bed didn't either. Emmanuel wanted Jazz back. He craved her. It was time to make up. But first he had to find out if she and Mario had rekindled their romance.

Emmanuel walked into his lonely bedroom and sat down on the bed. Just as he reached for the phone on the nightstand, it rang. He snatched it up quickly.

"Hello?"

As much as Emmanuel loved his mother, her timing couldn't have been lousier. She was in a very talkative mood. As usual, Carol Day wanted to fill her baby boy in on everything and everybody down in Georgia. Emmanuel removed his tie and shoes as he listened to his mother's nonstop gossip. It was going to be a long conversation.

*****

Gigi suddenly became fascinated with her black suede designer shoes the moment Jackson stepped inside the elevator with her. The two coworkers were alone surrounded by time, space, and silence. Gigi was uncomfortable and the elevator seemed exceptionally slow this morning.

"How do you sleep at night? The monster looking back at you in the mirror every day should give you bad dreams and day fright."

Gigi's head popped up and her eyes narrowed to thin slits in anger. "Who do you think you're talking to, little picture boy?"

"I'd rather be a modest photographer all day and every day than to be in your shoes. You're nothing but a miserable, desperate, pathetic female chasing after a man who wants nothing to do with you."

"You have no idea what you're talking about."

The elevator stopped on the seventh floor. The doors opened, but Jackson leaned over and pushed a button to close them again.

"What do you think you're doing?" Gigi tried to reach the button panel.

Jackson blocked her by placing his body in front of all of the lighted buttons. "Shut up and listen! You need professional help, lady. It's sad that you can't accept rejection. Congressman Day doesn't want you! You make him sick. He loves *Jazz*. Everybody knows it. He wouldn't have touched you with a ten-foot pole."

"If he's so in love with Jazz as you claim, please explain why he took *me* to his house for the night and invited me into his bedroom while his girlfriend was in New York."

Jackson doubled over, laughing hysterically. Then he stood erect and lost his smile. "Are you going to stick to that *lie*, Ms. Perdue? The only reason why you were in his house was because the congressman is an upstanding brother. He discovered you drunk out of your mind at the ball and saved you from being taken advantage of."

"That's ridiculous. Who on earth told you that?"

"It doesn't matter. It's the *truth*. The man didn't know where else to take you in the down pouring rain, so he drove you to his home. And instead of being appreciative, you made Jazz believe that you and Congressman Day had slept together. You should be ashamed of yourself, but you're not. Severely mentally ill people don't have a conscience. I wish he had dumped your ass at a homeless shelter."

Jackson pushed the button to open the elevator doors. He stepped out into the hall and walked away. He left Gigi standing there with her thoughts.

*****

"I wish I could go with you, sweet pea. I've never been to Dallas before. You and I could hit all of the clubs and do some shopping."

"I'll be so busy working that I wouldn't be able to show you around the city. I'm not coming back to Washington after my business is complete anyway. I'm going home. Grandma wants her baby under her roof before Christmas Eve. My flight from Dallas to Jacksonville will take off early Monday morning. I'll be back in D.C. after the New Year."

Ramone placed his fork on the edge of his plate and looked at his best friend across the table head-on. "I know you're trying to stay busy and be strong, but how are you *really* doing, Jazz? You and Congressman Delicious still haven't spoken yet. Is it officially over between you two?"

"I don't know." Jazz looked away. "I stopped reaching out to Emmanuel because he didn't return any of my calls. Tyrell said he's been real busy trying to tie up all his loose ends on the Hill before the Christmas break."

"Why don't you stop by his office tomorrow before you go to the airport? I'm sure he'll be glad to see you. I bet he misses you as much as you miss him. It's Christmas time. It's the season of love, peace, and goodwill. A little bit of romance and some good loving wouldn't hurt either."

"I'm going to do it, Ramone. I love Emmanuel so much and I miss him. It's time for us to talk so we can repair whatever is broken. I'm willing to do whatever it takes to make it happen."

"Good, because I'm tired of you walking around here looking like Pattie Pitiful. Plus I'm ready for a *wedding*."

Jazz laughed and held up her hands. "Pump your brakes, Ramone. Let Emmanuel and me get back together first, then we'll start talking about marriage and possibly a baby carriage.

*****

Emmanuel gunned his engine and peeled out of Black Diamond's parking lot. He had exactly forty-five minutes to get to the capitol before the national security breach hearing would begin. His plan to rise early to make amends with Jazz before going to work had fallen apart. She wasn't at her condo. It was the first place he'd checked. Then he went to Ramone's salon to interrogate him, but no one was there. Finally, he tried his luck at Jazz's job. Her car was nowhere in the parking lot. Unwilling to give up just yet, Emmanuel dialed the direct number to her office and even called the network's general line. Jazz was not in the building. A kind woman, a member of the clerical staff, informed Emmanuel that Ms. Dupree was out of town on assignment and would return to work after the New Year.

In his mind, the conversation he wanted to have with Jazz would be more effective if he could look into her eyes and speak from his heart. But due to the unforeseen circumstances, a phone call would have to do the trick.

"Jazz," Emmanuel spoke the one word to activate his car's voice controlled communication system.

After four rings, Jazz's sexy voice filled the air space inside the luxury vehicle, announcing that she was unavailable to take his call. She encouraged all callers to leave a detailed message after the beep. Emmanuel had a much better idea in mind. After the hearing at the capitol, he was going to pay Ramone a visit at his salon. By the time he left the place, he would know the city where Jazz was working and which hotel she had checked into. Emmanuel had grown tired of the misunderstandings and the frequent lapses in communication. It was time for him and Jazz to settle their issues once and for all. Before nightfall, he planned to have a long overdue face-to-face conversation with her no matter what.

*****

"What is going on up there?" Jazz stretched her neck to get a better view of the bumper-to-bumper traffic ahead of her. Cars were creeping slowly all around the capitol area. She blew her horn. "Come on! Move it!"

Time was not on Jazz's side. If she didn't make haste, she was going to miss her flight to Dallas. She'd had no luck seeing Emmanuel or getting anywhere close to his office. Her early arrival didn't seem early enough. The slow moving rows of cars were already wrapped around the building when she drove onto the scene. Phone lines on Capitol Hill were jammed too. Emmanuel didn't answer his private line either when Jazz humbled herself to dial the number. She then gave his cell phone a try, but her call rolled over to his already full voicemail box, making it impossible to leave a message. Jazz planned to call again from the plane before takeoff *if* she reached the airport on time.

Ramone's advice had sparked a fire. Jazz was on a serious quest. Come hell or high water, she had vowed that she would not spend Christmas without Emmanuel. She wanted off of the merry-go-round they'd been riding for too long. He didn't sleep with Gigi. She knew that now, thanks to Jackson. But Emmanuel needed to hear directly from Jazz's lips that her impromptu meeting with Mario at Brevard's Grill had been totally innocent as well. She wanted her man back because living without him was driving her insane.

Chapter Forty-Six

"We're closed! Go away!" Ramone screamed. He smacked his lips and continued punching the keys on his digital calculator.

His persistent after hour's visitor knocked on the locked door again, apparently, refusing to be turned away. Bravely and more aggressively, the uninvited caller kept a steady beat on the thick glass and tried to peer through the cracks in the blinds. The more the he knocked, the more annoyed Ramone became. He sucked his teeth and left his desk with a major attitude and a few choice words on the tip of his sharp tongue. He was shocked when he twirled the wand to open the blinds. A pair of puppy dog eyes was staring back at him.

Ramone deactivated the security system and disengaged the door locks. "Mr. Congressman," he greeted half surprised and half irritated. "What brings you to my establishment after business hours? Are you in need of a relaxer?"

"No. I prefer the natural look. I'm sorry for coming without calling first, Ramone. I know it's late, but I was in the neighborhood and I noticed the lights were still on. When I saw your car, I decided to drop in and say hello."

With his hands on his bony hips and his lips pursed, Ramone looked at Emmanuel like he had just grown a huge wart on his forehead. He was a seasoned politician. Surely, he could've come up with a more convincing and creative excuse. "I thought all lawyers and politicians were great liars. You suck at twisting the truth. Are you sure you chose the right professions?"

"I think so. Helping people and giving them a voice is my passion."

Ramone stepped aside and waved his hand, inviting Emmanuel into the salon. When they both were inside, he locked the door behind them. "Mmm, mmm, but helping certain damsels in distress can land you into a world of trouble. Do you catch my drift?"

"Nothing happened between Gigi and me that night. I did the right thing, but my kindness was abused. That's the real reason why I'm here. Jazz and I haven't spoken since we left Atlanta. I know she's out of town on assignment. I need to reach her as soon as possible. Our current situation requires a face-to-face conversation.

So I was hoping you would tell me where she is. I could hop on a plane and fly out to be with her tonight."

"I can't do that." Ramone folded his arms across his chest and rolled his neck for emphasis.

"Why not? I thought you approved of our relationship. Have you changed your mind because you want her back with *Mario Thomas*?"

"Oh, no, you didn't! The Blaze is a snake! *Okay*? Jazz is over him anyway. They happened to run into each other at Brevard's Grill the other day out of coincidence. He was in town for a speaking engagement. What you witnessed was a long overdue apology. Nothing more. Had you approached their table, you would've discovered that. You and Jazz have communication issues."

"You're right. We do. That's exactly why you should tell me where she is. I could rush there so we can work out those issues. Tell me where Jazz is, Ramone."

"No can do," he fired back, waving his finger. "I don't have permission to do that. It wouldn't be right. Besides, Jazz is *working*. But if or when she calls me, I'll let her know that you're hunting her down. I'm sure my girl will be happy to hear that. Then she'll probably give me the green light. When she does, I'll give you a ring."

*****

Too exhausted to practice any of her regular bedtime rituals, Jazz stripped down to her cream bra and panty set and slid under the bed sheets. Within minutes, she fell asleep. The flight to the Longhorn State and the fast pace of the day's events had been brutal on her body. To her credit, she had three successful interviews, a junior college speaking engagement, and a Christmas toy giveaway under her belt. Tomorrow would be just as busy and taxing, but in the midst of all the grinding, Jazz had something special to look forward to. Her former colleagues at Sports World International had invited her to join them live on their noonday show for a reunion. While she was prepared to read the script on the latest in sports news, Jazz was more interested in the camaraderie, trash talking, and joking that would came along with it. But afterwards, she would return to the more serious side of journalism at a holiday dinner for families who have lost loved ones to senseless gun violence. The program's sponsors had asked her to host the event, and she accepted.

Jazz was in need of a good night's rest after a long hard day in the Dallas-Fort Worth area. Hopefully, the sand man would be kind to her in her dreams so that she would be revitalized for the following days ahead.

*****

"Unc, you must've been mighty bored. I can't believe you cooked all of this good food. Grandma would be proud of you. This is a *nice* spread."

Tyrell circled the table for the second time, refilling his plate with food. Emmanuel stood in the doorjamb watching him with a smile on his face. Edgar and Fabian were seated in the great room stuffing their faces while they watched the football game. The Washington Warriors were in Dallas trying to oust the Stars out of the playoff pool. It was a great match up. The competition between the top ranked team in the division and its arch rival couldn't have been fiercer. Third place Dallas was trailing Washington by a touchdown. Two minutes and eleven seconds remained in the fourth quarter, and the Stars had the ball inches away from the forty yard line. It was third down, and both teams were receiving play instructions from their coaches on their respective sidelines after a time out called by Dallas.

"They're going to The Blaze. I'll put cash money on it," Edgar challenged everyone in the room.

Fabian shoved a forkful of baked bean in his mouth and shook his head. He chewed before he responded. "Nah, man, it would be a dumb move. Everyone expects the quarterback to hand it off to him. I say they should go long and hit that young wide receiver they got in the trade with San Francisco if they want to win. That dude can catch anything, and he's fast."

"I hope they fail no matter what they do. I don't want Dallas to win," Tyrell said dryly, walking into the great room with a plate in his hand.

Emmanuel followed his nephew and took a seat in the recliner. All four men sat quietly as the action on the gridiron resumed. The electricity from the crowd flowed through the television screen. Over seventy thousand rowdy football fans were cheering like maniacs in the Dallas Stars' home stadium. The crowd settled down when the center snapped the ball to the quarterback. A long pass over the middle intended for the young hotshot wide receiver was thrown over his head and out of reach. After a quick huddle, the Stars reset their formation on the field. They were going for it, unwilling to settle for a field goal. The two teams faced off, a struggling offense against one of the best defenses in the league. Dallas' quarterback dropped back, staying in the pocket before he faked a handoff to the closest runner. Then his intended ball carrier did a clever left sweep and took possession of the ball. With unbelievable speed and amazing agility, Mario 'The Blaze' Thomas took off, breaking through a host of defenders. He ran past the forty yard line, sprinting like lightning toward the thirty, the twenty, and was just shy of the ten when he was hit hard and low by a defensive player the size of a refrigerator. Down he went, backwards, landing in an awkward position with his right leg twisted like a pretzel underneath him. The huge hit man and another player from the opposing team landed on top of him in a human pile.

The crowd gasped and moaned at the misfortune on the field. They watched the three bodies with looks of horror on their faces. One defender got up fast to a boisterous round of cheers and applauds. The husky one moved slowly and stiffly, but eventually rose to his feet and limped to the sideline. Dallas' star running back remained on the ground grimacing and trembling in sheer agony. His coaches, trainer, and the game officials huddled above him. The commentators, in soft voices filled with fear, all agreed that the situation did not look good for Mario Thomas. When a gurney was brought out onto the field by medical personnel, the camera switched to a VIP skybox in the stadium. It zoomed in on a familiar face. Panic and desperation was evident in the woman's countenance.

"Hey, that looks like *Jazz*!" Tyrell leaned forward, nearly spilling his plate of food.

Edgar's eyes grew wide. "It *is* Jazz."

"Chill out, let's hear what the commentators are saying." Fabian grabbed the remote control from the coffee table and increased the volume on the television.

None of the other three guys noticed Emmanuel leave the room. They were too engrossed in the drama unfolding on the television screen. After waiting all weekend to hear from Ramone to learn where Jazz was away on assignment, Emmanuel became frustrated. The call never came. Either Jazz had failed to contact Ramone or she had, but didn't give him permission to tell Emmanuel where she was. It really didn't matter to him at the moment. He now knew her location and the information only infuriated him. There were questions galore swimming through Emmanuel's brain. But he was afraid to learn the answers to some. Of all the places Mr. McConnell could've sent Jazz on assignment, why *Dallas*? And why was it so soon after her so-called chance meeting with Mario Thomas? Emmanuel had a hard time believing that it had all been a coincidence after all. He figured that Jazz was confused and emotionally fragile due to all of the miscommunication between them since the incident in Atlanta. Emmanuel sure as hell was. Maybe Mario Thomas had sensed Jazz's vulnerability during their meeting at the restaurant and he'd lured her to Dallas somehow. And since she was already headed to the city on personal business, Black Diamond must've arranged for her to do a little journalism on the side, telling her story and promoting the network.

Regardless, Emmanuel was a broken man. He was estranged from the love of his life, and she was in the city where her ex-fiancé lay helpless on a football with thousands of his adoring fans pouring sympathy all over him. Jazz had probably jumped on the emotional bandwagon too. After all, she had once been madly in love with the baller, and in recent days they had made a reconnection of some mysterious kind. How could any brother compete with all that?

Chapter Forty-Seven

"Can we expect the congressman some time during the holidays, pumpkin?"

Jazz dropped her head to avoid eye contact with her grandfather. "No, Papa, Emmanuel won't be coming to Jacksonville for Christmas or New Year's."

"And why not?" Mrs. Anderson wanted to know. "The last time we spoke, he told me he would split his holiday break away from Washington between here and Atlanta."

There was no way around the truth. It was time for Jazz to come clean with her grandparents after dodging questions about her love life for weeks. They had their fingers crossed for a spring wedding, not knowing that she and Emmanuel were on the blink. In all honesty, Jazz didn't know if things would ever return to normal between the two of them. The idea of spending the rest of her life without Emmanuel made her sad to the core. Her eyes watered. She couldn't hold back the tears. The floodgates burst wide open.

"Oh, Grandma, Emmanuel and I aren't together anymore. I mean we took a break because we're having problems. I really don't know what's going on." Jazz picked up a napkin from the kitchen table and wiped her tears. "It's complicated, and I'm not sure if it can be fixed."

Mr. Anderson leaped from his chair, knocking it backwards. It fell to the kitchen floor. "I'm going to kill him! That lowdown, uppity son of a—"

"Frederick Douglass Anderson, don't you use that type of language in this house! Sit down, you old fool, and let the child tell us what went wrong between her and Emmanuel."

"I *know* what happened, Sallie Mae. He broke her heart just like that other fancy pants rascal."

"That's not it at all, Papa." Jazz blotted her eyes and blew her nose. "Emmanuel and I both made some mistakes. We lost faith in each other, and things went downhill from there. It's a long story."

*****

As the voices of thousands in Times Square counting down the New Year filled the room, Emmanuel leaned back on the stack of pillows piled high on his bed. Ms. Flora knew how to fluff them to perfection for his comfort. The ball was only seconds away from dropping. It was a tradition that Emmanuel had experienced once in person a few years ago. He watched the enthusiastic crowd of people on television, wondering what great expectations they had for their lives in the coming year.

Emmanuel had hoped he and Jazz would be preparing for their future together as husband and wife. He had been looking forward to watching her run around fretting over flowers, ice sculptures, and china patterns. Right now he didn't know what kinds of thoughts Jazz was dealing with. His stubbornness had held him prisoner over Christmas and the following days. He could've called Jazz in Jacksonville or kept his promise to her grandmother to visit them. Mrs. Anderson would've welcomed him with open arms. But every time Emmanuel thought about Jazz's trip to Dallas and the possibility that she had spent time with her ex while she was there, his heart grew harder than stone. She had attended Mario's game for sure. Everyone in America knew that.

But despite that very agonizing fact, Emmanuel still loved Jazz very much. He had come to the realization that he always would, which presented a major problem for him. Since his and Jazz's breakup, Emmanuel had come down with an incurable case of the blues. Nothing and no one seemed to help lift his spirits. That's why he had passed on the opportunity to stay in Atlanta to attend watch night service at church with his family. Instead, he decided to return to Washington to ring in the New Year in solitude. Ms. Flora had the rest of the week off to spend time with her children and grandchildren. Therefore, he'd ordered takeout food to keep him from starving to death. The refrigerator was stocked with a more than adequate supply of his favorite beer, and there were enough frozen home cooked meals in the freezer to feed an army. Emmanuel was set for his days of doing absolutely nothing in seclusion. He didn't want to talk to anyone and he refused to even think about work. Sleeping, eating, and pining over Jazz would be his activities until congress returned to session next week.

＊＊＊＊＊

"Congratulations, Jazz."

"What are you talking about, Gigi?" Jazz lifted her eyes to the lighted numbers on the wall above, willing them to move faster. Being in a slow moving elevator alone with the woman who had intentionally caused a rift between her and Emmanuel was not a good way to start off the first Monday in the New Year.

"I'm referring to your two Umoja Awards nominations of course. The one for the special feature you did on your hardship in Africa was no surprise. I can't say the same about your segment in the political documentary with your *ex*. I can't believe you got nominated for best appearance in a documentary for that."

It was Jazz's first time hearing about the nominations, but she refused to give Gigi the satisfaction of knowing she was the messenger of such fantastic news. She had to struggle to contain herself. Jazz wanted to break out in a hallelujah dance, but she scaled her happiness back to zero. She fought to suppress her anger too. Gigi's sly reference to her breakup with Emmanuel and the work they had done together was a low blow.

"Thank you," Jazz responded flatly to Gigi's back-handed acknowledgements.

"You're certainly welcome, dear. After all of the horrible things you went through last year, you deserve some happiness. I can't imagine being held hostage by rebels in a foreign country and losing my man in the same year."

"That's it!" Jazz stepped to Gigi woman to woman. "Do not let all of this designer fashion and cosmetics confuse you. I will kick your—"

The elevator doors sprung open and the bell chimed when it stopped on the fifth floor. Two cameramen and the network's most celebrated producer stepped inside, interrupting the confrontation. All three men greeted the two women, and they responded even in the midst of the heated standoff. Jazz pulled herself together and backed away from Gigi.

"Well, if it isn't Black Diamond's two-time Umoja Awards nominee. Congrats on the two nods, Jazz. I hope you take both trophies home."

"Thanks, Jake. I appreciate it. When I grow up, I want to have a bunch of awards in my display case just like you. How many nominations did you get this year?"

"Only three. The big one was for your special. It'll be cool if you walk away with best special feature and I snag best producer for it."

Jazz nodded and smiled. "That would be sweet."

The elevator doors opened again when they reached the seventh floor. Gigi rushed out ahead of everyone else. Jazz was tempted to run behind her and finish what she had started, but good sense prevailed. Giving Gigi a piece of her mind and kicking her butt wouldn't solve anything, although it sure would make Jazz feel better—*temporarily*. But at the end of the day, she and Emmanuel would still be separated by the constant controversy and miscommunication that seemed to plague them. So rather than giving chase to Gigi to serve her with the beating she rightfully deserved, Jazz squared her shoulders and wished her colleagues a pleasant and productive day before she left them in the elevator. She pasted a smile on her face and sashayed down the hallway like a runway model to the sound of sincere voices congratulating her on her two Umoja Awards nominations.

*****

Emmanuel picked up the silver foiled envelope Tyrell had placed on his desk. He waved it around nonchalantly and shot his nephew a puzzled look. "What is this?"

"It's your invitation for two to the Umoja Awards ceremony." A wide smile spread across his face. "Open it."

"I'm not going." Emmanuel tossed the envelope to the side of his desk.

"You have to go, Unc. You've been nominated for an award this year. They gave you a nod in the category of excellence in political leadership. The nomination alone is an honor, but I think you're going to win."

"In that case, you better put your tux in the dry cleaners and prepare an acceptance speech. You'll be attending the ceremony in my absence. Take Iris with you. I bet she'll have a ball." Emmanuel got up from the chair behind his desk and put on his suit jacket. "I'm on my way to budget hearings. I'll be back around eleven o'clock."

"Jazz will be there." Tyrell dusted imaginary lint from his jacket lapels and waited for his uncle's response.

"Why would Jazz be in a congressional hearing today?"

"She won't. She'll be at the *awards ceremony*. She received two nominations. One was for the segment she did on you in the political documentary. The special on her Swaziland experience is up for best special feature. Jazz wouldn't dare send anyone to receive an award on her behalf. She's the hottest female in black journalism today. Believe me. Black Diamond's sweetheart will be there."

Chapter Forty-Eight

"I think you should go with the red strapless mermaid gown or the champagne single sleeve sheath. You can't go wrong with either one of those."

Jazz removed a black velvet and gold lame floral print gown from the hook. She smoothed it out over her slender frame. It was strapless with a sweetheart neckline. A killer split ran up the right side all the way to the mid thigh area. The court length train gave the gown a sophisticated edge. "But this one makes me feel sexy. When I tried it on I felt like singing "Natural Woman". A sistah could turn a few heads in this dress."

Ramone gave Jazz his classic sour face like he'd been sucking a lemon. "Who do you want to look sexy for, honey? *I'm* your date for the evening. Surely, you're not hoping to impress *me* with your feminine wiles."

"I want to look good for *me*. It's been a while since I've attended a formal event. And it's not every day that your girl gets nominated for two awards from one of the most prestigious African-American organizations in the country."

"You do have a point. Your overall appearance must be on point that evening. The who's who in black Hollywood will be present."

"That's right. The Umoja Confederation of Excellence only recognizes the best in African-American music, movies, television, theater, literature, journalism, politics, and religion. Can you imagine little old country *me* actually winning one of those awards?"

Ramone stood from his chair in the tiny dressing room and stood next to Jazz in the mirror. "You're going to win *both* awards. Wait and see. I think Congressman Chocolate is going to win in his category too. Are you prepared to be in the same room with him? You can't expect me to believe that the thought hasn't crossed your mind."

"I try not to think about Emmanuel. It's too depressing, Ramone. Thoughts of him make me cry. Every time I look at the pendant he gave me or the picture we took at the Waldorf Astoria, I get physically ill. I've been praying for a miracle to bring us back together, but I think I screwed up too bad. Emmanuel doesn't trust me anymore. Without trust, we have nothing to stand firm on."

"What about *love*? You love that man with all your heart, and he loves you too. I know it beyond a shadow of a doubt. No matter what has gone wrong between the two of you, you were meant to be together. Don't give up on that miracle too soon. It may be just a few prayers away."

*****

"This is *Gigi Perdue*, damn it! I am a senior reporter at Black Diamond Television. Surely, you know who I am. One of my colleagues is covering the ceremony for our network, but I would also like to attend and have backstage access. Put me through right away to whomever I need to speak with in order for that to happen."

Gigi took a gulp of her Long Island iced tea as the phone rang several times in her ear. It rolled over to voicemail. Once again, she left a message for Sherriece Meriwether, one of the event's producers. Apparently, she was the guest and audience coordinator. Gigi's anger and frustration with the Umoja Awards' entire production team had reached the boiling point. They had been giving her the runaround for a week. The show was three days away, and she still hadn't secured a ticket and backstage pass.

Gigi had covered the grand affair for Black Diamond for the past six years. For some inconceivable reason, Mr. McConnell had decided to make some adjustments in her assignment selections this year, but the changes did not sit well with her. Tyra Tisdale had been asked to cover the Umoja Awards ceremony in its entirety. That would include the red carpet parade before the show and the exclusive after party. Gigi wanted very much to be a part of the glitz and glamour even if it meant she'd be among the lowly but lucky fans and seat fillers. That's how desperate she was about attending the ceremony. How else could she witness the fruit of her labor? She wanted to observe Jazz and Emmanuel in public for the first time since she had successfully destroyed their relationship. Perhaps, the former couple had crossed paths since their split at prior social events. Gigi didn't know for sure because she had purposely avoided all political functions, especially the small private ones where she

thought she would run into Emmanuel. She'd had no desire to
experience his wrath. The Umoja Awards was a major event. It would
be a nationally televised show on BDT. Only some cocky gangster
rapper, harboring a beef with one of his peers, would start a fight at
the Kennedy Center in front of cameras. Emmanuel was too smooth
of a guy to confront Gigi at such a lavish affair.

She saw the awards ceremony as the perfect setting to sit back
and enjoy the best in live entertainment while watching Jazz sink
deeper into a mud hole of misery after losing Emmanuel. The upbeat
attitude and fake smile she displayed around the office was an act.
Gigi saw straight through Jazz's daily façade. It was impossible to
have tasted the sweetness of Emmanuel Day and not suffer
withdrawals after having him snatched out of your life. He was like a
powerfully addictive drug. And there was no twelve step program or
medication that could help a woman shake her cravings for him. It
had only taken one dip into all of that chocolate masculinity for Gigi
to become helplessly hooked. Jazz had enjoyed several months with
him. She was probably on the brink of intense impatient rehabilitation
at the Betty Ford Center, and it served her right as far as Gigi was
concerned. Jazz should've stuck to her rule and avoided romantic
relationships with famous well-off men. But she'd chosen to venture
outside of the box. Now she was suffering because of it, and it pleased
Gigi to the highest. The old saying was golden. Misery did indeed
love company. However, Gigi couldn't get the full effect of Jazz's
despair at work and away from Emmanuel. The only way she could
witness it firsthand and celebrate their breakup was to see them in the
same room together. The Umoja Awards and its after party would be
the ideal occasion. Gigi was willing to do whatever was necessary to
be there.

*****

Sherry listened to Gigi's most recent voicemail message and
leaned back in her chair. She smiled at the sound of desperation
mixed with humility in her Southern drawl. She was almost begging
for a ticket to the ceremony. It reminded Sherry of how she'd felt all
those times she had pleaded with Gigi to relieve her of the verbal
agreement she had trapped her into. Sherry, the sweet but naïve

speechwriter, was a fool to get involved with the likes of Gigi Perdue. But *Sherriece Meriwether*, the social director for the Umoja Academy of Excellence, was full of confidence and steered clear of shady characters. Thanks to a letter of reference from Congressman Day, she was on a new career path and enjoying it very much. She and Fabian had worked through their issues, and life couldn't have been better.

"Amber," Sherry addressed her assistant over the intercom.

"What can I do for you, Ms. Meriwether?"

"Could you send me the final guest list for the VIP section for the ceremony by two o'clock please?"

"Yes, ma'am."

"Great. Also, I think I want extra security at the after party. There are no more tickets available, and we wouldn't want any undesirables attempting to crash the event. Take care of that for me please. Thank you."

"I'll do it right away. Will there be anything else, ma'am?"

"I think that we've covered everything. Thanks. You're the best."

"You're welcome."

Chapter Forty-Nine

"Work it, honey! Work it, I say! Work it!"

Jazz followed her BFF's modeling instructions and struck another sexy pose. This time she made a subtle move and slid her leg through the high split in her gown. Some photographers moved closer to the red carpet and snapped away. Men all around her, even the ones with dates, stopped and took notice. Jazz looked incredible. Ramone had to give his girl her proper due. The black velvet and gold lame floral print gown was lethal on her svelte hourglass figure. It hugged all of her curves just right. Gone were her usual curls. They had been transformed into soft waves. Ramone had relaxed Jazz's hair slightly with a little heat and brushed it back and away from her face. He'd added a single fresh gardenia to her mass of waves on the left side of her head, and it accentuated her soft facial features.

"How did I do?" Jazz asked, making her way to Ramone's side.

He placed her black and gold silk evening bag in her open hand. "You cracked the sky, darling. No wonder we're expecting snow later this evening. All that thigh action set the city on fire!" Ramone draped Jazz's mink stole over her shoulders to shield her from the chill in the air.

"I guess we should go inside and find our seats."

Ramone turned to offer Jazz his arm, but froze suddenly. "Uh-oh."

"What is it? Is something wrong with my makeup?"

"Your makeup is fine, sweetie. You remind me of a caramel goddess dipped in gold. I just spotted Congressman Chocolate at three o'clock. And he has a *date*."

Jazz closed her eyes, inhaled, and exhaled slowly several times. "This is my big night, and I will not cry or lose my temper. I can handle this. I will pretend that Emmanuel and his skanky date aren't even here."

"You must be a better actress than Angela Bassett, because the congressman, the skank, and Tyrell are making steps this way. Twirl and smile like you were just crowned Miss Universe, honey. Don't let him see you sweat. It's show time."

"Good evening, Jazz and Ramone."

Jazz spun around like a Naomi Campbell on a catwalk to face Emmanuel and his two guests. Before she could respond to his greeting, a pair of arms grabbed her and pulled her close for tight hug. It happened so suddenly that Jazz was unable to identify the person. The scent of the woman's perfume was familiar, though.

"Jazz, it is so good to see you, sweetheart. You look absolutely stunning."

All three men remained quiet as they watched the two women embrace lovingly.

Stepping back a few inches, Jazz met Mrs. Day's bright eyes with her own glossed with unshed tears. "It's wonderful to see you again too. You look fabulous. Pastel pink is definitely your color. Emmanuel has the prettiest date here this evening hands down."

*****

"Why didn't you talk to Jazz, Unc? You watched her rip the red carpet and then you walked over there and acted like a scared little punk. What's wrong with you?"

"What kind of conversation did you expect me to have with Jazz while she and Mama talked about dresses, makeup, and hairstyles? It wasn't the right time or place, Tyrell."

"Will you two hush?" Mrs. Day leaned over and scolded her son and grandson. "Smokey Robinson is about to sing, and you both know how much I love me some Smokey. Now zip your lips or I'll whip your behinds good."

Emmanuel was almost forty-three years old, but he still obeyed his mama without any back talking. He sat up straight in his seat in the VIP section of the Kennedy Center and cut his eyes sharply to his right. Jazz and Ramone were seated a row ahead of them on the far end. Emmanuel couldn't resist sneaking frequent peeks at them. The sight of Jazz posing on the red carpet, looking more beautiful than ever, had stirred up memories of happy times when their relationship was solid. He missed every little thing about her. She was his soul mate, making her irreplaceable. So much had taken place between them, and a lot of time had passed, but some things would

213

never change. Emmanuel was still very much in love with Jazz, and he wanted her back in his life.

*****

"And the winner is Jazz Dupree!"

The audience erupted with applause. Some people even stood up as Jazz rose to her feet gracefully. She covered her mouth with both hands apparently, in shock. Ramone jumped up and kissed her cheek and smiled excitedly like only a true best friend would. Gigi frowned disgustedly from her seat way up in the balcony among the commoners. She watched Jazz glide with great poise toward the stage and climb the few steps with the assistance of a handsome usher. He was the same usher that had escorted Gigi to her awful seat upstairs far away from the stars and important people.

Jazz was now giving a very emotional acceptance speech for her best appearance
in a documentary award, but Gigi was no longer paying any attention to the stage. She had completely tuned Jazz out. Her mind was reflecting on the moment that Sherry had come into the lobby and introduced herself as *Ms. Sherriece Meriwether*, the social director of the Umoja Confederation of Excellence. Her duty for the evening was to coordinate the audience for the awards show. Sherry smiled mockingly at Gigi and told her she could sit anywhere in the fourth or fifth rows up in the balcony, because no other seats were available. She also made it clear that the after party was an invitation only affair and no one without a ticket would be granted entrance.

*****

"I am deeply humbled by his honor. Thank you, Umoja Confederation of Excellence for acknowledging my commitment to service. I was born to serve, and it is my utmost desire to continue to serve and represent the people in my congressional district and others to the best of my ability. My mother, Professor Carol Scott Day is with me this evening. I owe this award to her and my father, retired

Attorney Thaddeus Day. They raised me right. All of those spankings and privilege restrictions were effective."

The audience laughed at Emmanuel's slice of wittiness, referencing his strict old fashioned upbringing. During the break of laughter, he focused on Jazz sitting close to the stage. The two crystal angel statuettes she had won earlier were sitting on her lap. She stared right back at him bravely, refusing to avert her eyes. It seemed like the stare off lasted for hours, but it was only a few seconds.

"It would be highly disrespectful and inappropriate if I failed to recognize Jazz Dupree's great work presenting me to the public in her network's political documentary. Her extended interview with me had an amazing impact on my last re-election campaign. It helped me secure another term in congress, and I'm thrilled that she won an award for her extraordinary effort. Thank you, Ms. Dupree for that and so much more."

Emmanuel's words warmed Jazz's heart. She wanted to jump up from her seat and run into his arms. She still loved him and she was helplessly hopeful that they would somehow find their way back into each other's lives. Jazz no longer cared about Gigi's schemes or Emmanuel's distrust in her regarding Mario. She just wanted her man back.

*****

"Jazz and Congressman Day, I need a few shots of the two of you together." Jackson motioned toward a corner in the press room swarming with stars and journalists. "That's a nice and cozy spot over there, and the lighting is perfect. Come on."

Jazz nodded, not trusting herself to speak. She was overly emotional and she feared it would be detected in her voice. She followed Jackson over to the small space on the other side of the room. Emmanuel was so close behind her that his body heat was sending fiery sensations to the bare flesh on her neck and back. Snow was in the forecast, and Jazz needed it desperately to cool her body down. It was the first time in many weeks since she had been in Emmanuel's presence, and the closeness was wreaking havoc on her nerves and hormones. Her attraction to him was still powerful even after being estranged from him for some time.

"Move in a little closer and let me see all three trophies," Jackson instructed.

"Like this?" Emmanuel asked, wrapping an arm around Jazz's waist. He held his trophy in his other hand next to both of hers.

"It's perfect. Now smile like a pair of winners."

Jackson took dozens of pictures of Jazz and Emmanuel together and individually with and without their trophies. He congratulated them repeatedly on their accomplishments. Then with a simple goodbye, he left them alone in the corner of the noisy and busy press room.

Chapter Fifty

Jazz and Emmanuel immediately turned to face each other and started talking at the same time. They laughed for no good reason except there was nothing else better to do in the awkwardness of the moment.

"Ladies first. Go ahead."

Jazz shook her head. "You should go first. I owe you the courtesy. You tried to say something to me that morning outside your house in Atlanta, but I refused to listen. Tonight I will."

"I didn't sleep with Gigi. The only times I touched her that night was when I carried her to my car and then again into my house. It was stupid of me to take her there knowing how twisted her mind is. My intentions were good, but they cost me you in the end. I'm sorry."

"I should've known better. I had no reason to suspect you of cheating on me with *Gigi* of all women. You're a better man than that. I must've been out of mind to assume that you had been unfaithful."

"I'm guilty of being distrustful too. When I found you with your ex at Brevard's Grill, I assumed you two were getting back together. And when I saw you at his game on television in Dallas, I was sure The Blaze had won your heart again. How stupid was that?"

"It was pretty outrageous." Jazz chuckled at the thought.

"By the way, I'm glad he's expected to make a full recovery."

"I am too."

"So where do we go from here?"

"I guess we should go to the after party to mingle with the other winners and guests. But I need to find Ramone first and…"

Jazz lost her voice and train of thought when Emmanuel eased his arms around her waist and pulled her body fully against his. She sighed and looked up into his piercing eyes.

"Let's skip the after party. We need to talk. Just give me a minute to find Tyrell and my mother."

"I'll meet you in the lobby after I get my purse and stole from Ramone."

*****

"It was a joy to meet you, Mrs. Day. You'll be hearing from me as soon as the wedding plans get underway."

"I hope they don't make us wait too long. I want a new grandbaby by next year."

"I don't think they'll waste any more time after tonight, ma'am."

Tyrell looked at the two new best friends and laughed out loud.

"Why are you so amused, boy?" Mrs. Day asked.

"I can't believe I let you two talk me into dissing Uncle Manny and Jazz."

"We had to do *something*. I was tired of my girl looking sad because she was missing your uncle. And I bet the congressman has been as mean as a lion since he and Jazz broke up."

"That's true," Tyrell admitted.

"So our actions were justified. Maybe we shouldn't have left them at the Kennedy Center without saying goodbye, but at least we gave their coats and Jazz's purse to Jackson. He promised to find them and deliver the items for us."

"We shouldn't have stolen their cell phones. It's snowing kind of hard out there. They may need them."

"For what, son? Your uncle doesn't need to talk to anyone tonight except *Jazz*."

"I don't expect they'll be doing much *talking* tonight, Mrs. Day."

"I like the way you think, young man."

The limousine stopped in front of Emmanuel's house. Tyrell and the driver helped his grandmother out of the car. She thanked Ramone again for coming up with the brilliant idea to abandon her son and Jazz at the Kennedy Center without their cell phones. Then she went inside to retire for the night.

*****

Gigi ducked behind an enormous potted tree in the lobby when Jazz and Emmanuel walked by hand in hand. They looked happy and deeply in love as they headed out the door of the Kennedy Center to brave the snow. There was a genuine smile on Jazz's face, and as usual, Emmanuel was showering her with lots of attention. He had bundled her in his heavy overcoat to make sure she was warm. All three trophies they'd won between them were cradled in the crook of one of his muscular arms along with Jazz's mink stole. The congressman and the award-winning reporter were a perfect picture of black love. Jazz was actually glowing like a bright flame in the middle of winter. Even if she hadn't won a single trophy, Gigi would have still considered her the big winner tonight. Jazz had something far more valuable than any crystal angel statuette. She had *Emmanuel*. Despite all the energy and effort Gigi had invested in destroying their relationship, Jazz and her man had weathered the storm.

*****

"At least they left your purse and our coats with Jackson so we didn't freeze on the cab ride here."

Jazz handed Emmanuel a glass of wine and sat next to him on the sofa with a glass of her own. "It was Ramone's idea. His name is written all over it. He wanted us back together. He begged me for weeks to call you."

"Why didn't you?"

Jazz shrugged her shoulders. "I was afraid I guess. I didn't know what to say to you, Emmanuel. I had accused you of the worst possible act of betrayal. Insecurities caused by my past relationship had resurfaced."

"You don't ever have to feel insecure with me. I love you and I would never jeopardize our relationship for anyone or anything. You're the only woman I want. I need you to trust me and believe in what we share."

"I love you too, Emmanuel, and I'll never doubt you again."

"I like the sound of those words, because you're stuck with this old man if you'll still have me."

Jazz placed her wineglass on the coffee table and shifted her bottom from the sofa to Emmanuel's lap. She wrapped her arms around his neck and looked into his eyes. "I'll die if I ever lost you again."

"In that case, you're going to live to be a very old woman."

*****

Tyrell left the great room holding the phone to his ear and walked into Emmanuel's home office. He closed the door behind him and sat down at the desk. "It's not possible, Unc. The city is dead because of the blizzard. There are thirteen inches of snow on the ground plus ice. The weatherman said another five to six inches is expected overnight."

"I need that ring."

"Why are you stressing over an engagement ring? You've been snowed in with Jazz at her condo for three nights and two days without any interruptions from the outside world. You two are *beyond* engaged by now. I know what y'all have been doing. Consider yourselves married already."

Emmanuel laughed at Tyrell's warped way of thinking, but he did have a point. He and Jazz had definitely reconnected. A few days of undisturbed isolation between lovers was a guaranteed remedy to heal a damaged relationship. The snowstorm for them wasn't a curse of nature. It was a blessing. Emmanuel and Jazz were no longer angry with Ramone, Mrs. Day, and Tyrell for the stunt they'd pulled after the awards ceremony. Their plan had been executed with the best of intentions in mind, and it had worked out in everyone's favor.

"Jazz is my wife in my heart," Emmanuel said after a brief pause. "But I'm ready to make it *official*. I need the ring to get the ball rolling. Did you find it?"

Tyrell leaned over and searched his uncle's bottom desk drawer. The ring box was inside in plain view. "I got it," he announced, checking out the brilliant diamond.

"I want you to call every courier and delivery service in the District and surrounding areas. Hire anyone who's willing to pick up the ring and bring it to me. If you can't find one, I'll walk all the way to Bethesda to get it myself."

"I'll see what I can do, Unc."

Chapter Fifty-One

"Why didn't you call me?" Ramone leaned over and whispered to Jazz.

"I didn't have a cell phone. Someone *stole* it."

Ramone draped Jazz with a towel and shampoo cape and reclined her chair. He bent way down to glare at her. "You have a land phone. I called it more times than I can shake my ass in a minute, but you didn't answer. Why didn't you check in with me?"

"Look Ramone, I didn't call you at first because I was ticked off with you for ditching me at the Kennedy Center. I got over it eventually because I realized why you did what you did. But I decided to pay you back anyway by ignoring your calls."

"How come you didn't give me a ring after you finished pouting?"

"I don't know," Jazz answered hesitantly.

Ramone's eyes narrowed, and he gave his best friend his famous sour face. "You're blushing. Don't get all bashful on me now, *hot tamale*. I can only imagine what activities you and Congressman Chocolate participated in to entertain yourselves while you were snowed in all that time."

"You will have to use your imagination because I'm not telling you anything."

"You don't have to, darling. Your secret is written all over your pretty little face. You and the congressman made up. I bet y'all melted all of the snow around your condo getting reacquainted."

"Emmanuel and I are definitely back together. We're even closer than we were before the misunderstanding in Atlanta. Something magical happened between us during the snowstorm. We promised to never let anyone or anything come between us again. We've been inseparable since the night of the Umoja Awards."

Ramone smiled as he lathered Jazz's hair with shampoo. "I'm happy for you. If any woman deserves a good man, it's you."

"Thanks, Ramone."

"Where are you two love birds going tonight?"

"We're going to a birthday party for one of his colleagues. Then we'll lock ourselves in at his place for the rest of the weekend."

*****

Emmanuel checked his watch for the hundredth time, and then closed the magazine he'd been flipping through. He tossed it on the coffee table. "Jazz, we're going to be late! We should've left twenty minutes ago!".

Jazz rushed into the great room dressed in a simple black cocktail dress with flowing butterfly sleeves. "I'm ready. I couldn't find one of my pearl and onyx earrings. I guess these gold and diamond hoops will have to do."

"You look sexy as usual."

"Thank you. You look very handsome. Midnight blue is my favorite color on you."

Emmanuel patted his thighs. "Come sit down for a minute. I want to ask you something before we go."

Jazz walked slowly over to the couch and rested her butt on Emmanuel's lap. "I thought you were in a hurry to get to the party. What's up?"

"The party can wait, but this can't." Emmanuel held the black velvet box within Jazz's reach. "Open it."

Jazz hesitated a few seconds before she took the box and lifted the lid. She gazed as if she were under a spell at the huge emerald shaped center stone. It was surrounded by a spread of tinier ones. The flawless diamond, sparkling brightly in a platinum setting, brought tears to Jazz's eyes. "It's the most beautiful ring I've ever seen in my life."

"I'm glad you think so, because from this day forward, I want you to wear it on your finger every minute of each day. I don't want you to ever take it off. It represents my feelings for you. I love you more than I thought I was capable of. There aren't enough words to accurately describe just how much you mean to me, but if you agree to become my wife, I'll spend the rest of my life showing you in every way. Marry me, Jazz."

"Of course I'll marry you. I've been waiting for you to ask. I'm going to treat you so good that every morning you'll wake up happy that you chose me to be your wife. I love you so much, sweetheart."

Emmanuel removed the ring from the box and took Jazz by her left hand. He slid the ring on her finger with ease. "It's a perfect fit."

Jazz sealed their engagement with a kiss on Emmanuel's lips. Then she leaned back to look at his handsome face. "I don't want to go to the party. I'd rather stay here and thank you for my ring and proposal all night long."

"I gladly accept your offer."

*****

Against their families' wishes, Jazz and Emmanuel decided not to have a party to celebrate their engagement. They chose to release a simple statement through Emmanuel's longtime publicist, Andrew Odom. Very few details were given because nothing had been finalized at the time of the brief announcement. The public was informed that Congressman Emmanuel Day, a democrat from Atlanta, Georgia and Black Diamond Television reporter, Jazz Dupree, were engaged to be married sometime in the spring. That was it in a nutshell. Since then, with Emmanuel's blessing and checkbook, Jazz had hired Jacksonville's most highly sought after wedding planner to the elite to coordinate the nuptials. Her grandparents had insisted that the ceremony be held at their family's church where Jazz had been christened as a baby. They wanted Reverend Obadiah Granville, their pastor of forty years, to officiate. Neither Jazz nor Emmanuel had a problem with the Andersons' requests. They both wanted a small intimate wedding with just their families and closest friends present. No members of the media would be invited with the exception of Jackson. He had been asked to be their photographer in addition to being an invited guest. The mid-May wedding would be private and off-limits to uninvited spectators. Security would definitely be tight.

*****

"Can we switch seats please?"

Jazz lowered the wineglass from her lips and set it on the table. "What for, Ramone?"

"The sunlight is bouncing off of that *humongous* diamond, and it's blinding me."

"Quit playing. I'm not swapping seats with you." Jazz shook her fist at him. She had no intentions of taking him serious. "We need to focus. Invitations must go out next week, and the second fitting for my dress is in a few days. Emmanuel can't go with me to Chicago. It would be bad luck anyway. I think *you* should make the trip with me. It'll be my treat."

"When are we leaving?"

"We can fly up Thursday evening and spend the night. My appointment with the designer is at twelve noon Friday. I thought we could do a little shopping afterwards and then catch a flight back home before dark. Emmanuel will have immigration reform hearings all day and a Department of Resources dinner that evening. I want to be in place to hear all about his day when he gets home."

"You're practicing to be a good wife already. That's smart, sweetie. I like it."

Jazz couldn't hide her emotions. "I have a good man, Ramone. Emanuel deserves the best, and I plan to make sure I give him the best of *me* for the rest of my life. I love him more than anything, and he makes me so happy. I trust him completely with my heart."

"Stop it, girl. You're gonna make me cry." Ramone fanned his face with his hand.

Chapter Fifty-Two

Attorney Maya Durant, a true blast from the past. The thought tumbled through Gigi's psyche. She hadn't heard that particular name in nearly a decade. Anyone who was close to Emmanuel was familiar with the exotic beauty of mixed heritage from New Mexico. When he'd first arrived on Capitol Hill, she was his exclusive companion. Every professional woman in the area envied Ms. Durant, including *Gigi*. They all wanted to take her place as Emmanuel's love interest. He was the hottest new congressman in his freshman class, and every sistah in the District and surrounding areas was lusting after him. Unfortunately for them, he was attached at the time, but only for a little while. The mystery behind Emmanuel and Maya Durant's sudden breakup only a few months after he'd landed in Washington had never been solved by curious minds outside his close knit circle. There had been a ton of rumors floating around, citing cheating and an overgrown ego on the congressman's part. Some people had blamed Maya's obsession with Emmanuel's position for the split. They had claimed she was more in love with the idea of being a congressman's lover than the man himself. Speculation had mounted for weeks, but a solid explanation never materialized. The only thing the gossipers knew for certain was that the couple had parted ways.

Upon Emmanuel's return to the singles' market, Gigi was the first woman in line to try to snag him. She chuckled and leaned back in her chair, reminiscing on all of the clever plays she'd made on him back in the day. Gigi had shamelessly used every trick in the book to hook Emmanuel, but fell short in the end. That one night was all she ever got out of him, and it would forever be sketched in her memory. It was the best night of her life although it had meant nothing to Emmanuel. Finally, Gigi had thrown in the towel. She was officially retired from her career of chasing after the congressman. He was engaged to be married to Jazz now, and she had accepted it as something that she could not undo. But in light of new information hot off the press, her curiosity had spiked off the chart. Gigi wondered what would happen if Maya Durant were to reemerge on the scene. Did she and Emmanuel have some unfinished business still lying on the table? Had he remained single all those years after their split hoping for Maya to trace her steps back to him? Gigi had no idea, but she would soon find out.

Mr. McConnell had given her an assignment to cover another round of immigration reform hearings on Capitol Hill. Various groups representing undocumented workers from all over the country were expected to appear before certain members of congress. They wanted sensible legislation to be passed that would secure a clear path to citizenship for the men and women from other countries who had been living, working, and paying taxes in America for years. Coincidentally, Maya Durant was the lead counsel for a group of produce farmers from New Mexico and parts of Arizona called Blended Hearts of America. She and dozens of members of the organization would be arriving in Washington Thursday afternoon to attend the hearings. Ms. Durant and the president of Blended Hearts of America were scheduled to testify before congress on behalf of the thousands of Hispanic farm hands seeking legal residency in the United States.

The combination of thrill and downright nosiness quickened Gigi's pulse as she envisioned Emmanuel and Maya Durant in the same room after so many years. Sure, there would be over three hundred other people present, but the two ex-lovers would be in close proximity of each other with memories and familiarity bouncing between them. Not even politics or business could make one's heart forget about certain things. And Jazz would be too far away to run interference. Thanks to Ramone's loose tongue bragging around his salon, Gigi had learned that he would be accompanying his best friend to the Windy City for a wedding gown fitting with the renowned Sir Hassan Amado.

"Oh what possibilities," Gigi mumbled into the still silence inside her office.

She swiveled around slowly a few times in her chair as the wicked wheels inside her head started to turn. Certain opportunities only came once in a lifetime. As much as Gigi had tried to forget her humble beginnings, growing up in a shack on the rough side of New Iberia, Louisiana, there were some things she couldn't escape. She knew all about hustling, scheming, and pulling strings. Her third and final foster mother, Mama Minnie, had taught her to never let a good idea or a slim chance pass her by. With Jazz headed for Chicago and Maya Durant en route to Washington, fate seemed to be on Gigi's side. Timing and opportunity together was a recipe for temptation if carefully planned out by the right person. Gigi was no stranger to tampering with other people's lives. If she could arrange a reunion with Emmanuel and Maya Durant, what would be the harm? If he was as deeply in love with Jazz as he claimed to be, nothing would happen. If he still had feelings for Maya, *anything* was possible.

*****

Emmanuel answered the phone on its first ring. It was Jazz. He'd been waiting to hear from her for quite some time. Her flight had landed at O'Hare International Airport almost three hours ago. Emmanuel was a bit irritated that it had taken her so long to check in with him.

"So you finally remembered you had a fiancé back at home missing you?"

"I'm sorry, sweetheart, but as soon as we stepped off the plane things went crazy. A couple of Ramone's friends picked us up from the airport and took us out to dinner. I guess I lost track of time. If you think Ramone is radical, you should meet his friends. Xavier and Chad are two characters."

"I'll pass. How was your flight?"

"It was smooth and on time. I started missing you right after takeoff."

"I don't think I believe you. You're away having fun with Ramone and company while I'm here preparing for the hearings tomorrow. I'm in bed reviewing a binder full of documents."

"I'm about to shower and relax for the rest of the night. Ramone is getting ready to go club hopping with his friends. I was invited to tag along, but I turned them down."

"Why did you do that?"

"I'd rather stay in and talk to you. I'll call you back as soon as I freshen up. I'm going to put on your big comfortable Morehouse t-shirt."

Emmanuel detected a hint of sexual taunting in Jazz's voice, and it caused blood to rush straight to his penis. "Where is your iPad?"

"It's in my briefcase. Why?"

"Don't bother to call me back on the phone. I'd prefer to see you."

"That won't be a problem. I'll hit you up on Face Time in thirty minutes."

*****

"Ms. Durant, I'm Gigi Perdue from Black Diamond Television. May I have a few minutes of your time please?"

Maya excused herself from a group of her colleagues and turned to face Gigi. She smiled and extended her free hand. "A few minutes are all I have, Ms. Perdue. How may I help you?"

Gigi shook her offered hand. "I'm aware of the reason why you and Blended Hearts of America are here today, but I'm curious. What impact do you expect your organization to have on key members of congress?"

"It's simple. We intend to provide proof that while there are thousands of undocumented workers from other countries in the United States, most of them contribute just as much, if not *more,* than some of our citizens do to our economy and to society as a whole. We need congress to introduce legislation that will allow these mothers and fathers to remain in America with their children who were born here. It's only fair that we keep families together by expediting the process to citizenship for law abiding immigrants."

"That sounds like a conversation you need to have one-on-one with Congressman Day. He's the highest ranking member of his party on the homeland security committee. I'm sure he would take the time to speak with you."

The sudden stiff body language and the drop of Maya's jaw were displays of nervous apprehension. Gigi picked up on it immediately. The sound of Emmanuel's name alone had knocked the wind out of Maya. Gigi was completely baffled by the response to her simple suggestion. She was intrigued, and curiosity had taken over all of her senses.

"Do you mean *Emmanuel* Day?"

"Yes, I'm talking about the one and only Emmanuel Day, the congressman from Georgia. Are you familiar with him?"

Maya shifted her eyes and fidgeted with the long straps on her burgundy attaché case. "We've met, but it was a very long time ago. I'm sure he doesn't even remember me."

"Well, you'll just have to remind him of who you are. I know for a fact that Congressman Day is very passionate about your organization's cause. He's been a champion for immigration reform for quite some time now. Why don't you arrange a private meeting with him?"

Maya shook her head from side to side briskly, rejecting Gigi's suggestion. Her long, black, silky tresses swung back and forth across her shoulders and back. "Oh, no, I couldn't do that. I know how hectic our representatives' schedules are. I'm sure Congressman Day is too busy to meet with me on such a short notice."

"I'll make the arrangements for you," Gigi offered with a sly wink of her eye. "I know the congressman's top aides *personally*. But don't tell anybody. Every Sally, Sandy, and Sue will be hunting me down for a hookup. Don't even let Congressman Day know that I arranged the meeting. Give me a number where I can reach you this afternoon. I'll call you with your appointment time and location in a few hours."

"Are you sure it won't be a problem? I really do need to connect with someone with influence within these walls, but I don't want to impose on the congressman." Maya searched her purse for a business card and handed it to Gigi.

"Don't worry about it. It's done. I'll be in touch."

As soon as Maya walked away out of earshot, Gigi removed her cell phone from her purse and turned it on. She dialed a number and waited for someone on the other end to answer.

"Guadalupe, it's me. Are you ready to earn your fee? Great. Make the call *now*. You better not screw it up either. I'll wait to hear from you."

Chapter Fifty-Three

"Good evening, sir. My name is Shelly, and I'll be your server. Can I start you off with a drink and an appetizer?"

"No, thank you. I won't be here long enough for anything other than a glass of raspberry lemonade."

"Great. I'll return shortly with your beverage."

Emmanuel glanced around the restaurant. The atmosphere was too romantic and cozy for a political meeting. He was surrounded by couples gazing affectionately into each other's eyes across candlelit tables. Tyrell had only agreed to the appointment with the president of Blended Hearts of America and its attorney because they had recently organized a chapter of the association in Georgia. They'd expanded in an attempt to protect undocumented peach, peanut, and watermelon farm workers in the Peach State.

Immigration reform had been one of the top issues on Emmanuel's re-election platform. His supporters were well aware of it. Therefore, they expected him to do anything within his power to influence other members of congress to get on board. Tyrell had made the correct judgment call by adding the president of Blended Hearts and their lead counsel to Emmanuel's schedule even though the late cocktail meeting would impose on his personal life. The secretary of the organization had called his office and insisted that he meet with them. In her heavy Spanish accent, she had told Tyrell that she would not take no for an answer. If Emmanuel hadn't missed the representatives from Blended Hearts' testimony at the hearing because of a conflicting lunch meeting, the persistent woman wouldn't have been so lucky. It was guilt and mercy that had caused Tyrell to give in. He had agreed to a short meeting between his uncle and the two individuals from the organization over drinks at the Glass House. The upscale restaurant was located just two blocks down from the hotel that the Department of Resources had held its dinner.

Emmanuel had walked the short distance to the Glass House after the affair, having arrived fifteen minutes ahead of the scheduled meeting. He intended to hear whatever the representatives of the organization had to say and offer a short and speedy response because

231

he was eager to get home. Jazz's flight should've reached Washington by now, and more than likely, she was en route to his house. Emmanuel wanted to spend some quality time with her before she fell asleep, but once again his job was getting in the way. He blew air from his cheeks as his mantra rang in his ears. *Politics is politics. It's a never-ending game.*

"Here is your raspberry lemonade, sir," the server announced. She placed the glass filled with the pale pink liquid on the table. "Are you sure I can't interest you in our appetizer menu?"

Emmanuel abandoned his thoughts of getting home to Jazz and smiled at his server. "I'm fine. Thank you."

Moments later as Emmanuel watched the bright lights on cars cruising up and down 16th Street, Northwest, the scent of expensive perfume and a soft voice pulled him away from his picturesque view of downtown.

"Hello, Congressman Day. It's been a long time."

*****

"What's up, baby girl?"

Jazz smiled when she recognized her friend's deep voice on the other end of the phone. "I just returned to town from Chicago. I had a fitting for my wedding gown. I don't think you and your camera will be ready for me on my big day. I am going to be the sexiest bride you ever laid eyes on, my friend."

"I'm sure you will. Are you at home yet?"

"No, I'm in the back of a Town Car on my way to Bethesda. Emmanuel sent a service to the airport to pick me up. He's so good to me."

"Where is your man right now? Do you have any idea?"

"Of course I do, Jackson. He had to attend a political dinner this evening at a downtown hotel. I bet it was boring. Hopefully, it'll be over soon. Then Emmanuel will come straight home to me. Why do ask?"

"I received some pictures on my cell phone a short while ago. They came over the ticker from the job. It's a little strange, but I can't determine who sent them. They're from an unknown source. Supposedly, the shots were transferred in real time."

232

Jazz's entire body froze perfectly still as tension seized her every muscle. She sensed that something weird was going on. "Who is in the pictures, Jackson? Tell me."

"I'd rather forward them to you so you can see for yourself. But you've got to promise me that you won't jump to any conclusions, baby girl."

"Jackson, you're scaring me! What's going on?"

"Promise me first, *please*."

"I promise."

"I'm about to send the pictures right now. Remember what I said. Draw no conclusions. I'll call you tomorrow."

*****

After an hour of waiting and guzzling down two-thirds a bottle of Moscato, Gigi's patience had dwindled down to zero. Adams had promised to call her if the on call producer wanted to make a move on the scoop about the engaged congressman being spotted in the company of his *ex-fiancée* while his current fiancée was away in Chicago being fitted for her wedding dress. It would be one juicy story on Black Diamond's hot topics blog or their Saturday morning celebrity news report. Gigi couldn't understand why no one at the network had taken the bait yet. If one of the reporters or producers didn't hurry up and pounce on the pictures and write a story, she would be forced to resort to extreme and risky measures.

*****

The sound of the key entering the door lock announced Emmanuel's arrival. Jazz's heart was filled with a myriad of emotions after an hour of soul searching and re-evaluating their relationship. The pictures Jackson had sent were blazing in her mind. The images were so vivid and fresh that Jazz could recall every single detail as if she had been there with Emmanuel and Maya Durant, his ex.

"Baby, I'm home! Where are you?"

Rushing from the master bedroom on bare feet, Jazz called out in a calm voice. "Here I am. How was your day?"

"It was long and full of surprises." Emmanuel placed his briefcase on the coffee table and approached Jazz with open arms. "I missed you," he said, pulling her close while kissing her left temple. "How was your flight?"

"My flight was fine. Ramone snored the entire trip. He had partied too hard last night and had to rise early to run around the city with me. He caught up on his rest, but now *I'm* tired. I was about to turn in when you arrived. Good night Emmanuel. I'll see you in the morning." Jazz wiggled free from his arms and turned to walk away.

"Wait a minute." Emmanuel took hold of her arm gently. "Can't you at least spend a little time with your man? I slept alone last night, and it wasn't any fun. And I want to talk. Tell me about your fitting. How did it go?"

Jazz yanked her arm away from his grip and took a backward step. "Is that really what you want to talk about, Emmanuel? Is my wedding dress all that important to you? Why don't you tell me about the dinner you attended this evening?" Jazz lifted her chin defiantly and folded her arms across her chest as she fought back tears.

"The dinner was a typical political affair with a bunch of movers and shakers trying to push their agendas. Is something bothering you, Jazz? If there is, you need to spit it out. We promised not to keep secrets from each other ever again."

"You're absolutely correct, Emmanuel. We did make that promise to each other, but only *one* of is honoring that agreement!"

"What are you talking about?"

"I think you're keeping secrets."

"I wouldn't do that, Jazz. I was just telling someone from my past about how transparent our relationship is. I sat and bragged about how we share everything with each other no matter how awkward it may be. Baby, please tell me what is going on."

The dam broke. Tears streamed down Jazz's face as she reached into the pocket of her pink bathrobe and removed her cell phone. She scrolled through the photo gallery and found the pictures of Emmanuel and his ex together. She handed him the phone.

Emmanuel's head jerked backwards. "Where the hell did you get these pictures from?"

"It doesn't matter. Why were you with *her* this evening and how come I had to find out from someone else?"

"It wasn't planned, and I had every intention of telling you about it tonight. You were in such a hurry to go to bed. Remember? I'm the one who wanted to spend time talking so we could catch up. Can we sit and talk now *please*?"

"I refuse to go through another round of foolishness with you, Emmanuel. My heart can't take it again."

Taking her by her hand and pulling her gently, Emmanuel led Jazz over to the sofa. "We've got to settle this trust issue tonight once and for all."

Chapter Fifty-Four

The phone lines at Emmanuel's office had been jammed all morning long with calls from journalists and bloggers seeking more information about the photos of him and Maya Durant. To everyone's surprise, particularly his and Jazz's, Black Diamond had posted the pictures along with a disgraceful story on its hot topics blog over the weekend. The spot was very popular on their main website. It was so unlike the network to report inaccurate information about anyone, especially one of its employees. Mr. McConnell was livid. He'd contacted Jazz before daybreak, advising her to take an additional day or two off work to avoid the embarrassment at the office. The old man was on a mission to sniff out the source behind the shadiness. No one in management had authorized the online article, but Mr. McConnell was not deterred in his investigation. Jazz was his award-winning star reporter, and she was engaged to a well respected member of the United States congress. Slander and vicious lies about the couple from within the walls of the network he had established as the most reputable and reliable African-American media empire on the planet was a diabolical offense. And the person who was responsible for it would pay the ultimate price for their sin. That was the promise Mr. McConnell had made to Emmanuel when he'd reached him by cell phone moments before he had arrived at the capitol that morning. He'd also offered him his sincerest apology for the notorious blog post and assured him that a public apology from the network would be issued by noon. The heat of the media mogul's rage had seared Emmanuel's ear during their brief conversation. Mr. McConnell's message was loud and clear. Whoever had overstepped their professional boundaries and posted the filth to the network's website would be dealt with accordingly.

*****

"This is Maya Durant. I'd like to speak with Congressman Day if I may. I've called his office at the capitol several times today, but I've been unable to reach him. Is he home by any chance?"

Jazz tightened her grip on the telephone and took a deep cleansing breath before she spoke. "Emmanuel isn't home, Ms Durant. If you leave your number, I'll have him call you as soon as he arrives."

"I would appreciate that…um…"

"It's Jazz."

"Of course it is. I would recognize that lovely voice in my sleep. Please forgive me for not greeting you properly. It's just that I'm so upset about that ridiculous article on your network's website. The gossip is spreading to other media outlets like wildfire. That's why I want to speak with the congressman. I owe him an apology for any trouble our meeting may have caused him. Thank God you're a beautiful, smart, and confident woman. Otherwise, those *lies* about your fiancé cheating on you with me could've ruined your relationship. That would've been awful because Congressman Day truly loves you. I could see it in his eyes every time he spoke about you Friday night."

"I know and I love him too. Thank you for caring, Ms. Durant. You're very kind."

"Please call me Maya. I'm one of your biggest fans. I admire your work."

"I'm flattered. Thank you, *Maya*."

"You're certainly welcome. Well, I won't hold you any longer. I just felt the need to touch base with Congressman Day. Please let him know that I would be more than willing to go on the record denouncing those dreadful rumors if he needs me to. It was very considerate of him to meet with me on a whim the way he did. I owe him and Gigi Perdue a great deal."

"*Gigi Perdue*? What does she have to do with any of this?"

"Oops! I promised Ms. Perdue that I would never mention it. She'll have to charge my loose lips to my head and not my heart. That sweet soul offered to arrange the meeting between the congressman and me. She even made reservations for us at the Glass House."

"Did she?" Jazz asked as calmly as she possibly could, trying to suppress the anger she felt stirring inside.

"She sure did. Apparently, Ms. Perdue is quite friendly with one of Congressman Day's aides. She pulled a few strings, and the next thing I knew, I was sipping coffee and pleading my case to him on behalf of Blended Hearts of America. And quite naturally, your name came up several times. The congressman even showed me a beautiful picture of you two together at a political function."

"Wow! I never would've guessed Gigi had a knack for bringing people together. I'll have to make a note of that for future purposes."

"You should definitely do that."

The home security system chirped, and the sound of the front door closing shut followed. Seconds later, Emmanuel entered the great room with his briefcase in tow.

"Emmanuel just got home. Would you like to speak with him?"

"Oh, no, girl. You go ahead and spend time with him. Let him know that I called, and tell him the nature of our conversation. It was nice speaking with you, Jazz. I really mean it. Congratulations on your engagement and your upcoming wedding. Goodbye now."

Emmanuel placed his briefcase on the coffee table and loosened the knot in his black and white polka dot tie. "Who was that on the phone?" He dropped down on the sofa next to Jazz and wrapped his arm around her shoulders.

"You will never guess and you won't believe what I just learned either."

*****

Jazz had expected some of her coworkers to act a little standoffish toward her once she returned to work. It was just human nature for certain people to feed into worthless gossip regardless of the source. Then again, Black Diamond's reputation for reporting unbiased, hard cold facts on every story gave everyone reason to believe that Jazz was being played for a fool by her fiancé. The rumor about Emmanuel and his ex rekindling their romance while she was planning her dream wedding was hard to ignore by most. The pictures and the bogus story had gone viral, but Jazz didn't care because she knew the truth. She and Emmanuel were very much in love and completely committed to each other. Gigi and company had jumped high over the bar of evil deception this time, but they would not get away with it. Mr. McConnell had launched a full investigation, and he had vowed that the person behind the unauthorized online article would be exposed and terminated.

Gigi was the guilty party. Emmanuel and Jazz believed it beyond a shadow of a doubt. But they had no idea how she had pulled the misdeed off. Producing and posting a story without proper consent had never been done before in the history of Black Diamond Television. Jazz's mind couldn't even conceive such a devious thing. Only a thorough investigation would uncover the details of just how low Gigi had stooped this time. Risking her job and compromising the reputation of the network in an attempt to sabotage Jazz and Emmanuel's relationship was lower than rock bottom. It was a hundred degrees below the surface of loathsome desperation. Gigi's wickedness had finally pushed Jazz over the edge. She was fed up with all of her mess, and she wanted it to stop immediately. Jazz could've stoked the fire by telling Mr. McConnell that Gigi had arranged the meeting between Emmanuel and Maya. She also could have informed him of her suspicion that the pictures sent to Jackson through the network's ticker had come from her too. Emmanuel had tried to convince her to throw Gigi under the bus, but she didn't want to. She preferred that Mr. McConnell make the discovery without her assistance. He was a wise old man and he was determined to crack the case. Jazz had confidence in him. Soon Mr. McConnell would learn all of the facts about the infamous blog post, and Gigi would no longer be an employee at Black Diamond.

It wasn't that Jazz wanted to see a fellow journalist lose a good job, and she definitely didn't think that Gigi could cause discord between her and Emmanuel again. Nothing and no one could separate them. Jazz had simply reached her limit with Gigi and all of her nonsense. There came a time in everyone's life when they had to face the consequences of their actions. Jazz's grandmother had told her many, many times that what you do in the dark would one day come to light. It took some longer than others to finally get caught in their mess, but in time, justice would always find its criminal. Gigi's days were numbered. Jazz only hoped that she would be exposed soon so that everyone could learn the truth. Then she and Emmanuel could put yet another scandal behind them and move on.

Chapter Fifty-Five

"Your phone is ringing off the hook. Maybe you should answer it."

Jazz opened one eye slowly and then the other one. The few candles burning in the dim bathroom provided just enough light for her to make out the handsome features in Emmanuel's face. The water's temperature in the Jacuzzi was perfect, and her muscles appreciate it. Emmanuel had poured honeysuckle-mango bath salts and bubble bath into the tub, and the aroma was heavenly. The cool jazz music floating through the state-of-the art sound system enhanced the romantic vibe. Jazz didn't care about anything else at the moment except her man and the moves he was putting on her. She sank deeper into the tub underneath the blanket of bubbles and lifted her leg. Wiggling her toes against Emmanuel's chest, she tickled him teasingly as the phone continued ringing.

"It's still ringing."

"Let it ring. I'll check my messages in the morning. It's probably an intern from the network calling with more information about the Wall Street piece I'm working on. It can wait."

"I don't know." Emmanuel took a sip from his champagne flute. "Whoever is trying to reach you isn't backing down. It must be important."

"Then by all means, answer the phone, sir, because *I'm* not going to."

After several more annoying rings, Emmanuel growled like an angry bear. Jazz watched him rise from the water as naked as he pleased. Bubbles and water dripped slowly from his body. He was the perfect male specimen. It didn't matter that Jazz was privy to personal viewings of his bare anatomy every day. The sight of Emmanuel fully exposed was always a fantastic treat that she didn't think she'd ever grow tired of.

"I'm coming," Emmanuel shouted, placing one wet foot on the floor and then the other. The scented bubbles and warm water sloshed all over the thick purple floor mat. "It better be a matter of life or death." He stormed out of the bathroom, making a wet and soapy path into the bedroom.

Jazz giggled before she took a sip of sweet champagne. She replaced the flute on the glass and wrought iron table outside of the Jacuzzi. Reclining, she pressed the back of her head deeper into the soft, bulky bath pillow behind her. The sound of Emmanuel's voice talking on her cell phone to the pushy unknown caller had a hint of concern in it. Whoever was on the other end of the call was threatening to ruin the romantic groove in progress, and Jazz didn't appreciate it. Emmanuel had surprised her with a scrumptious gourmet dinner. Her favorite dessert of blueberry parfait had followed the seafood feast, and it was delectable. Jazz had been too stuffed to follow the rose petal path to the master suite afterwards, so Emmanuel gladly carried her. The sights, sounds, and aroma she'd discovered in the master bathroom had put her on notice. She was well on her way to being seduced, but she'd had no complaints whatsoever.

"It was Jackson."

Emmanuel's announcement above the soft music startled Jazz. She opened her eyes and straightened her back in the water. Looking up, she asked, "What did Jackson call to say this late in the evening?"

"Things are somewhat chaotic at Black Diamond. It all began shortly after you left."

"What's going on?"

"Mr. McConnell's investigation exposed Gigi for posting the pictures and phony story about Maya and me on the network's website. He fired her on the spot. You and I knew it was coming, but apparently *she* didn't. Gigi thought she had covered her ass so well that she wouldn't get caught."

"That woman is delusional. How far did she go this time?"

"She used some young production assistant's computer, employee account, and password to do her dirt so that it would all fall back on him in the end. Jackson said the gossipers around the network claim that Gigi and the guy were having a fling."

"His name is Rashad Adams. I've heard about the special arrangement he and Gigi have. I can't believe she tried to feed him to the sharks."

"That's exactly what she tried to do, but the young cat refused to take a dive for her. Apparently, he drew the line at the bedroom door. The young man was able to prove that he wasn't even in the building the evening the pictures and story were posted. And he provided Mr. McConnell with technical evidence that traced the pictures back to a cell phone owned by Gigi. That's when all hell broke loose."

"Stop teasing me, baby. Tell me what's happening at the network."

Emmanuel lifted one long leg and placed his foot inside the Jacuzzi with a small splash and smiled. The other one followed. He sat down in the water facing Jazz still wearing that sexy smile that gave her stomach butterflies. "It's not important. Gigi's games and drama are not our concern. But if you can't control your curiosity long enough to enjoy the rest of the evening I've planned for us, you can check out the local news."

*****

"Gigi looked *worse* than hell, baby girl. I couldn't believe my eyes. She reminded me of a pig in a blanket because of the way they had her bound in a straightjacket and all. And she was naked as a newborn baby."

"Are you serious?"

Jackson nodded his head and snickered. He picked up a notepad and two pens from the table and walked toward the studio door. "It was like a scene out of a horror movie. She was screaming and jerking like a maniac. I think she was foaming at the mouth too. She had snatched off all of her clothes and locked herself inside her office. Everybody could hear her screaming and throwing things around, trashing the place."

"She was having a mental breakdown."

"I believe she was. She threatened to jump from her office window if McConnell didn't promise to rehire immediately. The standoff lasted almost three hours before the police finally stormed in and took her down."

"I knew Gigi had some serious issues, but I had no idea she was *psycho*!" Jazz followed behind Jackson. "It's hard to wrap my mind around it. All of the years I've worked here with her she seemed to be a smart, secure, sophisticated sistah who had her stuff together. She's very beautiful too. Gigi could've had any man she wanted."

"That's not exactly true, Jazz. I'm sure there were plenty of brothers out there standing in line for an opportunity to spend time with Gigi Perdue, but there was only *one* who could light her fire. Sadly for her, he was out of her league. I told you from the very beginning that she had the fever for the congressman. Now I realize it was more than just an innocent crush. Gigi was obsessed with your man. I hate to say it, but she probably still is."

"Hopefully, she'll get the help she needs so she can get over Emmanuel, because they will *never* be together. My heart goes out to Gigi, and I'll pray for her recovery every day. But I'm sorry. She can't have my man, Jackson."

"I know." He opened the studio door wide for Jazz. She exited with him a few steps behind her. "We better get to the conference room early so we can get good seats. I'm sure Gigi's termination and her reaction to it will be the topic of discussion. McConnell wants the network to squash it and move forward as quickly as possible."

"I do too. There is no time in my schedule to deal with extra drama. My wedding is thirty-three days away. All I want to do is concentrate on walking down the aisle and becoming Mrs. Emmanuel Day."

Chapter Fifty-Six

"Thanks so much for meeting with me on such a short notice, Ms. Dupree. In light of the circumstances, I'm surprised you even bothered to speak with me at all."

Jazz reclaimed her seat behind her desk. She nodded to the chair facing her on the opposite side of the stylish piece of hand crafted furniture. "Please have a seat, Mr. Perdue. I'll admit I was a bit iffy about speaking with you at first, but inquisitiveness got the best of me. Then after an in depth conversation with my fiancé, we decided that a face-to-face meeting with Gigi's brother was in order."

"Thank you. I'll get right down to business. Gigi and I were raised as sister and brother in New Iberia, Louisiana. We were foster children from two different biological families. Neither one of us knows anything about our birth mother or father. A sweet and caring older woman by the name of Minnie Perdue adopted us and six other children. I was ten at the time, and Gigi was only seven. We'd both been bounced around the system all of our lives. Thank God we both found a permanent home before we turned teenagers. Nobody ever wants to adopt the older kids."

"I've heard snippets about Gigi's unfortunate childhood, but I never learned very many details. I'm sorry she had a hard time as a youngster, but it seems like Minnie Perdue did a decent job once she adopted her."

"Mama Minnie did the best she could on a fixed income and an eighth grade education. We didn't have a lot of material things, but we were loved, nurtured, and very well fed. And those of us who studied hard and performed at the top of our classes in school were able to go to college on a free ride thanks to the state of Louisiana's child welfare system. The only two out of the eight of us that took advantage of the opportunity were Gigi and me. I made good grades and I was a star baseball player throughout high school. I went to Louisiana State University on an athletic scholarship. Three years later, Gigi took off for Loyola University in New Orleans to study journalism."

"What happened after college?"

"I played pro ball until my right knee completely gave out after thirteen successful years. Thanks to my business degree and some smart investments, I was able to enter corporate America as a real estate developer. Then I settled down and got married and started a family. Life has been good, but I never forgot where I came from or who helped me. Mama Minnie lived with my wife Ceola, our two boys, and me in comfort until the day she died. Gigi was nowhere to be found. She was too busy trying to run away from the past. She had dreams of becoming rich and famous and marrying and even richer and more famous man."

"Your story is very enlightening, Mr. Perdue."

"I'm sure it explains Gigi's obsession with Congressman Day and why she repeatedly attempted to tear down his relationship with you. I warned her about such unhealthy behavior toward men back during her college days. She stalked all of the star ballers and student government officers that she thought would become prosperous and well-known someday. We had a falling out when I made it to the major league. She chased one of my teammates to the point that he no longer wanted to be my friend."

"How is your relationship with Gigi today?"

"Up until she was hospitalized a few days ago, we spoke maybe once or twice a month. She flew down to Houston to visit my family and me for a few days during the Christmas holidays last year. I was surprised, but happy. I love my sister in spite of her problems. I'm all she has. That's why I came to see you. I was hoping that you and Congressman Day would spare Gigi of any criminal charges she may be facing for the terrible things she's done to you. She went out of her way to try to assassinate your fiancé's character with those pictures and article. She made the network look bad in the process. Miraculously, Mr. McConnell has no plans to file any complaints against Gigi with law enforcement. It would mean a great deal to me if you and the congressman would have mercy on her as well."

Jazz looked at the framed picture of Emmanuel and her sitting on top of her desk. During pillow talk the night before, they had agreed that Gigi's constant plots to separate them weren't worth filing any criminal charges against her. They were annoying hiccups along the way if anything. Only a disturbed woman would waste so much time and energy pursuing a man who had avoided her like a deadly virus for a decade. Emmanuel and Jazz had decided that Gigi didn't need to go to jail or be sued for slander. Her case was better suited for an impatient mental health facility.

"Prison won't help Gigi. It's not the place for a woman in her condition. She needs professional help to deal with her issues. Emmanuel and I won't file any criminal complaints against her. But we won't put up with any more of her foolishness either. We don't wish to have any contact with Gigi ever again. Therefore, we felt the need to protect ourselves with restraining orders."

"I totally understand your actions. However, you could've saved yourselves some time and money."

"What do you mean?"

"As soon as Gigi is released from the hospital, I'm moving her to Houston to live with my family and me. My wife and I think she'll be better off there with us. We'll make sure she receives the necessary services to make a full recovery. Thank you for being compassionate and understanding," he said, standing from his chair and extending a hand."

Jazz stood also and shook Mr. Perdue's hand. "You're very welcome. I'm glad you came to talk to me. Most of my questions about your sister have been answered now. Thank you."

*****

The Dupree-Day Wedding Reception; Alexandria Ballroom - Jacksonville, Florida…

"So as the *man of honor* to Jazz, our very lovely bride, on this joyous day, I ask all of you to raise your glasses in a toast to the newlyweds." Ramone turned away from the guests to address Jazz. "Sweetie, may every day for the rest of your life with Congressman Day be filled with joy, peace, contentment, and more mind-blowing loving than you can handle. And I pray that all three or four of my god children will be as beautiful and smart as both of you. Cheers!"

Through laughter and chimes of glass touching glass, Emmanuel leaned in and whispered to his wife. "Did he say three of four god children?"

"He was only kidding, Emmanuel. You know how sensational Ramone can be when he has an audience. Don't panic."

"Who's panicking? I'm as cool as an ice cube. Making three or four babies with you is doable. I can handle the task with pleasure."

Jazz searched Emmanuel's eyes, totally tuning out the toast being made in their honor by his best man, Tyrell. The raw desire in their depths told her he was serious about his last statement. "I'm sure you could, but let's stick to our plan. Two babies will be perfect for us. That way we can continue on with our careers, parent our little ones, and still have enough quality time for each other."

"Suit yourself. But if you ever change your mind, remember I can rise to the occasion. No matter how many little Days you want pitter-pattering around our two homes, I can make it happen."

"I'll keep that in mind, sweetheart."

Just then, the wedding coordinator appeared at the ornately decorated table for two. "It's time to throw the bouquet, Mrs. Day. Please come with me. You're next, Congressman. Some lucky single man needs to catch that garter."

Jazz winked at Emmanuel. "I'll be right back. Try not to miss me too much."

*****

Gigi closed the latest edition of Jet magazine and stuffed it under her mattress for safe keeping. A nice orderly, one of her fans, had sneaked it to her in exchange for her autograph and the promise of a future date. The young man knew everything about Gigi. He was fascinated by her charm and good looks. That kind of flattery was pleasing to her ego. Even a psychiatric patient could use a little attention and admiration.

Gigi needed healthy doses of each after seeing Jazz and Emmanuel's wedding picture in her smuggled magazine. They looked happier than ever decked out in their expensive designer wedding attire. Jazz was a stunning bride, and as expected, Emmanuel was the world's most handsome groom. The picture made Gigi sick to her stomach. She wasn't supposed to even think about them or say their names in the privacy of her hospital room. It was unhealthy to do so because she had not made enough progress in her recovery process to deal with her obsession with Emmanuel yet. Gigi was still trying to sort through the abandonment issues from her childhood and feelings of rejection and worthlessness she had experienced as an adult.

In her psychiatrist's professional opinion, she had a long road ahead of her if she wanted to become mentally healthy again. It was up to Gigi to participate in individual and group therapy and take her medications as prescribed. Her problems as a result of her past obsessions with men and her present one with Emmanuel could be cured through intense treatment. But honesty and acceptance would be key factors. Only Gigi knew if she would make a full recovery or not. Basically, her sanity was in her hands.

Epilogue

Eighteen months later...

Garcelle left her desk and rushed over to Jazz as soon as she entered the office pushing the baby carriage. She leaned over to get a good look at four-month-old Harmony Emanuelle Day. "My goodness! She's getting bigger and prettier every time I see her. She looks just like my boss, but that's *your* complexion, Mrs. Day."

"Our little princess is growing so fast, and everyone says she's the spitting of Emmanuel. I can't argue with the truth. She is definitely his daughter. Has he made it back from his committee meeting yet? His baby girl and I had some spare time today, so we stopped by to take him to lunch."

"He hasn't returned yet, but I expect him shortly. Have a seat while I get you a cup of that ginger tea you like so much."

Jazz sat on the sofa to wait for her husband. She selected a magazine from the end table closest to her and started skimming through it. Moments later, a few of Emmanuel's staff members entered the office behind Tyrell. They all hurried over to greet Jazz and sneak a peek at the baby. Little Harmony was sound asleep while the group stood above her. Jazz smiled and watched Tyrell lift his sleeping cousin from her fancy carriage to show her off to his coworkers. Harmony was now the star of the Day family. Neither politics nor journalism was a match for her. Emmanuel's popularity was steadily growing as the leading contender in all polls in his race to become Georgia's first African-American United States Senator. But his daughter's flame still shined brighter than his. Jazz's explosive ratings as the lead anchor on "Mornin' Mix", Black Diamond's daily morning news show, shot even higher after Harmony's debut appearance. Fans went bananas when the adorable baby girl, whose birth they had all been anxiously awaiting, arrived on the set of the award-winning show at eight weeks old. Little Harmony, dressed in a frilly lavender and mint green outfit with a matching headband and a pair of diamond studs in her tiny earlobes, had won the hearts of viewers. Like her mommy, she was a natural in front of the camera, smiling and cooing for the entire viewing audience to see. And she didn't cry or even whimper once during her seven minute guest appearance. Since that day, Harmony has been considered the most celebrated member of the Day family by far.

Emmanuel was her number one fan without a doubt. His little girl was the center of his universe. That's why as soon as he entered his office and saw her nestled in the crook of Tyrell's arm, he headed in their direction. He gently removed Harmony from her cousin's arms and cradled her with care. Jazz walked over to join them.

"We came to take you to lunch if you have time."

Emmanuel leaned down and pressed his lips to Jazz's temple. "I'll make time for you two. Give me a few minutes to have Tyrell adjust my schedule."

The End

About the Author: Honey was born March 7, 1968 in Macon, Georgia. She is the middle child of five born to very loving, devoted, and supportive parents. In the third grade, Honey developed a passion for creative writing. She used her gift in school, church, throughout college and beyond, writing and editing political speeches, essays, and skits. However, she did not pursue her dream to write professionally until many years later. "Judge Me Not", her debut novel with Jessica Watkins Presents, was released in March 2015 and received outstanding reviews from readers across the country. Honey is happily married to her husband of nearly eleven years. They reside in McDonough, Georgia where they are raising their nine and a half-year-old son.

CPSIA information can be obtained
at www.ICGtesting.com
Printed in the USA
LVHW01s1953180618
581092LV00017B/1907/P